Sep 2015

TOR BOOKS BY CARRIE VAUGHN

Kitty Saves the World

CARRIE VAUGHN

TOR®

A TOM DOHERTY ASSOCIATES BOOK
NEW YORK

KITTY SAVES THE WORLD

Copyright © 2015 Carrie Vaughn, LLC

All rights reserved.

A Tor Book
Published by Tom Doherty Associates, LLC
175 Fifth Avenue
New York, NY 10010

www.tor-forge.com

Tor® is a registered trademark of Tom Doherty Associates, LLC.

ISBN 978-0-7653-6870-6

Tor books may be purchased for educational, business, or promotional use. For information on bulk purchases, please contact the Macmillan Corporate and Premium Sales Department at 1-800-221-7945, extension 5442, or write to specialmarkets@macmillan.com.

First Edition: August 2015

Printed in the United States of America

0 9 8 7 6 5 4 3 2 1

For my family.

The Playlist

Traveling Wilburys, "End of the Line"

Patsy Cline, "Walkin' After Midnight"

Bob Geldof, "The Great Song of Indifference"

The Fabulous Glittering Aquanazis, "The Song That Will Get Us That Parental Advisory Sticker"

Everclear, "Strawberry"

Ian Cooke, "Fortitude"

The Pogues, "If I Should Fall from Grace with God"

Celtic Legacy, aka Kiltic, "Amazing Grace"

Johnny Nicholas, "John the Revelator"

Musica Antiqua, "Sheep May Safely Graze"

Pandora Celtica, "The Leaving"

Jane Siberry, "Calling All Angels"

Anonymous 4, "Angel Band"

Kitty Saves
the World

Chapter 1

M Y STUDIO space felt like a favorite pair of jeans, worn and comfortable, maybe disreputable, but while wearing them I was sure I could conquer the world. Here behind my microphone, monitor and status lights glowing, I was invincible.

"Welcome to *The Midnight Hour,* the show that isn't afraid of the dark or the creatures who live there. Thanks for joining me this evening. I'm hoping to have a rollicking good time, so let's get going."

Over the years since I'd started working at KNOB after college, and since I'd launched my radio show, we'd replaced the chairs, upgraded equipment, updated screening procedures, and syndicated to almost a hundred markets across the country. Details had changed, but this still felt like home. It would always feel like home, I hoped. We still played CCR's "Bad Moon Rising" as the intro. My sound guy, Matt, still engineered the whole show from his booth. I could see him through the booth window, head bent over the board. A big guy with short black hair and a laid-back attitude, he'd been with me almost from the beginning, as soon as the calls got to be too much for me to handle and we syndicated and suddenly had a mountain of technical issues. The show and I wouldn't have made it this far without him. I should probably tell him that.

"My guest this evening is a regular on the show, my good friend Dr. Elizabeth Shumacher, who heads up the Center for the Study of Paranatural Biology at the NIH, and my go-to guru for cutting-edge science and research on the conditions we know as vampirism and lycanthropy. Welcome back to the show, Dr. Shumacher."

"Thanks, Kitty, I'm happy to be here." Her voice came through my headphones; Dr. Shumacher was doing the interview from an affiliate radio station in Washington, D.C.—very late at her time, which meant I owed her one. On the plus side, I could interview her while in my jeans and T-shirt, sans makeup, hair tied up in a scrunchy. One of the many reasons I loved radio—I didn't have to dress up.

In my chipper radio-host voice I said, "I understand there's some new research indicating that scientists may have learned the origin of vampirism, which in turn may lead to discovering the source of lycanthropy. What can you tell me?"

Shumacher was the consummate scientist, talking evenly and articulately about everything. I'd met her a few times in person; she was a middle-aged woman who

embodied calm and confidence. I liked her and was lucky she kept letting me drag her onto the show. We needed people like her to cut through the legends and fear and get to the truth.

"It's far too early to be making sweeping statements about the discovery of anything. But we have some promising leads developing, which ought to point us to some fruitful new lines of inquiry."

"Which is scientist speak for, you're not going to stick your neck out, which is fine, but I'm not going to let you off the hook that easily," I said. "What exactly is this research about?"

"For some time, there's been a popular working hypothesis that vampirism, and perhaps lycanthropy as well, are transmitted through a variation of retroviral infection. Think of it as a kind of nefarious gene therapy. Gene therapy can be used to replace a portion of a patient's faulty, mutated DNA with healthy DNA. Viruses are often used to deliver healthy DNA, since they're naturally designed to attach to human cells, inject their own DNA, and reproduce quickly. Only in the case of vampirism, healthy human DNA is replaced by the DNA markers indicative of vampirism."

I got just enough of what she was talking about to know it was dangerous. But I wanted to *understand*. It was half the reason I did the show in the first place. The other half came from a vague hope that I might actually be able to help people. Just a few people. I wasn't trying to change the world.

"So vampirism—it's like catching a cold, except instead of just a runny nose, it transforms the host into another state of being entirely?"

"It's a bit more complicated than that," she said, sounding amused. She understood the need to paraphrase for the lowest common denominator audience. I'd read the papers she'd sent me—twice—and had to do some translating of my own. We'd get there. "Most people have antibodies that repel cold viruses—the symptoms of the cold are the result of the body's immune system fighting off the infection. It's my thought that vampirism was never common enough for human beings to develop antibodies to fight against, and so it's able to transform the host DNA without resistance. The next step is to confirm this hypothesis by identifying and isolating the transmitting virus."

"How close are you and your colleagues to doing that?"

"Well . . ."—and this was where I could tell she was self-editing—"not as close as we'd like. Samples are not all that easy to come by."

I said, "If it's a virus, do you think you might ever be able to develop a vaccine to protect against vampirism or lycanthropy?"

"Really, the transmission of these conditions is so difficult, and the chance of any one person becoming infected is so small, the development of a vaccine probably will never become a priority. I know the focus of many of my colleagues is on treating and potentially curing those already afflicted."

This was getting into *very* interesting territory indeed. "How close are you and your colleagues to finding a cure?"

A pause, almost too long for radio. The back of my neck itched, wanting to jump in and fill the quiet, but I didn't want to push her. When she finally answered, Shumacher sounded as uncertain as I'd ever heard her. "These are difficult, elusive questions we're dealing with, Kitty. All we can do is keep working and see what we find."

In other words, they didn't have much. They used words like *virus* because the concept was descriptive and provided a working model. But people like me were called *supernatural* for a reason. An ineffable part of the problem remained out of reach.

"All right, I'm going to open the line for calls now. If you have a question for Dr. Shumacher or a comment on this discussion, you know what to do."

I already had a dozen calls lined up in the queue. Excellent. Even after years of this, I lived in fear of looking at the monitor one day and seeing it blank, empty. If my audience vanished, the show would be done. This was not that day. At heart, people wanted attention, and if they had to call into my quirky fringe show to get it, so be it.

For the first call, I tried to pick one that sounded sane. Or at least balanced. One with a substantive comment, not too far out there. Sometimes I picked well.

"Hello, Martin from Boston, you're on the air."

"Oh hi, Kitty, thanks for taking my call. Yeah, I

have a question for Dr. Shumacher. She said getting samples was hard. So if I'm a vampire and I want to participate—I guess I'm asking if there are any studies I could sign up for, to help out?"

"Dr. Shumacher?" I prompted.

"Yes, a number of researchers are conducting a variety of studies at any given moment, and they're often looking for not just vampire and lycanthrope volunteers, but uninfected humans for experimental controls. It should come as no surprise that these communities are often difficult to reach out to, and that's one of the reasons our options are sometimes limited, so thank you especially for asking. We have a website you can check to find various calls for study volunteers . . ."

See? I was performing a public service. Contributing to the community. It wasn't all prurient exploitation.

I picked up the thread. "Thanks, Martin, for putting yourself out there for science. I hope others will check out that website. We'll put the link on *The Midnight Hour* site as well." I looked through the window, and yes, Matt was writing down the reminder, because I would likely forget. I was caught up in the flow of the show, and nothing could stop me. "Next caller, hello, what do you have for me?" This was Nadia from Tucson.

A woman spoke, her voice earnest, searching. "Hello, Kitty, yes—I have a question for both of you, if that's okay."

"It's what we're here for, ask away."

"All this talk of science, it seems like it's missing something. Vampires, werewolves, there's more to

them than just curing an illness, isn't there? I guess I want to know where the mystery of it all is. The magic."

I deferred to my guest. "Dr. Shumacher, you want to tackle this one?"

"I'm not sure that 'science' and 'magic' are such distinct categories as people sometimes make them out to be. I try to keep that in mind when I do my own studies, that this is all part of nature, no matter how strange it seems. I'm studying nature."

I added, "I've heard a lot of variations of the saying that magic is just phenomena that science hasn't explained yet."

Shumacher said, "I became a scientist because the natural world fills me with wonder. I think DNA is magical—how does all that information come to be stored in a collection of molecules? How does it come to be expressed? Learning the answers to those questions doesn't make me any less filled with awe."

"Yes, exactly," I said. "I've seen a lot of weird things in my time. Ghosts, channeling, fairies, you name it. It doesn't matter how weird things get, I'm not going to stop asking questions and trying to figure out how things work. Otherwise, we're sitting alone in our dark caves, waiting for something to come along and eat us."

Nadia didn't sound convinced. "Yeah, okay—but what if you never find real answers? What if it really is just magic?"

"As if 'just' is a word you can use with magic. It's 'just,' you know, the universe."

She kept pressing. "Surely there are some questions

that will never be answered—why vampires are immortal, why werewolves are controlled by the full moon. It doesn't make any scientific sense."

"And it never will, if we stop asking questions," I said. "Maybe it's magic, yes, but we still need to figure out how magic works, don't we? Moving on, before we get too philosophical, my next call comes from Providence. Hello!"

The caller was male, fast talking, and clearly short on patience. "Kitty, longtime listener and all that. I've been a fan for a long time, but why do you always fall for these so-called scientific explanations? You know it's all a smoke screen, don't you?"

The screener's comment on this call was "opposing viewpoint." I had a feeling what that viewpoint was going to be. Doing the show as long as I had, I'd heard just about everything at least once. But I was always willing to be surprised.

"Oh? A smoke screen? Do tell."

"This isn't about science, or magic, or anything like that. It's about who controls our souls!"

Of course it was. Sometimes I thought I'd be better off if I hung up on these calls. Usually, though, I had way more fun letting them run on. Sure, I liked providing altruistic public service when I could. The rest of the time, I wasn't above ratings-boosting conflict.

"This is a good and evil thing, I assume is what you're getting at."

"You know the stories: vampires and werewolves, lycanthropes, witches, all the rest of it—they're a perversion of God's perfect human form. They're not nature, they're a twisted mockery of nature! Your doctor there said basically the same thing—these monsters rewrite our DNA, DNA made in God's image. How can corrupting that not be a sign of true evil?"

"Because . . . I don't feel evil?" It got too easy to point and laugh at these guys. When they didn't make me feel utterly exhausted.

"That's the whole point," the caller from Providence said, and even he sounded tired, like he'd had to explain this one too many times. "You're a pawn. You're being used. Maybe you didn't start out evil, but your DNA, your very being, your *soul* has been warped. And why? Tell me that? What purpose does it serve? Think about it a minute and you'll realize the answer."

If I wasn't playing dumb, I was at least playing stubborn. "Does there have to be a purpose? Do you know what the purpose of a cold virus is?"

"No?" the guy said, nonplussed.

"Dr. Shumacher?" I asked.

She said, gamely, "Well, the purpose of a cold virus is to make more cold viruses and then to spread. Reproduction. Biologists feel that this is the base purpose of most life on Earth."

"There you go," I said. "It's a function of reproduction. Does it have to be more nefarious than that?"

"Yes!" he exclaimed. "Because this isn't biology, this is about the war in Heaven, and the rebellion of Lucifer, and his entire purpose is twisting God's creation and bending it toward evil! Spreading that evil!

When you say this is all science and biology, you're confusing people, turning them from the truth! Vampires, werewolves—you, even!—you're a symptom of original sin! You're being *used*!"

"You know," I said. "There was a time when I'd say this rant never gets old. But I've changed my mind— this is getting old. You can't call someone evil because of some aspect of their identity they can't control. I'll say it again: being a vampire or a werewolf doesn't make a person evil. Doing evil things makes you evil."

"You're deluded, you're a tool of Lucifer—"

I cut off the call. Because I could. "There's definitely a tool here but it's not me. Dr. Shumacher, do you ever get this kind of response to your work?"

"We have an intern whose entire job is filing the hate mail we get at the center."

Oh. I didn't know that. "That . . . do you find that depressing? This antiscience attitude? This outright hatred?"

"I think it highlights the need for education. I don't think people are antiscience—they're scared. They know now that vampires and werewolves exist, but they don't know what to do about it, so it's easy for them to believe the worst. I know you've done your best to get as much information out there as you can, Kitty. But, well, not to throw any kind of shadow on what you've done, you know very well that sometimes backfires. Any hint of conspiracy, people get more scared, not less. And vampires and conspiracy are almost synonymous."

She wasn't the first person to call me on that. Last

year I'd stood up before an international conference and declared the existence of Dux Bellorum and the Long Game, a cabal of vampires with a nefarious mission of world-domination. Maybe that hadn't been the most responsible thing to do. But I'd been at a loss—Dux Bellorum was real and I didn't know how else to stop him. Speaking truth into a microphone was the only thing I knew how to do.

Dux Bellorum—Roman—was a vampire, a soldier of the Roman Empire in the first century who had become a vampire and decided to spend his immortality learning arcane lore and building an empire of his own. He'd traveled the world in search of magic and followers, whom he marked with an enchanted coin. I had a handful of the coins, collected from his minions and former minions, scratched and marred and flattened to destroy the magic in them. He had dozens of allies—the Master and Mistress vampires of cities around the world—and through them he exerted control over the entire supernatural world. Maybe even the mortal world as well, and I had begun to suspect that Roman didn't just want to take over the world—he wanted to destroy it. Or at least damage it to such an extent that taking it over would be made easier. All the signs over the last few months indicated that Roman was on the move, that his endgame was in play.

I had evidence that he'd caused Vesuvius to erupt and destroy Pompeii, using a spell called the Manus Herculei. I believed he was preparing to use that spell again. I kept a map in my office with every volcano that had been active in the last thousand years marked with red thumbtacks. There were volcanoes all over the world. We'd never be able to stop him.

I'd been trying to track down Roman for years, ever since he came to Denver and decided I was an obstacle. There *was* a conspiracy, but it wasn't about good and evil and the supernatural; it was about power and egos. The usual stuff. The supernatural didn't fundamentally change people; it just gave them power.

I'd blown all this up in public because I figured the more people were watching for him, who knew about him, the less likely he'd be able to pull off anything terrible. Turned out, a lot of people just stopped taking me seriously. I was just like the crackpots calling into my show.

"I blame *Dracula*," I said, deflecting the issue entirely, because I had a show to run. "All right, let's take another call. Hello, you're on the air."

An authoritative male voice came on the line and lectured. "I think you're ignoring the *real* controversy here, which is how the World Health Organization is planning to start incarcerating werewolves in concentration camps to serve as food for vampires, to spare the human population . . ."

And that was *The Midnight Hour*.

MY PHONE rang as I left the KNOB studios. Normally, after-midnight calls would be a cause for worry, except the caller ID said it was Cormac. He usually called at strange hours, so I wouldn't know if this was an emergency until I actually talked to him.

"Hey!" I said brightly, hopped up on postshow adrenaline.

"You going to New Moon tonight?" he said, without any extraneous social preamble. Not his style.

Many times after the show, I'd head to New Moon, the bar and restaurant my husband, Ben, and I owned, to burn off said adrenaline with a drink and company. Sometimes Cormac, Ben's cousin and our friend, joined us. He rarely gave warning ahead of time.

"Yeah," I said. "Ben should already be there."

"I'll meet you there," he said.

"Why? What—" He clicked off without explanation.

Well, that was Cormac, man of mystery. He'd found something, obviously. And now my stomach was churning, wondering what it was and what can of worms it would open.

Chapter 2

Worry about what trouble Cormac had gotten into squashed my postshow buzz, so I walked into New Moon distracted and frowning. After midnight on a Friday the place was busy, but past peak crowd. Seeing lots of people here ordering lots of food and drink usually gave me a warm fuzzy feeling—a busy restaurant was a successful restaurant. Tonight, I cut through the crowd without noticing, looking for a familiar face.

First up was Shaun, the restaurant's longtime manager and part of our werewolf pack. Family, practically. Early thirties, confident and sensible, he had close-cropped black hair, brown skin, a shining gaze, and a smile that lit up when he saw me. People he didn't like never saw that smile; I was glad he was on my side.

"Wild show tonight, Kitty."

"I don't know how you listen to it with all this racket going on."

"You kidding? It's one of our Friday night attractions. *The Midnight Hour* drinking game."

How did I not know about this? And why was I not surprised? This was what I got for never being at New Moon during my own show. "A drinking game? How long has that been going on?"

He shrugged. "Maybe a couple months."

"So what, it's like someone calls in asking how to get bit by a werewolf, take a drink. I hang up on a religious rant, take a drink."

"Exactly!"

"How often does this result in cases of blood poisoning?" He just grinned. I should have been laughing, but I wasn't. It was just one more thing.

"What's up?" he asked. "You're nervous."

The muscles across my shoulders were tight. I must have walked in here looking like a wolf on the prowl. "Distracted. Hey, while I'm thinking of it—thanks. The reason this place works is you. So thanks." Now I was sounding maudlin.

Shaun shrugged, a way to brush past the sentimentality. "I love it here. Dream job, you know?"

The bartender pushed over a glass of my favorite beer. Personalized service. I could hug the guy. "Cheers all around," I said, and lifted the glass in a toast.

Ben, suit jacket over the back of a chair and the first couple of buttons of his shirt undone, was waiting for me at the back table, "our" table, where we held court and seemed to spend an inordinate amount of time.

Sometimes plotting, sometimes just hanging out. This was our den, our refuge, our tribe.

Why did it all suddenly seem fragile?

He stood when I approached, and I set the glass down so he could fold me in an all-encompassing hug, his arms tight around me. I leaned my face against his neck and breathed deep, taking in his scent, soap and skin and the sweat of the day, the wild and fur of his werewolf side, as familiar as my own self.

"How'd it go tonight?"

"So you weren't here for the drinking game?"

"No, I had a call from a client. There's a drinking game?"

"Apparently." I tried to sum up tonight's far-ranging show, and couldn't. "The usual, I think. It's so hard to tell from that side of the mike. And how are you?"

His expression was drained. "It's been one of those days."

Ben was a criminal defense lawyer. When he said "one of those days," he meant it, and I likely couldn't imagine how bad it could really get. Because of client confidentiality he didn't go into details, but he spent a lot of his professional life with people who were hitting bottom or on the way there.

I pulled back, tipped his chin toward me, and kissed him. I felt the tension leave him, and his arms settled more firmly around me. That only made my own tension more evident.

"What's wrong?" he asked.

"That obvious?"

His smile was kind, and he brushed a strand of loose hair back behind my ear. "Seems like a little more than your usual after-show jitters."

"Cormac's on his way over. I think he found something."

Ben sighed, pursed his lips. All that tension returned. "Right. Good thing we have beer."

The man himself arrived maybe ten minutes later. I could smell him when the door opened, his distinct scent of leather jacket and close apartment living. Also, an undercurrent: herbs and lit candles—a magician's tools. This, I associated with Amelia. His ghost, a Victorian wizard woman who'd died—or "died" rather—over a hundred years ago. And, I had to admit, his partner.

He came straight to the back table, trusting we would be here. We had a chair waiting for him across from us.

"Hey," Ben said in greeting. "What's up?"

"You're not going to like it," Cormac said. Which was a hell of a greeting. I'd have asked, How bad could it be? But this was Cormac, and my imagination failed me.

He pulled his laptop from a courier bag slung over his shoulder and opened the screen, turning it to face us. Ben and I leaned in close to look. I needed a few minutes to make out what I was looking at—an e-mail thread, maybe a dozen messages deep.

Earlier this year, we'd posted online a mysterious coded book of shadows that potentially contained information about what Roman planned—and how to stop him. We hoped crowd sourcing might help us decode the writing when all else failed. Finally, Cormac managed to translate the book. That was where we got confirmation about the volcano thing. In the meantime, dozens of people had sent him messages. This thread of conversation didn't seem to have much to do with the book, but the correspondent must have contacted Cormac with enough information to warrant a response.

I read on. The unknown correspondent knew about Amy Scanlon—the author of the coded book of shadows—and asked a lot of questions about what Cormac knew about her: who she was, whom she was working with, what she was doing. The pointed inter-rogation was enough to raise the hairs on my neck and the hackles across my shoulders. This guy knew some-thing, but what? Cormac's replies were vague, leading without giving too much away. He kept his own iden-tity safely hidden. Then the discussion got into really arcane details about some kind of dueling magic and spells.

"What exactly have you been getting up to?" I said, accusing. He'd spent time in prison, and as an ex-con he wasn't supposed to carry—or handle, or even think about—guns anymore. He'd been pursuing magic as a replacement, which seemed to miss the point to my thinking.

"Just keep reading."

I did, and got to the last few e-mails in the sequence. The unknown correspondent seemed to be offering Cormac—or whoever he thought was writing to him—a job. Cormac replied, "I don't know anything about you. Who are you?"

The answer came back: "I am called Roman."

I stopped breathing. That had to be a coincidence. It couldn't possibly be a coincidence. I checked the date on the e-mails—he'd been sitting on this for almost two weeks. I could murder the guy. But he'd done it. Somehow, he'd drawn Roman out of hiding. Now what did we do?

Before I could say or do anything, either yelling at Cormac or fainting dead away, Ben said, "Shit. You've got to be kidding."

That seemed like a reasonable explanation. Cormac, suddenly developing a prankster sense of humor and having one over on us. We looked at him, waiting for the punch line.

"Be nice if I was," he said, and seemed amused. Or at least fatalistic to a dangerous degree. Not that he was ever one to freak out about something like this. "But I'm pretty sure it's really him."

"What did you tell him?" I demanded, breathless. Truth was, I was in awe. We'd been looking for Roman all this time, I'd had friends die trying to go after him, and all we had to do was put out bait?

Cormac leaned over, tapped a couple of keys, and brought up the reply: "My name is Amelia Parker. Let's do meet."

Which wasn't a lie. But it was such a complicated truth, the mind boggled. This felt like juggling dynamite. I waited for the inevitable explosion. But there wasn't an explosion, just the three of us leaning over the computer screen, staring in wonder.

"I have no idea what to do with this," I murmured. "What are we going to do with this?"

"I say we set up a meeting," Cormac said, calm and steady. Discussing a battle plan and not freaking out. "Agree to meet with him and set a trap. Stake him while his guard is down."

"You make it sound simple," I said. A million things could go wrong. Other people more powerful and more experienced than we were had tried setting traps for Roman, had tried staking him while his guard was down. They hadn't succeeded. While we were setting a trap for Roman, he could just as easily be setting a trap for us. In fact, that seemed the most likely scenario. We were getting suckered into something.

"No, this could work," Ben said, studying the computer screen as if it might reveal more secrets. "Even if he picks the location, we'll have time to scout it out and set up an ambush. It may be our only chance to physically confront him."

As if setting traps for two-thousand-year-old vampires was like setting up a drug bust. "Ben, you're the one who's supposed to be all skeptical and negative."

"When are we ever going to get another opening like this?" he replied.

"There's a problem," Cormac said.

"Only one?" I shot back.

"I can't go. Roman knows what I look like, he knows I'm with you and that I'm not anybody named Amelia Parker. The minute he sees me he'll know it's a trap."

A simple problem to put an end to a simple plan.

Would it be wrong to be secretly relieved that Cormac was not going to be marching straight up to Roman to put a stake in his heart? "So what do you want to do?"

"Find someone to be Amelia," he said.

"What, throw some poor innocent woman in Roman's path?" I said.

"Whatever it takes," Cormac said. "Maybe someone from your pack—Becky, she's pretty tough. Might not matter that she's a werewolf."

"We're not using Becky as bait." I wanted to get up and pace.

"Kitty, calm down," Ben said, touching my hand. "I thought this was what we've been waiting for. Why so worked up?" From anyone else, the question would have sounded condescending, but his expression held only concern.

I shivered, trying to work out the tension. "I just have a bad feeling about this. It can't be that easy."

"I don't expect it to be easy," Cormac said. "But it's a chance."

The front door opened, letting in a taste of the night air outside. Usually I ignored it—the scents that came with the breath of air were generic, anonymous, strangers coming and going, or familiar smells of people I knew and expected to be here.

But I caught this scent and looked up, because I recognized it, and it was totally unexpected. My hand closed on Ben's arm and I stood.

"Tina!"

A striking brunette, Tina McCannon was lean and

photogenic, one of the stars of the TV show *Paradox PI*. We'd met when the show came to town a few years ago, and I roped her and her colleagues into an interview, which turned into a live ghost-hunting session and a Ouija board séance that set New Moon on fire. We fixed it. Turned out, Tina was good at ghost hunting because she really was psychic. A year later, we both participated in a cabin-in-the-woods reality TV show that went very south very quickly. We survived, when not many of the original participants did. Made for a tight-knit club. She'd been one of my go-to resources on psychic phenomena ever since.

Tonight she was in jeans, T-shirt, and jacket. She paused at the doorway, searching. Her gaze lit up when she found me.

"Kitty!"

I squealed as we came together in a big, noisy hug there in the middle of the bar. I might have been a werewolf, but I had a monster-sized sentimental streak. The last time I saw Tina she was recovering from a gunshot wound in her gut. My friends and I, bound by our scars. And Ben and Cormac wondered why I worried so much.

"This place looks so much better when it isn't on fire, doesn't it?" she said.

Yes, yes it did. "I didn't know you were going to be in town, why didn't you call?"

"I knew you'd be here. I *am* psychic," she added, a twinkle in her eye.

"Er. Right. Come in, sit. What's up?"

Over at our table, Tina and Ben shared a friendly hug and traded mutual well wishes. Cormac looked on expectantly, patiently. I had to think for a minute—he'd been in prison when she came through town, hadn't he?

"Um, Tina—this is Cormac."

She blinked at him, then donned a sunny smile. "Hi, I'm Tina," she said redundantly.

He smiled thinly, took a sip of beer.

"Um," Tina said, leaning toward me. "There's something weird going on with his aura."

"There are two of them," he said.

"Cormac and Amelia," I said.

That weird subtle change came over Cormac as he spoke in a suddenly refined voice. "Hello, I've heard so much about you. Delighted to finally meet you. Um, Cormac would rather I step aside for the time being. But yes."

"Oh. Hi. Yes, nice to meet you, too." She nodded sagely, like she encountered this sort of thing all the time. And maybe she did. "So, I take it he's—they're—in on everything."

Ah, how to explain Cormac and his role in all this in a dozen words or less? Without making him sound like a maniac?

"You could say that," Ben said. Nailed it.

I made us all sit, and Tina asked a server for a glass of water.

"How are you? What brings you to Denver?" I asked.

"This was kind of last minute," she said, wincing as if chagrined. "That's why I didn't call. I just got in my car and drove."

"From L.A.?" I said.

"Yeah." That wince again, like she knew it sounded crazy and couldn't explain it to herself, much less me. "I need to talk to you."

"You couldn't have called? Not that I'm not happy to see you—but what's wrong?"

"Would it be weird if I said I didn't feel safe calling? I keep looking over my shoulder like someone's following me. I just . . . I needed to see you, to make sure it was you, you know?"

That made a scary amount of sense. I exchanged a concerned glance with Ben. Cormac studied the inside of his beer glass. It was that feeling again, that something was about to happen. So, it wasn't just me.

"There's something in the air, I think," I said.

"Kitty—when was the last time you heard from Anastasia?" she asked.

"That's . . . a long story," I said. They were all getting to be long stories. Anastasia was a vampire, some eight hundred years old, from China. She was also a survivor of that terrible reality show.

I'd last seen her in San Francisco's Chinatown—the last time I confronted Roman, come to think of it. What happened to her after that . . . I wasn't exactly sure. It involved Chinese gods and goddesses, ancient spells, and interdimensional tunnels. "Would it mean anything to you if I said I think she's gone to another plane of existence?"

"That . . . that makes sense. I keep feeling like I'm hearing her voice. At first I thought maybe something had happened to her. Can you call it dead when it happens to a vampire? They're already dead—"

"I call it dead," Cormac said.

"I usually have a really hard time sensing vampires because they're in between, not dead or alive. I've never channeled one who was, you know, *dead* dead. This didn't feel like any of that."

"Anastasia accepted an employment opportunity offered by a divine being," Ben said helpfully.

"Oh. Well, okay then." Very little fazed Tina. "I think she's been trying to tell me something. I'm just not sure exactly what. But coming here, seeing you— seemed like the right thing to do. I can't get any more specific than that." She looked back and forth between us, and at Cormac's laptop—we'd obviously been in some kind of conference. "Something's about to happen, isn't it?"

Worse yet, I was sure several somethings were about to happen. At once, and spectacularly. I just didn't know what, and Tina's sudden appearance with ominous messages didn't help the feeling.

Meanwhile, Cormac's gaze had finally settled on Tina, and he was studying her thoughtfully. Like he was sizing up an elk he was about to shoot.

"What?" Tina said.

"She'll do," he answered.

"What?" I repeated.

"We need an Amelia," Cormac said. "She'll do."

Oh good God, he had to be kidding. "No," I said. "No no no. We can't ask her to do that."

"Do what, what is he talking about?" Tina asked.

Tina knew about Roman, the Long Game—most of it, anyway. She was one of the people I called when I had questions. One of my allies. But she didn't know what she'd be getting into with this. It was too dangerous, and I wasn't going to put her in danger. Not again.

I didn't say anything. Ben didn't say anything. Cormac was the one who explained. "We have a chance to take out Roman, but we need a woman to front the trap. Someone he doesn't know."

Direct and to the point. He wouldn't have it any other way.

"No," I said. "Absolutely not. It's too dangerous. And besides, Roman knows Tina—he's seen her, she was with me when he was in Denver that first time."

"Then she knows exactly what we're up against," he said, without a speck of hesitation.

"Not to mention she's on a famous TV show!" I shot back.

Now Tina had that same thoughtful, determined look on her face that Cormac did. "You'd be amazed how many people don't recognize me without makeup and my hair done." Sure enough, no one in the bar was looking her way now. In her casual jacket and jeans, her hair tied back, cosmetics free, she looked different. Inconspicuous.

"Roman would recognize you," I said. "Ben, tell her—"

"Do you think I can't do it?" she interrupted.

I slumped and set my head in my hands. "That's not it. It's . . ." I didn't want anyone to get hurt. Anyone *else*. I didn't want any more people to die because of this. Cormac and Ben would tell me that this was the whole point—to confront Roman so no one else had to die. The risk was worth it. We weren't going to solve anything by sitting here and stewing. Here, we finally had a plan. So what was my problem?

"I don't like any of this," I said simply, sullenly.

"I'm here for a reason," Tina said. She put a hand on my arm, a simple gesture of comfort, like she knew that a gentle touch from a friend calmed werewolves. "I knew I had to come see you. This must be why." Being psychic, believing in magic—that made everything so easy, didn't it? Everything became a matter of fate. I didn't much like fate. "If not me, then who? Who else are you willing to put in danger?"

I couldn't answer that.

Cormac said, "You won't have to do anything but stand there. I'll take care of the rest." He was probably trying to sound reassuring, but it came out ominous.

"Sounds like fun," Tina said, bright eyed, a picture of cheerful enthusiasm.

Ben gathered my hand in his, squeezed. "It'll be fine. It's a good plan."

I wasn't sure I'd go so far as to call it a good plan. But it was the best plan we had.

Chapter 3

AFTER E-MAILING back and forth a few more times, Cormac and the mysterious correspondent identifying himself as Roman set up a meeting in Albuquerque in three days. I was suspicious enough to start questioning whether this person even was Roman, or was actually one of Roman's minions trying to draw us out, or some entirely new player trying to pull one over on us. Any possibility seemed likely when they all seemed outrageous.

Roman originally asked for a meeting in Las Vegas, which was out of the question. The city was one of Roman's strongholds, its vampire Master one of his dedicated servants. I had allies there—the magician Odysseus Grant, especially—but I couldn't risk it. I wanted neutral ground. We came up with excuses and alternatives, without dropping any clues that Amelia had anything to do with Denver, and therefore me.

This was turning into real cloak-and-dagger shit. I

hated it, but Cormac seemed determined. Driven. He was finally hunting again, the biggest prey of all. He was very excited about Tina playing the part of Amelia. At least, as excited as he ever got about anything, emotion revealing itself as a glint in his gaze.

He explained over dinner at our place. "Roman's not stupid. He may only have her name, but he'll dig up what he can on Amelia Parker, and he'll know that she's dead. He'll already be suspicious no matter what we do, but he'll also be curious. When he sees Tina, maybe he does recognize her—but he knows she's psychic, and he might think that she's channeling Amelia, or that Amelia possessed her. It'll make sense to him, and even if he thinks there's some connection with Kitty, he'll want to check it out. It's the best kind of bait: too good to pass up, but not too good to be true."

Tina stayed in our guest bedroom. We spent some time catching up on news. Her show was still going strong in its eighth season, and her cohosts, Jules and Gary, were doing well, though she confessed they'd started checking out urban legends and rumors that made the more science-minded Jules bristle. None of them were ready to quit yet. I talked her into recording an interview for *The Midnight Hour,* which seemed excessively normal next to all the other weirdness going on.

After she'd started hearing voices, she'd spent some time trying to contact Anastasia using her toolbox of channeling techniques, which included Ouija boards and automatic writing. But our Chinese vampire friend had gone quiet. She'd nudged Tina, Tina was here, and that was that.

I wondered if Tina was having trouble talking to her because Anastasia wasn't really dead—or not fully dead. Tina knew how to contact the dead, but Anastasia was something else. I suggested this to Tina, who turned thoughtful at the suggestion.

"It feels bigger than that," she said, her gaze vague. "Like we're all tools for a greater force."

And didn't that sound ominous? I wasn't a fan of destiny as an excuse for these things. Like magic, it was too easy a target to blame. I wanted more control over the situations I found myself in. I wanted to believe we had a chance. In the meantime, all we could do was wait, and prepare. Three days seemed like a very long time when you were trying to save the world from a powerful vampire.

Three days was long enough to introduce complications.

I was at KNOB wrapping up work on the next episode of the show the day before we were set to drive to Albuquerque, when my cell phone rang. The caller ID said it was Detective Jessi Hardin. I shouldn't get a sinking feeling in my stomach when the police called, but I felt that every time I got a call from Hardin. She was head of the Denver PD's Paranatural Unit, and she rarely brought good news.

"Hi," I said cautiously.

"I can sense the dread in your voice in one syllable," she said.

"Can you blame me? Maybe if you ever called offering, like, prize money or wishing me happy birthday or something."

"Mercedes Cook is back in the country. I thought you'd want to know."

My mouth went dry and for a second my brain stopped thinking because it was too much to deal with. Mercedes Cook—another old and powerful vampire, one of Roman's minions, and this couldn't be a coincidence.

"I don't even know what to do with that," I said finally.

"Watch your back, I imagine."

I'd been watching my back for years now. I was tired of it. "How'd you find this out? Where exactly is she?"

"It was luck," she said. "She didn't show up on any of the security cameras, but we've gotten pictures of her in every Interpol office in Europe and in quite a few agencies outside it. An officer spotted her at the airport in Frankfurt boarding a private jet. And I don't care how supernatural and scary you are, your private jet still has to file a flight plan when it uses major international airports. She landed in Atlanta. This was last week. After that, we don't know."

Still, a little information was better than nothing. "Does her professional schedule show anything?" Mercedes Cook made her name as a Broadway performer and world-class singer. This was before she made her name as the world's first celebrity vampire. She'd been keeping a lower profile lately—no shows, no concert tours announced for the near future.

"No," Hardin said. "She doesn't have anything planned. She'd be easier to track if she did."

"Yeah, that's the point, I imagine. I'll ask around; maybe someone else has heard something." Sometimes it felt like all I could do was share information. Little more than gossip. It had to be worth it, it just had to.

"Anything else going on?" she asked. An innocent question, but I felt a spike of anxiety. My first impulse was to brush her off. Everything was fine, just fine. But it wasn't. I wouldn't be doing anyone any favors by not telling her.

"Actually, something's come up. You might be able to help out . . ."

ONE SET of people I hadn't told anything to: my family. Ben and I had dinner with my parents, my older sister, Cheryl, and her husband and kids every other week or so. We'd been scheduled for dinner in a couple of evenings, but the trip to Albuquerque meant I had to cancel. Since I couldn't tell my pleasant, easygoing mother that I was on my way to trap and assassinate the two-thousand-year-old mastermind of a global vampire conspiracy, I made up something about a onetime chance to interview a very important person for the show. Mom made impressed and encouraging noises and didn't ask questions. Bless her.

But she did want to know if we could have dinner tonight instead, and I couldn't say no. So there we were, Ben and me sitting in the car in their driveway, getting ready to go in. Cheryl and Mark and the kids were already here. The lights in the front window were blazing and warm, welcoming. Domestic bliss.

"Remind again me what our cover story is," Ben said.

"I've gotten a chance to interview a Hopi medicine woman who's only going to be in Albuquerque this weekend. We're making a vacation out of it." I sounded disgruntled.

Ben sat back, sighed. "Vacation. Sounds nice, doesn't it?"

"We can still call the whole thing off."

"How about this: we get through this standoff with He Who Must Not Be Named, then take that vacation you're telling everyone about. Deal?"

I tried to imagine the weight that would come off my shoulders if we could really and truly get rid of Roman. It sounded like heaven. "That's a deal."

"All right, then. Eye on the prize." He patted my leg, and we hauled ourselves out of the car for our evening of domestic normalcy.

The noise started as soon as we opened the door. "Kitty!" my mother announced, sweeping out of the kitchen to plunge at me for a big hug. I could explain to her that to a wolf, a too-enthusiastic hug looked like an attack—arms out, forward movement. But she wouldn't get it, so I tamped down Wolf's growls and accepted the love as it was intended. Ben, too. We'd both had a lot of practice at this. Then came Dad, solid and benevolent, who like Mom had never really processed the me-being-a-werewolf thing, so we let it go. Brother-in-law Mark, then sister Cheryl, who out of all my family had some idea of how weird my life had gotten, and when I told her not to ask questions, she usually listened to me.

"Kitty!" The loud squeals came from Nicky and Jeffy, niece and nephew, who roared in from the living room and attempted to tackle me. Nine and six, they'd gotten articulate and willful enough to be interesting. So I had Jeffy hanging on my arm, trying to pull me to a pile of plastic cars and trucks, insisting he had to show me something, and Nicky standing there, looking up at me, very serious—her "I'm a grown-up" face. "Aunt Kitty, Mom said I should tell you about the thing that happened at school last week."

"Oh?"

"The teacher gave us some homework to write a story about someone in our family, and so I wrote about you, but the teacher didn't believe you really were a werewolf, she said I was making it all up and called Mom to tell her that I was lying, and, well, Mom told her that it was all true. And now the teacher looks at me funny when I come into class."

I looked over Nicky's head to Cheryl, questioning. She gave a silent, grim nod, confirming the story.

"Wow," I said. "That's cool that you picked me to write about, but I'm sorry you had to deal with that."

"It's okay. I just don't understand why she has to be like that."

"Neither do I, kid. Your teacher probably never thought that someone she sees every day might know a werewolf. You gave her something to think about, and she didn't like that."

Nicky's nose wrinkled. "I can't wait until this year is over and I get a new teacher."

I smiled and gave her a hug. I remembered years like that.

The grand entrance continued with small talk and assurances that everything was fine, nothing was wrong, we were doing well, work was going well, and so on. I asked Cheryl about her new job, and was pleased at how her eyes lit up. With both her kids in school now, she decided last year to head back to work and promptly had a midlife crisis. Her IT credentials were out of date, and she was daunted by the thought of going back to school. Instead, she switched gears and now managed an art gallery on Broadway. Back to her alt-punk roots—she wore jeans to work. She explained how it was the best of both worlds—a job that made her feel useful, the chance to get her foot back in the real world, but still enough time to be there for her kids. Seeing her happy made me happy.

It was like I had two packs, human and wolf. An embarrassment of riches, and that much more to protect and worry over.

After a pure comfort food dinner of pasta and chicken Parmesan, we retreated to the living room for talk and drinks. I watched Ben with the kids. Nicky was telling him a story about a school field trip to the Museum of Nature and Science, while Jeffy was trying to get him to help color a page in his superhero coloring book. Ben didn't just tolerate them, he engaged, asking Nicky questions while somehow simultaneously giving Jeffy advice about what color Spider-Man's mask should be. I never would have expected it, except in hindsight. He wasn't a lawyer for the money—he'd gotten into the field wanting to help people. He was thoughtful. He listened. It didn't matter if the person in front of him was six or sixty. The kids sensed it, and they gravitated to someone they felt would take them seriously. Watching them gave my heart a room-sized glow.

I wanted kids. I'd wanted kids for a few years now—pretty much since I learned I couldn't carry a baby to term myself, I'd wanted one. The paradox of denial, wanting precisely what you can't have. Usually the feeling was abstract. I'd wanted kids because it felt right. But the thought "*Ben would be a great dad*" popped into my head, and my heart ached and tears welled.

We'd talked about adoption. After this trip, after this confrontation, after we didn't have to worry about the Long Game anymore. We could make it happen.

Grandma came in and announced ice cream, the kids screeched with delight and bounded to the kitchen, and Cheryl shouted after them to calm down, leaving Ben and me looking across the living room at each other. His smile was bemused, and I had no idea how I looked, but he must have suspected what I was thinking, because he came over, put his hands on my shoulders, and kissed my forehead.

"That bad, huh?" I said, wiping a stray tear.

"I've never seen you look so happy and sad at exactly the same time," he said.

"I will be so damned relieved when this is all over."

"Yeah. Come on, ice cream will make you feel better."

And it did, at least briefly. Rocky road. Sometimes it was the little things.

As we left, I made sure to give everyone extra-big hugs, even though Jeffy wiggled and escaped as soon as he could. Cheryl was the one who pulled back, her brow furrowed. "Is something wrong?" she asked.

Oh, was it. I almost gave into an impulse to fall sobbing into her arms. Instead, I offered her a crooked smile. "No more so than usual," I said, which wasn't a lie. Usually I said something like, I'm a werewolf, of course something's wrong. But she already knew that.

"Well. Be careful." She brushed a loose blond strand out of my face, and suddenly I was thirteen again and wishing I could be just like her.

If Roman ever went after them . . . And that was why we were going to Albuquerque. That was why the risk was worth it.

THE KIDS had early bedtimes, so we were back on the road by nine. After dark, I could finally call Alette,

Mistress of Washington, D.C., and arguably one of the most powerful vampires in the U.S. She knew where the bodies were buried—or where they weren't, in some cases.

One of her people answered the phone—I hesitated to call them human servants, even though most vampires would. She had housekeepers and drivers and bodyguards, people who looked after her during daylight hours, people who were devoted to her. But many of them were her own descendants. She'd had children before becoming a vampire, and she still took care of them. She was a however many greats grandmother to them all, and they knew it and loved her for it.

Once I said who I was, I didn't have to ask to speak to Alette.

"Mercedes Cook is back," I said.

"Yes, so I've heard," Alette replied in her prim English accent. I kind of suspected she had.

"Any idea what she's up to?"

"What is she ever up to? She's gone to ground, I'm afraid. You should keep vigilant, of course."

Exactly what Hardin had said. "I think Roman's on the move. We're going after him, Alette. We've got a plan. It's—it's a good one, I think."

She hesitated a moment before answering. "Well. I know you wouldn't act on anything less."

"That's probably more of a vote of confidence than I deserve."

"If he's moving on his plan, he likely summoned Mercedes Cook here to be part of it. When you confront him, you'll make provisions for facing her as well, won't you?"

"How many vampires is he likely to have with him at any given moment? I've only ever seen him by himself. He has followers, but he seems to travel and act alone. He finds his minions where he goes."

"That's one of the mysteries, isn't it? I have no idea who else he might have along. You might be facing an army."

I groaned. "I'm thinking part of the plan should be a well-defended escape route."

"See, I knew you'd have thought this through," Alette said pleasantly. I wished I could see her face, to see, and smell, what kind of anxiety she was hiding.

"All these years, it all comes down to this."

She chuckled. "As someone who has lived quite a number of years longer than you, my dear, it rarely all comes down to 'this.' You'll make yourself sick with worry if you aren't careful."

"Too late," I grumbled.

"Just remember, you are Regina Luporum and we all have great faith in you." I couldn't tell if she was making fun of me.

Regina Luporum: Queen of the Wolves. Based on the legend of the wolf who mothered Romulus and Remus, she was a werewolf who'd helped found Rome, who'd defended her kind against all comers. A twenty-eight-hundred-year-old Babylonian vampire bestowed the label on me; a three-thousand-year-old vampire made it stick. Destiny, indeed. Sometimes I wasn't sure I believed in her at all. Other times, I *needed* to believe in her. Believing that someone like me had done something like this before made it seem a bit more possible.

"I still don't know what I think about that."

"Well, if the rest of us do, it doesn't matter what you think, does it? Kitty. Katherine. Do be careful."

"You'll let me know if you hear anything through the grapevine?"

"Oh yes, certainly. And I won't say anything about what you're up to until I hear from you."

"Thank you, Alette. For everything."

I hung up before I could hear any more wishes for good luck. We'd either have it or we wouldn't, at this point.

"You okay?" Ben asked, glancing at me. I was leaning forward, my head in my hands. I wanted to *run,* to let it all go. But I had work to do.

"She's one of the most powerful vampires I know. Why am I doing this and not her?"

"Because Roman's been targeting you?"

Right. I was the one with the radio show.

We continued on to New Moon. I had one last meeting tonight.

ANGELO WAS already there. I'd called and asked to see him so I could warn him in person—without warning him. I'd told Detective Hardin what was going on, and I'd told Alette, because I trusted them. I didn't trust Angelo.

I would have told his predecessor, Rick.

Lurking in the back near my usual table, Angelo was clearly uncomfortable, scowling at his regular food supply, all the people off-limits to him here. He could only be here at all because I'd invited him. He leaned against the wall, his hands shoved into the pockets of a suit jacket, which he wore over a turtleneck.

He called himself the "acting" Master of Denver. But really, he was in charge, since none of us had heard from Rick, the previous Master, since last year when he ran off on a religious quest, joining a secret order of vampire priests at the Vatican. We'd all been a little shocked at that one. That description wasn't fair—it made him sound crazy. I didn't think he was crazy. But he'd been around for five hundred years and took the long view of things, and he thought he could do more good as a vampire priest than he could staying here and helping me. Than protecting Denver, which after all was only one city. I would have loved to have him here for this. I could have asked him for advice—he was one of the few people who'd ever successfully stood up to Roman. He'd know what to do now, and whether or not this trap we were setting was a good idea.

But I didn't even have a phone number for Rick. I was on my own, and all Denver had was Angelo, who preferred being a minion and hadn't looked happy once since stepping up as Master.

Ben stopped at the bar to talk to Shaun and get us drinks while I approached Angelo.

"Hey," I said, trying to sound upbeat.

He glared at me. He looked young, but by my guess he was a couple of hundred years old. He cultivated the stylish ennui a lot of vampires did, but I never forgot they studied everything around them, and they remembered.

"What's wrong?" he asked.

"Why should anything be wrong?"

"You look like you're being hunted. Well, you are, given all the trouble you've been stirring up, but you don't usually look it."

My lip curled. "Have a seat."

Grimacing to show how beneath him this was, he pulled out a chair and flopped into it, sprawling. I sat a bit more primly, hands folded in front of me.

"Mercedes Cook is back in the country," I said. "I don't know for sure that she's headed for Denver, but she might be."

His foot started tapping, a show of nerves. "Great. Excellent. Well then. You remember what happened the last time she came through town, don't you?"

I said, "She orchestrated a civil war to try to destroy Rick but ended up destroying Arturo instead." Arturo, previous Master of Denver before Rick. Roman had never been able to get his hands on this city. *My* city.

"She still likely has her eye on the city. You know that, don't you?"

"Yes."

"What am I supposed to do?"

"I don't know, Angelo. What do you want to do?"

He turned away. "I want to stay out of it. I want to

stay safe, and I want to stay out. It's your fault for bringing this down on us."

Ben arrived then, beers in hand. "I guess you told him," he said, eyeing Angelo warily.

"She probably won't even come to Denver," I said. "What are the odds?"

"I can console myself that she'll likely attack you before she comes after me. Canary in the coal mine. Early warning system." He smiled as if this pleased him.

I winced. "I'm not going to be here. I've got some work to do in Albuquerque. An interview for the show." Could vampires smell lies? I worked hard not to look into his eyes, not to let him capture me with his hypnotic gaze, and thereby control me.

He pointed at me. "There's a reason vampires do not have day jobs—so to speak. Playing the Long Game is a full-time occupation."

"I'm not playing. I'm trying to throw the board over."

"Oh, you're playing, whether you like it or not. Be aware, when you go away on this trip of yours, the city might not be the same when you get back."

He almost surprised me into meeting his gaze. Instead I picked a spot on his swept-back hair and glared. "Well. That's ominous."

"It's supposed to be!" He swept a hand through already mussed hair. "I'm not strong enough to stand up to Mercedes Cook. I'm just telling you."

I thought he was, but he was scared, a vampire raised on terrifying stories of the Long Game and Dux

Bellorum and what happened to weak vampires who got in the way.

"You just have to hold the fort for a few days. You can do that."

He stood, stared down at me. "I'm looking at you, and it feels like I'm never going to see you again. You're such . . . my goodness, you're trying so hard, it's like watching a child try to build a cathedral. You're like Joan of Arc. You're doomed."

"Angelo—what's gotten into you?"

"Oh, don't worry about me." His smile was tight, cruel. "I've looked after myself this long, I'm sure I can manage for a while longer. Good evening to you all."

He stalked out of the place like he was on a mission.

"What the hell was that all about?" Ben asked, watching after him.

I wanted to rush over to Psalm 23, the vampire-owned nightclub and hunting ground, and find someone to ask what was wrong with Angelo. But I didn't have time.

"Let's finish our drinks and get out of here."

I tried to sip slowly, to enjoy the atmosphere, looking around at this thing we'd made. Ben and I started the place to be neutral ground, a safe haven where the members of our pack could gather as human beings, where they wouldn't be inclined to let their wolfish instincts overwhelm them. The plan had been a success, and being here usually gave me a warm feeling of pride. But tonight, this all felt suddenly fragile. Mercedes

Cook and her cohort would like nothing better than to come into Denver, take over the vampire Family, and shut this place down.

That was what I fought for, and why I wanted to stop Roman. Good to have the reminder.

Finally ready to leave, I nudged Ben. "Go on ahead. I'm going to talk to Shaun."

"You want company for that?"

"Naw. Don't want to scare him."

He nodded. "Right." He squeezed my hand, looking as grim as I felt.

Leaning on the bar, I waited for Shaun to finish pouring a couple of glasses of wine for a pair of after-work professionals, a man and woman who seemed to be deep into an evening of flirting. I wished them well.

"What's up?" he said, coming over.

He was another manifestation of my good luck: if I hadn't been able to win him over when I came back to Denver, I never would have been able to confront the old abusive pack alphas, and I never would have been able to take over the pack and build what we'd done here.

I said, "Hey. Shaun. I just wanted you to know—if anything happens to us, you've got New Moon."

"Yeah, I've got you covered until you get back—"

"No. I mean, it's yours. It's in the will and everything. Ben did the paperwork, and I thought you should know. I hope you'll look after the pack, too, but that's going to be up to everyone else."

His expression was slack. "But you're coming back."

"That's the plan. But, you know, just in case." I'd fed Shaun and the others the interview story, not the real story. Not because I didn't trust them, but because I didn't want them following me, trying to help. I wanted to protect them.

"What's really going on?" he asked. He could smell the anxiety on me. We'd known each other for years, human and wolf. We'd seen each other naked. I couldn't hide.

"I can't say," I said. "I'm sorry."

"Kitty—" He glared, and it was a challenge. I just stood, looking back calmly, waiting for him to settle. After a moment, he dropped his gaze.

"See you in a couple of days," I said, and brushed his hand before turning to follow Ben out.

Chapter 4

WE MET at Cormac's place at dawn.

He had a second-story studio apartment off the Boulder turnpike and I-25. I sometimes worried about him being stuck by himself in a run-down place in that part of town, but he didn't seem to mind. I wasn't sure he even noticed. It was out of the way, nobody bothered him. *I* was the one who wanted the nice house in the country. He probably didn't understand that any more than I understood him.

Tina hugged her jacket around her against the morning chill as we went to his door. The sky was gray, misty, but it looked like we'd have a dry drive south. It would take about seven hours—we'd get there before nightfall, in time to scout the area before Roman made an appearance after dark. We assumed he'd have non-vampire minions keep watch for him. Our plan was to avoid them as much as possible, and distract them from Tina otherwise.

"Come in," Cormac called after Ben knocked.

"Should you be leaving your door unlocked?" I said as we pushed in. I'd never get used to this, the tiny kitchen in one corner; the slept-in futon with makeshift bed stand; secondhand bookshelves filled with books, boxes, jars, and artifacts; an open closet leaking clothes, and a table stacked with just about everything. It all seemed so temporary. The place smelled old.

"I knew you were coming," he answered. He was busy. Two crossbows sat on the rickety kitchen table. Several spears—five-foot lengths of wood sharpened to nasty-looking points—leaned against the wall nearby. He was packing a bundle of a dozen or so steel-pointed, wooden crossbow bolts into a leather quiver. "I could use some help loading this."

Each of us took an armload and managed to get it down the stairs to the parking lot without dropping anything. It was a bit disconcerting seeing Ben handle the spears easily, clasped in an arm, leaning against his shoulder, perfectly balanced. He kept a gun at home, and in the glove box of the car. He'd taught me to shoot, but I didn't enjoy it. I forgot sometimes that he'd grown up with them. Heavy weaponry would never be second nature to me the way it was for these two. I wondered what *exactly* the rules said about ex-cons and weapons possession, if it was just guns Cormac wasn't allowed to own anymore or if it was anything. He didn't seem too concerned.

"Um, I should probably mention Detective Hardin wants to come with us."

A crossbow in each hand, Cormac looked at me sidelong. "Why'd you tell her what we're doing?"

"She asked?" I said. "I thought she could help. Run interference if the cops get involved."

He grumbled, but didn't argue. Ben and I exchanged a glance; me encouraging him to back me up, him being noncommittal. That was the thing with Ben: he was never going to take sides between us.

Ben went to the trunk of the sedan, but Cormac called out, "I'm taking the Jeep."

"There's not enough room for all of us in the Jeep—"

"I'll follow you down, in the Jeep."

The Jeep had Cormac's stash of surprises; of course he wouldn't leave it behind. He arranged things the way he liked while we watched. "I just need a couple more things."

We went with him back up to his apartment. Turned out, Cormac had collected his weapons. Now Amelia had to collect hers.

Cormac stood back from the table, his arms crossed, frowning under his mustache. The items seemed arcane to me—of course they did. Leather bags filled with who knew what, a couple of books, several amulets on chains laid out. A metal box with the lid open. I stepped forward to see what he'd taken from it, items that had obviously caught his attention.

One was a bronze coin strung on a leather cord, damaged by slashes and hatch marks beaten into it with a hammer. One of the coins of Dux Bellorum, talismans that Roman gave to his followers to identify them, to mark them. I was pretty sure this one had belonged to Kumarbis, the three-thousand-year-old vampire who'd created Roman.

The second item was a pair of goggles, dark glass set in leather on a well-worn strap.

"Is that what I think it is?" I asked.

"Yep."

I'd ripped those goggles off the head of a demon. A real, honest-to-badness demon summoned from some other realm to wreak havoc, an imposing warrior woman with more weapons slung about her person than even Cormac could manage. I was sure she was working for Roman—or for whomever Roman was working for.

Dux Bellorum—the leader of war, the general. But as Cormac once said, who was the Caesar?

"Have you figured out if they do anything?"

"Nope," he said. "But that doesn't mean they don't."

I picked them up. Didn't put them on, because that would have felt really weird—best not meddle with items stolen from very dangerous demon women. But I held them to the window, looking distantly through the shaded lenses. They were almost opaque. I couldn't see a thing.

"You want to see what Tina makes of 'em?" Cormac asked, nodding at the psychic.

I offered them to her. Wisely, she approached with caution. "You want to tell me about them first?"

"I'm more interested in what you can tell me," Cormac answered.

She raised her hand, and I set the goggles across her palm. She wouldn't close her fingers around them. Eyes shut, her brow furrowed and her lips pursed. Not just worried, she seemed almost in pain.

"No," she murmured. "I don't think I want to go there." She hurried to set them back on the table, then backed away. Hugging herself, she shivered.

Cormac shrugged and put them back into the box.

I didn't recognize the third item on the table. It was a Maltese cross, a couple of inches across, made of polished bronze, simple and roughly made, strung on a leather cord.

"What's that?" I asked.

He held it up. It glinted in the faint morning light coming in through the window blinds. "That is an amulet that turns magic spells back on themselves."

Huh. "That sounds useful."

"Yeah, could be."

"And where did you pick that up?"

He turned a rare, wry grin. "Long story," he said. Experience told me that was all I was going to get out of him.

He considered the items on the table for another long moment, and finally murmured softly. If I hadn't been a werewolf I wouldn't have heard it at all. "Bring everything. We never know what we'll need, so bring it all." The diction was careful, formal, different from his usual curt speech. "Right, then, in you all go." He—she— packed the items back into the lockbox.

Tina leaned close to me. "That's Amelia, isn't it?

That's who I'm pretending to be?" Her daunted expression no doubt came from thinking about trying to replicate that precise, old-school diction.

"Just be yourself," Cormac said, and it was definitely him this time, brusque and to the point. "Roman won't know the difference."

She seemed thoughtful. "It's not straightforward possession, is it? There are two people there, two beings. I've never seen anything like it."

"Amelia and I worked out a deal," he said.

"Deal—what kind of deal?"

Cormac was loading items from the table—the lockbox, various satchels of crystal and herbs and jars presumably containing potions and whatnot—into a duffel bag and pretended to ignore her. Tina knew better than to push.

We piled outside while Cormac put on his leather jacket, took one last look around the apartment, and locked the door behind him.

I was about to call Hardin when her car, an unmarked sedan, pulled into the parking lot. I went out to meet her.

"This feels like the start of a movie where everything goes horribly wrong," she said in greeting. She had both hands wrapped tight around a tall cup of coffee. She smelled of office work, too much coffee, breath mints.

"It does, doesn't it?" I said, grinning. "You're just in time to get in on deciding what car you want to ride in."

"Tina's with me," Cormac said. "We can figure out just how we're going to play this."

That meant the rest of us were *not* with him.

"Detective Hardin, I don't know if you remember Tina McCannon?"

The two women shook hands and exchanged polite greetings before Tina turned to join Cormac at the Jeep.

"You going to be okay?" I asked her quietly.

"Sure." She shrugged. "He's kind of cute, you know."

"Then have fun." Should I warn her? Should I warn *him*?

Cormac, the man himself, shut the Jeep's back door and gave us a cursory glance before climbing in the driver's seat.

"You did tell him I was coming," Hardin asked.

"Yeah. Briefly."

She pursed her lips, considering. "Separate cars. Good idea. I'll be asleep in the backseat if you need me." She stomped off to Ben's car and climbed into the back.

"Keep your phones on," Cormac said through the lowered window, then started the engine and pulled into the drive. Tina waved back at us.

"This is going to be a very long drive," Ben observed.

I sighed. Yes, it was.

SEVEN HOURS, a couple of stops for gas, and a terrible fast-food lunch later, we pulled into Albuquerque in the middle of the afternoon. Apart from a week a few years ago when I was on the road, I'd never spent time here.

The place was an unlikely city in the middle of a very wide desert. Kind of depressing.

Tina pulled me aside at one of the stops. She seemed to be surviving the drive with Cormac, but she obviously needed to talk. We walked across the gas station parking lot with the excuse that we needed to stretch our legs. She'd put her hair up, and was still bundled in a sweater and jacket. I wondered if the heater in the Jeep worked. She was right on the edge of saying something, trying to find the words. I waited.

Finally she said, "Anyone who has any kind of relationship with him is going to have to have a relationship with both of them. Does he know that?"

I looked at her, part astonished, part horrified. "Are you considering it? A relationship? With Cormac?"

"I don't know—he's got that rugged thing going. But I'm kind of thinking he's already taken."

I had absolutely no response to that. They were both grown-ups, they could do what they wanted. But I shied away from trying to actually picture the reality of the pairing. I'd had my chance with the guy. Long time ago now. But he still looked at me sometimes in a way that made me wonder.

Let it go.

"Do you ever hear from Jeffrey?" I asked. Jeffrey Miles, another professional psychic, a good friend, and another victim of that damned reality show. Like Tina, he'd been shot, but he hadn't recovered. Tina could communicate with the dead—sometimes.

She smiled, but the expression was sad. "Sometimes I

think I do. Just the feeling that he's looking over my shoulder. Nothing in words, you know?"

"Yeah. I have my own ghosts looking over my shoulder. We could maybe use a few guardian angels looking out for us on this one."

This seemed to cheer her up. "Maybe Anastasia's out there keeping an eye on us."

Wasn't that a nice thought? Ben waved us back over to the cars, he and I switched driving, and we continued on.

We arrived in the city with a few hours of daylight left to scout, to choose our ground. To set the trap.

Cormac and Amelia had negotiated a meeting place at the southwest edge of town, at Petroglyph National Monument. I couldn't decide if this was good or bad. My impulse toward safety wanted us to meet in a very crowded restaurant or shopping mall, surrounded by lots of people, witnesses who meant everyone would be on good behavior, maybe impede potential fireworks. On the other hand, if there were going to be fireworks, best we go where no one would get hurt, yes?

Both Cormac and Roman, I gathered, wanted a location where they had a good line of sight, with few to no places to hide. Their mutual suspicion wasn't, apparently, suspicious. Powerful magicians always acted this carefully, with this level of paranoia, Amelia assured us. Powerful magicians, and hunters. Cormac fit right in.

The place was bleak, dried-up sage and scattered juniper on a chalky plain, lined by low mesas of volcanic rock. The tract housing across the highway seemed unlikely, and a dusty smell tickled the back of my throat. The spot they'd chosen was a parking and picnic area a quarter mile or so from the visitors center. Nice place for a weekend outing, I thought. It would look lonely and desolate after dark.

We wanted to scout the site, but didn't want to be seen scouting the area. Roman would have his own people out here, and they had the advantage—they knew us, and we didn't know them. Ben and I walked the perimeter of the immediate area, taking careful stock of the scents as we went. We weren't walking side by side, but staggered, a few paces apart, both of us looking in different directions—wolves on the hunt.

"No lycanthropes," Ben said after a minute. His chin was up, his nose working, taking in the air. "Wolf or otherwise. I'd have thought this region would be filled with werewolves, there's so much open space. Nobody'd bother them."

"A few are around, but they're not organized. I asked Rick about it once. He said there's too much competition, too many other kinds of magic. Native American peoples maintained more of their traditions here. The Spanish and Mexican *curandero* traditions stayed strong. There's too much magical protection against things like werewolves. At least, there's a reputation for it. Keeps the riffraff out." As far as I knew, Albuquerque didn't have a Master vampire. That may have been part of why Roman agreed to meet here.

"Huh. I want to get the hell out of here, but I don't

think it's from any magical protections keeping me out."

"Yeah, I know what you mean." I smelled lizards and rattlesnakes, and the dust made my skin itch.

We didn't smell anything unusual. If Roman had followers in the area, they were well hidden, or so entirely human that we didn't notice them.

We met up with Hardin, who'd stayed by the road, and walked back to the cars. I caught her patting her jacket pockets and scowling. "I picked a hell of a week to try to quit smoking," she muttered. "I'm going to be reaching for a pack for the rest of my life." Finally, she stopped looking for the absent cigarettes, crossed her arms, and scowled.

After our survey, we retreated to an innocuous fast-food restaurant for another bad meal and last-minute planning. The mundane noises and goings-on around us seemed out of place, disconcerting. How could things possibly be *normal*? The place smelled like rancid grease. Most fast-food restaurants did. Cormac was the only one of us who ate much; the rest of us picked at fries and stared sullenly at a diagram he was drawing on the back of a napkin.

Cormac had sketched out the general layout of the parking lot, picnic tables, and outbuildings, and marked X's where everyone would start out. We'd keep the Jeep hidden, since it was recognizably Cormac's. Hardin would drive it off site, then keep watch over the outskirts of the area. Ben's sedan was nondescript enough it could stay—ostensibly Tina would have had

said, handing Tina the mirrored cross amulet. "He tries throwing anything at you, this should protect you."

"Should?" she said, uncertain, running her fingers over the smooth surface. I wondered what she saw in it. "Wow, this is really old," she murmured.

"You can still back out of this."

"No, I want to stop this guy as much as you do."

Cormac nodded, satisfied.

"We likely to get hassled by the cops?" I asked Hardin.

"I checked in with a friend at the local PD, and they do regular car patrols along the highway, but it's not one of their high-crime areas. We should be okay, unless one of the locals calls in weird activity."

"It's worth the risk," Ben the attorney said. "They can't pin anything worse than misdemeanor trespassing on us if we get caught in the park after dark, if we're not doing anything more illegal than that."

"Is conspiracy to murder a vampire more illegal?" I asked. The excuse we'd give to anyone who called us on why we were at the park after dark was way down on my list of things to think about right now.

"Hey, assuming we get him, there won't be a body and no way to prove what happened."

That was logical. Didn't make me feel any better.

Cormac glanced at his watch, then out the place's big picture windows, as if he didn't trust what the watch had told him and needed external confirmation. The sun was setting, casting a muted orange light across the sky. "Let's get going. Everyone good?"

No. I was not good. But I wasn't going to get any
better than I was right now, so I supposed I was good.
Nobody else said anything, yes or no. My limbs were
stiff with tension.

We should Change, my Wolf said from behind
the bars I kept around her most of the time. *We can be
stronger. This is a hunt, let me hunt.*

It's not the time for that, I murmured.

But it might be, before the night is over.

If it came to that, yes, it might very well be time for it.

Chapter 5

A STARK DESERT sunset haunted the sky, unfiltered light across a washed-out landscape granting a red tinge to the dust. The breeze had the chill of spring and smelled chalky. The wildness of it called to Wolf, but I shivered and crossed my arms, unwilling to expose myself, uncertain what else lay out there.

Ben and I were hidden in a stand of junipers near the mesa, too far away to be of any use if things went bad. Hardin waited at the other end of the mesa with a pair of binoculars. I could smell her, but her nervous energy seemed eager, full of anticipation. She was a hunter, too.

Tina had driven herself over in Ben's sedan, the only car in the parking lot right now. I hoped Roman wouldn't notice the Colorado plates and grow suspicious.

The reason Cormac wasn't worried about hiding: he had some kind of spell or potion or thing from Amelia. It didn't make him invisible, but it somehow convinced onlookers that he wasn't there. I didn't understand it, but I also didn't see him, so it must have been working. I smelled him, his leather and determination, but only because I knew he was there.

It didn't matter, because Roman the vampire would sense all our heartbeats. He'd smell our blood on the wind. He'd read our minds across the distance. We weren't fooling anyone. Cormac insisted we didn't have to fool him—Roman would stay because he'd be curious, no matter what, and Cormac only needed one clear shot.

I tried to tell myself to stop worrying.

Tina sat at one of the picnic tables, her back very straight, her hands folded on the surface in front of her. She looked like an arcane practitioner, a modern psychic channeling a Victorian woman. She must have learned something about Amelia on the trip down.

"What if *he's* wearing body armor?" I'd said, cranky.

"You ever see him wear body armor?" Cormac countered.

I hadn't. Huh.

We wouldn't see him approach. Roman was a vampire, and they had strange ways of moving, of hiding in shadows, of making themselves invisible. Roman would simply appear, maybe standing off a moment to take stock. We wouldn't see him until he wanted to be seen. Yet another of our disadvantages.

We waited half an hour past the agreed-on time. This was okay; we expected it. He wanted Amelia—

Tina, all of us—off balance. He wanted the higher ground, the control. The desert air grew cold, and as time passed Tina hugged her coat around her.

I smelled Roman before I saw him. An even colder twist in the already chill air, a sharp odor that smelled dead, but not rotten. A heart stilled, but preserved. A corpse, but one with a mind, will, and motion. Close, and getting closer. Ben's nose flared; he smelled it, too. Tina looked across the park the same time I did—she felt it.

I couldn't risk saying anything to warn the others. The sound would carry. We had to wait and see what happened.

He appeared, a shadow taking form, breaking off from the night beyond the orange glow of the lights in the parking lot. He was dressed in black, long coat flapping around him, arms loose at his side. His dark hair was close cut, militaristic, and he walked with purpose across the asphalt.

He stopped about twenty paces away from the picnic table, as if giving Tina time to notice him.

Tina stood, mouth open, and I was glad we'd forgotten to warn her that Roman would likely appear out of nowhere. He'd have expected her to be surprised, and so she was. He actually smiled at her, a thin and somehow calming expression. Setting her at ease after the pain of so much anticipation. In our few encounters, I wasn't sure I'd ever seen him smile with anything other than disdain.

He came closer until he stood across the table from

her. He could have reached out and touched her. She was frozen, staring—had she forgotten not to look into his eyes? I couldn't tell from here. She smelled afraid.

"You're Tina McCannon," he said. "Not Amelia Parker. Or—are you? It's my understanding you're able to channel the dead." He waited for an explanation.

Now, *now* she should get out of the way, let Cormac take his shot—

Before she could answer him, a shiny black town car pulled into the parking lot. Incongruous, suspicious, it stopped without turning into a marked slot. Somebody having a look around before getting chauffeured to the airport? Seemed unlikely. I braced to run—but I didn't know which way to go. Help Tina, stop Roman—or what? She should duck, Cormac should shoot *now*, while we were all distracted.

The car also attracted Roman's attention. He looked over, frowning. So, not part of his plan, either. The uniformed driver got out, stepped over to open the passenger door, and stood at attention as Mercedes Cook emerged.

She looked like something out of a film clip, pale and beautiful, shining with her own light in the dark. Her red curls framed her ivory face and fell to her shoulders, and she wore a long, thick shawl over a black calf-length dress, an outfit that would have looked brilliant in New York City but seemed far too glamorous for this obscure stretch of desert. She glared across the space to Roman, her red lips turned in a smile. I started to dash forward—all I wanted was to get my teeth around her throat. Ben grabbed my arm, held me back.

Mercedes strolled across the asphalt, chin up and haughty, focusing her attention on Roman. Tina was backing up. Probably smart.

The actress looked down her nose. She had stage presence in spades and brought it all to bear, commanding attention. But the way her hands clutched her shawl, the tightness across her shoulders—she was angry, or scared, and trying to hide it.

She stopped and regarded Roman. I got the feeling that each of them was waiting for the other to speak, and neither wanted to break that silence.

"I'd heard you were here," Mercedes said finally. She gave Tina the merest dismissive glance. "Recruiting."

"Yes. And?" Roman said in a tone of annoyance.

That didn't seem to be the response she wanted. "You could have asked me first."

"That wasn't necessary," Roman said, his lip curled.

Mercedes rounded on him. "Not necessary? You need me, sir! You'd not have gotten this far without me!" Her fists were clenched; her bravado seemed to be masking terror.

"If not for you, I'd have found another tool," he said, eyeing Tina as if to say, *like this one.*

What in the world was going on here?

I wasn't going to find out, because Tina dropped, covering her head and hiding under the picnic table, and

Cormac appeared from behind a nearby shelter, aiming the crossbow. He fired.

Roman turned to look, as if he'd heard the weapon's string vibrate. He stepped, and almost dodged it. Stumbling back, he immediately straightened and glared at his attacker. He did not, alas, turn into a pile of decayed ash. The bolt hung from his right shoulder, a full handbreadth from his heart. The hit wasn't going to kill him. So close.

Snarling, Cormac dropped the bow and swung the next off his shoulder, already loaded, and fired again. But Roman was running. I didn't see where he went—he was a shadow, and all the shadows in the park seemed to get bigger, to swallow him up.

This time when I launched myself in a run, Ben didn't stop me. In fact, he was right on my tail. I headed for Tina with some high-and-mighty notion that I could get in front of her and take whatever bullet was coming. I could take damage, she couldn't, and we had to keep her safe. Ben aimed for Cormac. He had a stake in each hand.

Wolf could run faster. Wolf had better weapons for this. But I didn't have time to shift.

Ben arrived at Cormac's side and took a defensive covering position while Cormac winched back and reloaded the first crossbow.

Tina looked back to see me skid to a stop next to the table. I reached out with my hand, which she grabbed, and I pulled her out from under the table and shoved her behind me, backing away in an attempt to escape.

I expected Roman to appear in front of us—he'd be moving so fast I wouldn't see him. He'd be a blur, a shadow shifting when a light turns on. I took short breaths, smelling as much as I could, tracking patterns in the air, which was suddenly filled with vampire. Calm, keep calm. I knew where Mercedes was, and I could only spot where Roman had gone if I could breathe and catch his scent. Standing tall, I hoped he'd go for me instead of Tina. A stray crossbow bolt wouldn't kill me.

But Roman didn't come after us. When he appeared again, a running blur, he went to Mercedes. She was ready for him, her teeth bared, her expression lethal. He made to slip behind her, arm around her neck for a quick snap and takedown, but she ducked, whirled past his shoulder, and got her mouth to his neck, fangs ready for a deadly cut. She wanted his blood, and therefore his power. If he'd been an inch slower, she might have had a chance, but his arm was up under her chin, shoving.

After that, I couldn't follow the movements, which might have been choreographed, a dance instead of a fight, arms reaching, bodies slipping around each other. They dodged every strike the other offered, as if they could both predict a dozen or more moves ahead of what the other had planned.

Mercedes was the kind of person who recruited other people to do her dirty work. She usually watched from on high, her hands immaculate while chaos churned beneath her. I had assumed she couldn't fight. My mistake. They were both old. Ancient, experienced, powerful. As much as I'd dealt with vampires, I hadn't really understood.

"If they'd finish each other off, that would be *ideal*," I murmured. I wasn't macho. I didn't have to get in the killing blow. It would be enough to watch.

Cormac must have thought this was a possibility, because he turned the newly loaded crossbow toward the car driver, who had a wicked three-foot-long spear in one hand and a semiautomatic pistol in the other. The pistol was up, aimed at Cormac and Ben.

"Ben, he might have silver!" I yelled, because he'd put himself in front of Cormac, thinking he could take the bullet. He couldn't, not if the guy had silver bullets. I didn't want Ben to test that.

"Police, drop your weapon!" Now Hardin was in on it, her own gun raised in one hand, her badge and ID held up in the other. Never mind that she was Denver PD, not Albuquerque, and didn't have jurisdiction here. The driver didn't know that.

He looked at her, bug-eyed.

A woman screamed—Mercedes. My first thought was, aha, at last and good riddance, Roman had ripped her head off or drained her borrowed blood. But no— they stood apart now; she was clutching her throat, and he was holding an object: a coin on a leather cord. He'd ripped it from around her neck and threw it to the side like it was trash.

"This was never about you, and it was never about power." He said this calmly, in the tone of someone laying off an employee. Mercedes stared at him, eyes round and in shock. She'd probably never been rejected in her life.

"You can't do this," she said, her ordinarily powerful voice gone reedy as she struggled for breath. "I have been loyal, for centuries I've followed you—"

"You overstepped yourself in London. You should have known."

Mercedes's expression turned stricken. "No. Oh no, no—"

Violence hung in the air, nasty and imminent. I bared my teeth, and Wolf tore at my gut. *Change, attack, fight—*

No, this wasn't our fight. We were caught in the middle of something else entirely.

The wind changed, a slap on my face, and I smelled brimstone, heat, fire, anger. I dropped to a crouch, nose up, searching for this new enemy. Meanwhile, Tina screamed. It happened in a second—the wind, her scream, and me turning to look up into the face of a tall woman, monstrously tall, and powerful. She wore leather and weapons, spears and daggers, swords and javelins, all wood and silver, all made to fight monsters. Dark-tinted goggles strapped over her short-cropped hair covered her eyes, even in the dark. She backhanded Tina across the face, sending her flying a dozen feet. Air left her lungs with a gasp.

Then the demon turned to me and sneered.

Chapter 6

TINA LAY still. Unconscious? Maybe she just had the wind knocked out of her. I hoped. Meanwhile, the demon transferred a weapon—a long spear tipped with a sharp metal point, no doubt laced with silver—from her left hand to her right. I'd met this demon before, and her sole purpose was hunting creatures like me.

"Got new goggles, I see. Nice." I winced. My mouth ran faster than my legs. Last time we met, I'd managed to rip her goggles off—Cormac had them now. Any light at all, even the dim streetlights of the parking lot, left her blind and slowed her down—briefly.

She didn't credit me with an answer, just drew back in order to impale me. The impaling wouldn't kill me—the poison of the silver in my bloodstream would. In the back of my brain, Wolf howled, furious. We could shift, we could attack, we'd driven her off before, we could do it again—

In the time it would take me to turn, run, shift, anything, she'd have me pinned to the ground. I backed away, delaying.

"Do you have a name?" I said, my voice rising. I couldn't disguise my fear. "I keep running into you and I don't know what to call you."

"Won't matter in a second," she said. Her voice rumbled like breaking wood.

I could run. And she could throw that spear. I could charge her, get inside her range. But it would only take a scratch from that silver to kill me. Plus, she had a dozen daggers. No room to fudge this. I sat up from my crouch, bracing to do . . . something. Like, talk more.

"You told me you don't work for Roman, then why are you here, covering his ass? Who do you really work for?"

"You'll never know," she said, and prepared to launch.

"No!" Tina sat up, wobbly. A cut marred her forehead and blood streamed down her face. Metal rivets on the demon's glove had cut her badly. My heart sank, seeing what she was trying to do. She should run away, just get out of here—

The demon turned, Tina charged, grabbed her arm—trying to turn the spear away from me. The demon shook her off easily, smacking her again for good measure, and again Tina fell hard.

But it was enough of a distraction. I grabbed the spear, dropped my weight, and wrenched the weapon out of the demon's hands. Turned the point back on her, stabbed. She smacked it aside with her leather-armored arm, but I kept hold of it. She kicked, and I dodged, but not fast enough. I was fast, but she was a demon from hell. The blow struck my gut, knocked the wind out of me, but I kept my feet.

I had to get close enough to take those goggles—that had worked last time. I braced for the next attack, but the demon suddenly looked up, as if at a call or an alarm. Lips curled, teeth bared—wolflike—she ran, grabbing another spear off the collection of them strapped to her back. This one was sharpened wood, not silver. It couldn't hurt me. She had a different target now.

I ran after her.

Mercedes called a name—her driver, I assumed—and made to retreat to her car. Stricken, the driver looked back and forth between Hardin and his mistress—and the demon.

Cormac stepped up, ignoring Mercedes now to face the demon—shifting his focus to the baddest bad guy. He held a cross in one hand and a burning torch in the other. And where had he gotten a torch? Ah, he'd made one, out of a crossbow bolt and a scrap of cloth. Maybe doused with fluid from a lighter. He had a whole warehouse of useful items in his pockets.

The demon ignored him and continued after the vampire.

Mercedes sprinted, but the demon was faster. A thrusting spear stabbed through her back, driving her off her feet. The point planted in the ground.

"No!" Mercedes growled, an unmusical noise coming from her throat. She grabbed the spear protruding from her chest and twisted, as if she could wrench herself off it. But she was already crumbling. Her hands fell apart, her arms turned to dust. She kept saying *no*, grimacing with bared teeth, lips moving after sound ceased.

The decay of the grave, many hundreds of years of death, caught up with her all at once. Her body, even her clothing, dried, shrank, fell in on itself, and crumbled. Even dying, she was still angry, still fighting, hate and fury written on her face, until her face vanished. Crumbled to dust.

Gone, just like that.

The moment of shocked stillness that came after lasted only a breath. Cormac—Amelia—marched on toward the demon, chanting in Latin. Fearless, as always. Even years after him leaving prison, seeing him weaponless was still odd. Before prison, he'd have had a shotgun in hand, firing over and over, a relentless assault. And it wouldn't have worked, not against the demon.

The demon sneered, hefting another spear from her collection—this one tipped with metal. But she didn't move forward to meet him. She took a step back.

"It's a litany from an exorcism," Tina said. Her voice was hoarse, obviously in pain. She was still bleeding horrendously from the cut on her head. "But since he's not an ordained priest I don't know if it'll work."

I tore off a piece of my shirt and put it on the wound. She hissed, but held the makeshift bandage in place.

Cormac kept on, and again the demon stepped back.

Straightening, she lowered her weapons, waited—and a whirlwind rose around her. Made of smoke and fire, stinking of ash and brimstone, it swirled liked a curtain, a cape. Biting sand reached across the park, and I ducked against it. When the storm collapsed, the demon was gone. A strategic departure. The wind roared for a second, then faded to nothing.

The park turned still, quiet, as if nothing had happened. Not a clump of sagebrush was out of place, not even smashed from all the fighting. The pile of ash that used to be Mercedes had blown away in the whirlwind.

Roman was gone. *He* was the one who'd taken advantage of the distraction to get out. His work here was done, evidently. I supposed I could comfort myself that he deemed us enough of a risk that leaving was a better option than sticking around to finish us off.

Either that, or we simply weren't a threat at all.

Time for roll call. "Ben? Hardin?" I helped Tina to her feet, and we met up with the others.

Ben came over, put a hand on my cheek, leaned in to smell my hair, and I took a deep breath of his scent, which meant home, safety. Maybe things would be okay. His T-shirt had provided the scrap of cloth for the torch. I looked at his shredded shirt, and mine, and had to chuckle. What a pair.

"You're psychic—can't you see these things coming?" Ben demanded. He was fuming. I hoped Tina realized he wasn't angry at her, he was just angry. Burning off anxiety.

"It doesn't work that way!" she shot back. Then, quieter, "You know it doesn't work that way."

"Is everyone okay?" I asked, cutting through.

No one answered right away. I would have been worried, except I could see them all, Ben and Cormac, Tina and Hardin. All awake, all conscious, all catching their breath as we gathered at the edge of the parking lot.

Ben said, "You stopped that thing, right? It's not going to come back?"

He hadn't ever seen the demon before. Cormac and Hardin had. I'd faced her down twice.

Cormac sighed. "I didn't stop her. She decided I wasn't worth fighting. Just like last time." He threw down the torch and stomped out the flame.

The driver of the town car had fallen to his knees, dropped his gun and stake, and held his face in his hands, crying. Mercedes's human servant, grieving. I almost felt sorry for him. Hardin stood nearby, gun holstered and handcuffs in hand, but she seemed to reconsider arresting him. Finally, she picked up his gun from the pavement.

"Get out of here before I change my mind," she said, backing off.

He looked up at her, his expression stark. Made his own calculations and climbed to his feet like a creaking old man. "This isn't over," he said. "You'll pay for this."

"We didn't even kill her!" I exclaimed. He glared at me. It obviously didn't matter.

Hardin crossed her arms. "I'm about to change my mind."

He hurried into his car, started the engine, and swung around on squealing tires.

"Not sure that was the best idea," Cormac said.

"What did you want me to do, shoot him?" Hardin answered.

Cormac raised a brow as if to say yes. Hardin shook her head and turned to the rest of us, focusing on Tina, with the wadded-up cloth clamped on her head. The bandage was soaked red, and blood was still dripping.

"That's going to need stitches," Hardin said.

Tina closed her eyes, sighed. "Ashtoreth," she said. "I don't know if that's her name, or a type of demon. But if you want to call her something, it's Ashtoreth." That was how the psychic thing worked. Flashes of insight, slivers of knowledge. Hardly ever the whole picture. It wasn't predicting the future, it was untangling puzzles.

The name didn't mean anything, but I had a stack of reference books and an Internet connection at home that I was sure would have a listing. But right here we had Amelia, a walking reference library.

Cormac spoke—the words were Amelia's, more precise, less brusque. "The name is a derivation of Astoreth, a Canaanite goddess cast as a demon by later Judeo-Christian mythologists wishing to discredit pagan religions. Some alchemists and demonologists began to use the term to refer to a collection of female or hermaphroditic spirits. She appears in Milton: 'With these in troop came Astoreth, whom the Phoenicians called Astartè, queen of heav'n, with crescent horns.'"

I didn't have the whole thing memorized like Amelia did, but I'd read *Paradise Lost*. This sounded like the listing of demons, the followers of Lucifer. As if this could get any more ominous. This still didn't tell me anything more about her. It didn't give me anything useful about *stopping* her. She was little more than a metaphor. I couldn't do anything about it, I could just handle what was right here in front of me.

I hunted over the ground where Roman and Mercedes had had their confrontation. The place had gone back to desolate and peaceful so quickly, it was hard to imagine that anything had happened here. I wasn't sure I'd be able to find it—but there it was, a dull glint against the pale desert earth. Mercedes's coin, a bronze circle the size of a nickel, old face and writing barely visible.

"Does someone have a hammer we can use on this thing?"

Cormac did, in the back of his Jeep. As we had with all the other coins of Dux Bellorum we'd found, we put it against the concrete and smashed the hell out of it, until the face and writing were mangled smears of bronze, negating its connection to Roman.

"Okay, now we go to the doctor," I said, pulling Tina toward the car.

So, we hadn't stopped Roman, but we'd all gotten out alive. For now, I counted this one a victory.

* * *

WE RECONVENED at a local urgent care. After some discussion, Tina and Hardin went in by themselves, because Hardin thought the whole troop of us would have looked suspicious, and two people could keep their stories straight better than five of us. Especially if one of them was a cop. Not that "tripped and fell" was that hard of a story to keep straight. That was what they were going to say, not "smacked by a demon in the middle of a vampire war." Damn, this needed to be a movie. No one would believe it.

While we waited for them, the three of us claimed a booth at a Denny's down the road. The coffee was terrible and delicious at the same time. I had finally stopped shaking from spent adrenaline.

"Well?" I said finally.

"Could have gone worse," was Cormac's curt assessment.

I snorted. Technically, he was right—we could all be dead.

Cormac added, "My second shot would have got him if that other vampire hadn't shown up."

I let loose. "And what was that all about? What the hell was going on there?" Whatever it was, we didn't have a clue, and wasn't that always the case. This was just such a dramatic revelation of it.

"Dissention in the ranks," Ben said. "We ought to be happy. Maybe the Long Game isn't as far along as we thought."

Cormac said, "In case you didn't notice, if this was

a sign of dissention, Roman pretty much quashed it. Him and that demon."

What all this suggested to me: not only was the Long Game far along, Roman was getting ready for the home stretch, weeding out his own ranks. Our attempt at an end run had failed. And if Roman really was focused on stopping his opposition—

"We have to get back home," I said. "Right now."

Chapter 7

FIRST THING, I called Shaun, and got sent straight to voice mail.

"Shaun, call me, it's important." I sent a couple of texts for good measure. I called New Moon next, even though it was after closing and no one would be there. I left the same message.

Ben and Cormac had ordered a plate of bacon, but I wasn't hungry. I nibbled on the same piece because it was something to do.

"He's probably gone to bed," Ben reassured me. "Turned off his phone for the night."

"He doesn't usually turn off his phone."

"I'm sure he's okay," he said.

"We really need to get going," I insisted. Cormac didn't say anything.

Ben stopped me from calling Cheryl. She was probably fine, he kept saying, and wouldn't appreciate being woken up at this hour.

However, it was a perfect time to call the vampires.

Angelo wasn't answering his phone, either. Trouble was, I didn't know if that meant something was wrong, or if he was just ignoring me. Surely as tense as things had gotten, he wouldn't just ignore me.

Hardin called—Tina was patched up. We drove over to meet them in the parking lot of the urgent care. Tina looked awful, a bandage over her face, a splint on her nose, arm in a sling. She moved slowly.

"Are you okay?" I asked. Why did we only ever ask that question when things were clearly not okay? A bit wobbly, she leaned on the trunk of the sedan.

"Oh yeah, few weeks it'll all heal. I got some of the good drugs." She tried a weak, sleepy smile. Her voice was muffled, nasal, from the bandages. And the drugs, probably.

Hardin announced the litany: "Five stitches on the forehead, cracked nose, dislocated shoulder, and a couple of cracked ribs. No concussion, thank goodness. I keep telling her the appropriate response to questions is, 'You should see the other guy.'"

And this was why we shouldn't have dragged a normal, nonsupernaturally strong, untrained person into this. "I'm really sorry. I never should have asked you to come—"

"I offered," Tina said. "I had a choice. It could have happened to any of us. Kitty, it's okay. Don't apologize."

I'd keep apologizing forever and it wouldn't be enough.

"We're heading back to Denver," I said. "Right now.

I'm worried Roman's going to take the fight back home."

"What exactly are you expecting to happen?" Hardin asked.

"If I knew that, I wouldn't be worried," I said. Roman was on the move. Mercedes was on the move, or at least she had been. That demon—Ashtoreth—was out and about. We must have kicked over someone's sand castle to get that reaction.

I wanted to be home, to brace for whatever happened next. Roman always kicked back.

Of course, getting back home "right now" involved a seven-hour drive on no sleep. I argued with myself—maybe we should stop, hole up in a hotel room, get some rest before leaving. Surely everything would be okay.

But I called Shaun again, and he still wasn't answering. I scrolled through the contacts list on my phone. I knew a lot of people. Usually that gave me a warm happy feeling. I had friends, a support network. Right now, though, I'd put every single one of those people at risk.

Hardin declared that she would drive the sedan, with Tina resting in the backseat. They could travel at an easy pace and stop if they needed to. Ben, Cormac, and I would speed back in the Jeep. Our pack of three.

Before we left, Hardin called her department. She walked a little ways out and I only heard her half of the conversation, but when she returned, she seemed confident.

"I've got a note to the patrol cars," she said. "They're keeping a lookout; they'll let me know if they see anything funny."

I sighed, relieved. Allies. Everything was going to be fine. I was probably freaking out over nothing. We weren't important or dangerous enough for Roman to want to strike back at. Yeah, right.

CORMAC DROVE, Ben rode in the passenger seat, and I was crammed into the tiny back, along with crates and containers filled with who knew what arcane gear. Maybe just road flares and a spare tire kit. What did I know? A few hours into the trip, crossing into Colorado and still heading north, dawn broke, and I called Cheryl.

"Kitty, what is it?" she said, and I melted with relief. Finally, someone answered their phone. She sounded awake, but tired. I probably should have checked the time first, but she'd be up—she had kids, right?

"Hey, Cheryl, is everything okay? Like, with you and Mom and Dad and everyone?"

Now she sounded confused. "Um, yeah? Except Nicky got detention yesterday. Nine-year-olds shouldn't be getting detention."

My brow furrowed. Well, that was a distraction. "What did she do?"

"Near as I can figure, she started a fight with a kid who was flipping girls' skirts up with a stick at recess."

Did that kind of thing actually happen? "Huh. Good for her, I say."

"I know, right? That's what I told the principal."

"At least tell me the skirt flipper got detention, too."

"Yes. That's the only reason I'm not going nuclear on them."

"Well, I say give her a cape and a mask and let her go. But other than that there's nothing . . . *weird* going on, right? No strangers lurking around, no bad vibes."

"No?" she said, but didn't sound sure. Probably because I didn't know what the hell I was talking about.

"Okay. Will you call me if you see anything, you know, weird?"

"Like werewolf weird?" she said.

"Yeah, I think." Time to wrap this up before I scared her. "Sorry. Gotta run. Love you."

"Okay, you, too—"

I clicked off, then called Shaun again. Still no answer. I tried Becky next. She was another longtime member of our pack, a tough woman I could usually count on to know what was up.

No answer.

I left a message, sent a text, then tried another of the werewolves. The numbers for everyone in my pack were on my phone, and I went down the whole list. No one answered, no one texted back. Maybe everyone was having a hoedown while the alphas were away. Then I tried New Moon again. Still no answer. I had to consciously slow down my breathing.

"Kitty?" Ben murmured. He'd been napping in the Jeep's passenger seat.

"Nobody's answering. New Moon isn't answering. There's something wrong."

"There's a logical explanation." His sureness was forced. "Maybe you just caught everyone at a bad time. What is it, six in the morning?"

Almost everyone kept phones nearby. *Someone* would answer, even at the crack of dawn.

Cormac glanced at me in the rearview mirror. "We're still two hours out of Denver; we can't do anything about it right now. Just hold on."

Ben reached back and held my hand. "I'm sure there's a logical reason why no one's answering their phones."

"I can think of several," I said flatly. "All bad." I squeezed his hand back. The touch helped.

When my phone rang about a half an hour later, I jumped, flinching so hard I banged my knees on the back of the front seats. Hardly noticed, because I was too busy grabbing my phone, looking to see who had finally called back. Shaun, I hoped.

Caller ID said Detective Hardin. The other car had fallen an hour or two behind us. Tina was hopped up on painkillers and they were taking it slowly to avoid her getting motion sickness. I answered, hoping she hadn't gotten seriously sick.

"Detective, what is it?" I asked, gripping the phone hard enough my fingers hurt.

She took a deep breath. I imagined that was the same kind of deep breath she took before telling someone their loved one had been in an accident. "Kitty. I just got a call from one of the patrol officers."

"Something happened," I said simply. It couldn't be anything else.

She said, "There's been a fire at New Moon."

Chapter 8

IT HAD to have been more than a fire, the way one of the brick walls was blown out. There must have been an explosion. Debris fanned out, and the remaining structure looked like it had had a bite taken out of it. Inside was gutted, blackened, covered in ash. Smashed glass and shards of wood and metal had settled like a postapocalyptic snow. Furniture was in shambles. The air smelled smoky and sour, the reek of soot settling in the back of my throat. If I started coughing, I'd never stop. The New Moon sign, simple letters with a painted crescent moon, had disappeared—fallen, destroyed. The place didn't have a name anymore. It all seemed so stark in the sunlight.

We'd had a fire before, a couple of years ago. Tina and her *Paradox PI* crew had been there for that one. We'd been able to clean it up and reopen fairly quickly after. This—I didn't think we'd be getting over this. This wasn't a bar anymore, it was the set for a horror movie I wasn't interested in seeing.

Something had destroyed my second home, my pack's heart.

Fire trucks still surrounded the block, and the street was soaking wet from the work of the hoses and fire retardant. A handful of firefighters continued working, tromping through the ruins, looking for hot spots, or just making sure it was all well and truly destroyed. Yellow caution tape surrounded the site some thirty feet out from the building. Bystanders stood beyond, gawking, taking pictures. I wanted to chase them out of my territory. I wanted to howl to the skies.

Ben, Cormac, and I stood together, staring. We'd gotten through the cordon set up by the fire trucks when Ben explained that we were the owners. After parking as near as we could, we walked, my mind a blank because how could I know what to expect? No matter what, the reality would look worse than anything my imagination could cook up.

After a minute of staring, I turned around, took a deep breath, and gave a shuddering sigh. I could get through this. I had to get through this. Without a word, Ben wrapped his arms around me, pulled me close, and I clung to him. We stood like that for a long time.

Ben found the firefighter in charge. He introduced himself—Captain Allan—and offered condolences.

"No one was hurt," he said. "We think it happened

in the early morning hours, around 4 a.m., after every-one had gone home. No one was inside when it hap-pened, fortunately."

"Good, thank goodness," I murmured. Because if anyone, if Shaun, if any of the pack had been in there . . . Werewolves were tough, but they didn't sur-vive being at ground zero of explosions.

I thought back, plowed through my scrambling thoughts. By 4 a.m. we'd left Albuquerque, and enough time had passed for a certain demon to zap herself from Albuquerque to Denver. Or for someone like Roman to pass along a message, to enact some kind of revenge.

"We're still looking into the cause, but that fire burned very hot. That indicates some kind of acceler-ant. This may be arson. You know of anyone who might want to hurt you by burning your place, Ms. Norville?"

I laughed. I just laughed, hand over my mouth, tears streaming. The captain didn't seem at all surprised—he was probably used to people cracking.

Ben stayed calm, put his arm around my shoulders, anchored me. Explained, in a calm and lawyerlike manner, "She hosts a talk radio show that attracts fringe types. There's a pretty long list of people who might do something like this."

From the start of the show, I'd kept a folder of threats I'd received, for just this kind of situation. But I was pretty sure the attack didn't come from someone in that folder. What would the captain do if I mentioned demons from hell?

Allan was still talking, and Ben seemed to be listening attentively. Stuff about paperwork and insurance claims and what would happen next and making sure they had contact info. Logistics-type stuff. I'd gone back to numb. This was just a building, just a thing. An important thing, but the problem of what to do with it would still be here tomorrow.

Shaun and the rest of the pack still weren't answering their phones. That was a bigger problem right now. Usually, New Moon smelled like pack, a wild scent of wind, pines, granite, a mix of wolf and people, distinct and familiar. All I smelled now was the fire.

The pack hadn't been here when the place went up, and that was good. But where were they?

The fire captain was about to turn back to his work, but I stopped him. "Captain Allan, is it okay if I take a walk around?"

"It's not safe to go inside, but if you stay away from the walls, then go ahead." He smiled kindly, if tiredly. My request must have been normal. It boggled me to think how much he must have had to deal with people in my situation.

Before I started my trek around the ruins, Detective Hardin called to say she was taking Tina straight to our place. That was good—Tina had slept for most of the trip and was still out of it.

"How bad is it?" Hardin asked.

I didn't know how to put it into words. I had the

phone to my ear, staring at the ruins, and felt like I was watching a movie happening to someone else.

"It's gone," I said. "It's all gone." My voice was flat.

"I'm sorry, Kitty," she said—kind, sympathetic. Maybe the nicest I'd ever heard her.

"Thanks," I murmured, and we hung up.

The air smelled awful, of burned plastic and ashes. I'd never scrub the smell out of my nose.

"What do you think?" Ben asked. Cormac and I were standing next to him; he was talking to both of us.

"Real fishy," Cormac said. "But I don't think the plan's changed. You want to find out who did this, my money's on Roman. And that demon. Wouldn't have taken much—sabotage the gas line, some kind of gasoline bomb."

Ben sighed. "Right. Maybe the investigators'll turn up something interesting."

"I'll be back in a minute," I said, moving off, keeping my gaze on the wreckage of the building, like it was another predator and I was waiting to see which way it would jump.

I stepped slowly, breathed calmly, searching for—I didn't know what. I didn't know enough about explosives or fire-starting techniques to think I'd be able to smell anything under all the ash. I hadn't had enough experience to develop a catalog of those smells. It couldn't hurt to try, to see if anything jumped out. But mostly, I wanted to say good-bye. File this spot into my memory before walking away.

On the side of the building that looked like it had been blown out, I thought I smelled brimstone. Just a whiff, like the exhaust of a car that had backfired a block away, or the rubber from a squealing tire. Might have been my imagination. But I could see her, Ashtoreth, one of her storms blazing around her, powerful enough to knock down walls, blowing gas lines and leaving fire in her wake.

We had to figure out how to stop her. Not just banish her, not drive her off. Stop her. She'd appear again, and next time, I wanted to be ready. Like Cormac said, the plan hadn't changed.

I continued to the back of the building and swung around to the front again, where I spotted two men standing just outside the caution tape. They didn't look like the rest of the gawkers, and they didn't seem to be acting like investigators, even though they wore dark suits and sunglasses and seemed very official and government-like. They were the same height; one was a white guy with brown hair, the other had olive skin, black hair, short and curly. Their frowning made them seem old. I tried to get a scent off them, but the burning smell was too overpowering.

Because of the sunglasses I couldn't tell if they noticed me staring at them. I stopped, surprised and somehow drawn to their incongruous presence. Were they cops? Insurance adjusters? One of them leaned in to murmur at the other, and they seemed to give the building one last look-over before turning to walk away. I frowned. I'd been about to go up and talk to them. I was maybe a little sensitive about strange Men in Black poking around.

Eventually, I made my way to the front of what used to be New Moon. The fire captain shook hands with Ben, gave me a sympathetic smile, and walked away. Cormac was standing back, arms crossed, frowning.

Ben put an arm around me, and I slipped easily into his embrace. "He thinks the building's a complete loss. Insurance should cover us, financially at least." We only leased the building. Technically, that wasn't our problem. But it was going to be a mess to sort out.

"I can't think of what to do about that right now," I said. "If I think about it I'll start crying." Rubbed my face again, took another deep breath. Moving on. "This happened in the middle of the night. Angelo must know something. If Roman or one of his people is in town causing trouble, Angelo should know—"

"He'll be asleep," Ben said. "We can't ask him until nightfall."

I wasn't going to sit around on my ass for the next few hours until dark. "Then in the meantime we need to figure out what's up with Shaun and the others."

Something had very decisively destroyed New Moon, the pack's human center. Had it also gone after the pack? My shock and grief were falling away, and fury rose up to replace them.

* * *

SHAUN AND the others still hadn't called back.

We hadn't picked up the pack's fresh scent at the remains of New Moon—none of them had been here since closing time. We had to find their scent somewhere else. And follow it. Before heading out, we took Cormac's Jeep back to his place to finish out the round of musical cars. After dropping off Tina, Hardin had returned here to trade Ben's sedan for her own.

"There's got to be some way to track that demon," Cormac said. "Amelia wants to do some poking around, now that we have a name to go with it."

"Assuming Tina was right," Ben said.

"Tina's got a good track record," Cormac answered.

"You two seemed to get along pretty well," I said, obviously leading and not even caring.

Cormac glanced at the rearview mirror. "I'm pretty sure she gets along with everybody," he said, deliberately dodging.

"Well, yeah, but. You know," I said, because it was vague.

"She's too smart for that," he answered.

I was about to ask if that meant he liked her or not, when Ben leaned in, interrupting. "We have to find the pack." He'd gone stiff, sullen. Tapping a hand on his knee, shoulders bunched up. We had to *do* something, get out and bleed off this anxiety. Find Shaun and the others.

"You can do that better than I can," Cormac said. "I'll go after the demon."

"You can't take her down by yourself," Ben said. "You've tried it, what, twice now?"

"Yeah, but she won't surprise me next time." His lips curled in his wicked hunter's grin. "Third time's the charm."

What did that mean, when you were playing host to the soul of a wizard?

Chapter 9

DENVER SEEMED suddenly dark. A layer of clouds hung low, bringing a chill and threatening a spring snowstorm. No storm was coming; the world just felt heavy. Even the traffic on the freeway seemed muted.

We went home. The house was fine, and part of the weight that had settled on me lifted. Our enemy hadn't touched every part of our lives, only the most visible. With the new shape of our world a little more firmly established, we could move on.

Tina was comfortably asleep in the guest room. The temptation to crawl into my own bed was huge, but I wouldn't be able to sleep until we figured out what happened with the pack. We stopped long enough to change clothes and get some food—heated up leftovers, devoured standing in the kitchen. A second wind, fueled by calories and anxiety, kicked in.

Our house was at the southwestern edge of town, backed up on open space—quick, if limited, access to the wilderness of the foothills. Late afternoon, the sun ought to be lowering toward the mountains, backlighting the pine forest. But clouds obscured the tops of the hills. The sky would just keep getting darker until night fell.

Ben and I went outside and walked slowly, skirting the edge of our yard to the tangled scrub oak we hadn't made time to tend at the end of the property, and through a narrow gap that gave access to the meadowland beyond. The air was clear, dry despite the clouds. If anything had happened back here in the last few days, we'd smell it.

The yard smelled like us and our territory. We'd claimed it, marked it, and our scent was strong and indisputable. Any being with a good sense of smell would know this place belonged to us.

"Anything weird?" Ben asked, calling across the yard. I shook my head. Edging past the shrubbery, I continued searching. Our territory, our markings, extended out, all the way to the mountains. Nothing had disturbed that. This place still belonged to the pack, and the scent markers I sensed were generic, lingering. I didn't smell the individual wolves. Shaun and the others hadn't been out here, at least not in the last few days.

The whole pack didn't often come out here. We had places in the mountains and east on the prairie where we went on full-moon nights. Together, we walked for twenty minutes, half an hour, a mile or so from the house. Still nothing. I looked into the hills as if I could see through them to find a message written in stone.

When we didn't find any sign of our pack at its human center, we needed to check the places the wolves called home.

"Ready for a drive?" I asked.

"Yeah," he said, already heading back to the house. "Let's get some coffee first."

FIRST WE checked Shaun's apartment—no one was home. His scent was rich around the doors, in the stretch of parkland behind the building. But I couldn't tell how recently he'd been here. We checked a couple of other pack members' places in nearby neighborhoods. It was part of our job as pack alphas to know where everyone lived, to make sure everyone was okay.

I didn't know if they were okay. I just knew that they *weren't here.* So we had to search for them.

We took I-70 west, into the mountains. We had a patch of national forest land we called ours. At least, we used it a whole lot. Our den in the wild, the place our wolf sides would feel most at home. We were taxpayers, we had as much right to use the land as anyone, right?

Our usual spot was at the end of a winding dirt track beyond even the service roads. Ben pulled over; we didn't see any other cars.

"They're not here," I said softly. "There'd be cars."

"That just means they didn't drive."

That was a lawyer answer. He was right—they might

have shifted somewhere else and traveled here after. In wolf form, we could run fast and far.

I got out of the car and started walking. Spring had started to seep into the mountains. Patches of snow still marked the ground, distant peaks were still snow-capped. But shoots were coming up from the ground, and birdsong was plentiful and purposeful. The air had a touch of warmth instead of the undertone of chill it had in winter. We'd still see a few more snowfalls, but they'd melt quickly, and on the other side of them the world would be green and growing.

This place was as familiar as New Moon. For our wolf sides, this was home. Close enough to Denver to be convenient to where most of the pack lived, but far enough away to not attract attention or bother anyone. Here, the forest opened out to high-country meadows, and a bare, rocky outcrop on the hillside offered shelter. We could leave our cars parked unobtrusively at various trailheads and turnouts and gather in peace.

Usually I felt better here. This place smelled like home, the scent of the pack thick and welcoming. I knew the area so well, had been coming here almost every month for years. But now it felt unfamiliar, like returning to the apartment you lived in ten years ago. I recognized it, but felt detached.

"They haven't been here," I said. The last time anyone had been here was the last full moon, a couple of weeks ago.

Ben had come up behind me. I felt him, smelled his

scent on the air. "Would they come here if there was a problem? Or would they go somewhere less obvious?"

"If there's a problem, why hasn't anyone called us?"

"There's a logical explanation. Look at it this way— the place doesn't smell wrong, does it?"

I took a few more steps out, nose up, smelling. No, nothing smelled wrong. No fear, danger, anxiety, adrenaline, or blood. It smelled exactly the way it should have smelled. Normal.

"We should go east next," I said.

Ben nodded. Our eastern den, the spot on the plains we went to when the mountains were snowbound, would take three hours to drive to. I'd be at this all night if I didn't watch the time. That'd be okay.

Dusk would come soon, and I could finally track down Angelo.

"Let's get going," Ben said.

East, we drove past farmland, some newly plowed fields, and some still covered with the stubble of last year's harvest. Prairie, gullies filled with cottonwoods, and flatness that was in contrast to the mountains. Dusk fell, but that didn't matter. We needed our noses, not our eyes. Our den out here was a dry creek bed lined with cottonwoods, grasslands surrounded by ranches but remote enough to be relatively safe.

We didn't come out here often, but the place still smelled like us. We caught a few other trails, cattle passing through, a few pronghorn antelope, some coyote, but they didn't stay long. They knew this was our spot.

Still no sign of Shaun and the pack. Ben came up next to me and put his arms around me. I leaned hard into his warmth, and he kissed the top of my head.

"I was supposed to keep them safe," I said.

"Don't bring on the guilt yet. We still have a lot of looking to do."

We headed back into town.

NIGHT FELL on our way back to the city, and we drove straight to Psalm 23.

I was a mess, sleep deprived, and in need of a shower. Somehow the change of clothes hadn't gotten rid of the smoky, ashy smell that seemed to live inside my lungs now. I'd never forget the smell of my destroyed building.

Angelo still wasn't answering his phone. His minions weren't, either. Maybe he was in the same trouble the pack had gotten into. On the other hand, maybe he knew what had happened to them.

I hadn't showered, and after a day—no, two days— of running around, I wasn't really fit to go out. When I found him, Angelo would wrinkle his nose at me, but he'd do that anyway.

Ben found a parking spot a couple of blocks away from the nightclub, which even on a weeknight was pretty good luck.

"Let me do the talking," I said as we walked to the entrance.

"When have I ever not let you do the talking?"

"Courtroom appearances. Senate hearings."

"Well, yeah," he said. "Is this a courtroom appearance?"

"It kind of feels like it."

We turned the corner, and the club's low-key printed sign, dimly lit, came into view. Ben said, "Everything here looks normal, at least."

Psalm 23 was the kind of place with bouncers and velvet ropes and a long line of young, well-groomed people in slinky cocktail dresses and silk shirts and tailored slacks waiting outside, not quite able to hide their desperation to be cool. You could go your whole life and not realize that Denver had this kind of nightlife. One of the reasons this particular club had lasted so long, with relatively few changes in identity: the vampires owned it. It was their hunting ground. Because why go looking for food when you can set bait and lure it in? Vampires didn't need to kill their prey—a few swallows of blood kept them alive and kept the streets clean of bodies that raised too many questions. If they could make the experience alluring, enjoyable, and terribly hip—why, they'd never run out of willing victims.

And that was why vampires hung out at trendy nightclubs.

When Rick was Master, I could often find him here, tucked away in the back, quietly surveying his realm.

Ben and I had both rounded the corner from scruffy

into disheveled. He had a pretty good start on a beard. We walked past the line of pretty young people, ignoring their stares. The bouncer was one of the Family's younger vampires—younger meaning decades old rather than centuries old. A tough-looking black guy, Braun wore a suit and glowered professionally. We stopped, Ben looking over my shoulder at him.

"Hi," I said. "I need to talk to Angelo, is he here?"

Braun didn't say anything. Usually, the bouncers here, particularly the vampire ones who didn't seem to like werewolves—or maybe it was just me—on principle, argued for a minute as a matter of form, then stepped aside to let me in.

"Well?" I said, crossing my arms and glaring without meeting his vampiric gaze.

Still nothing. The guy was a brick wall, blocking my way.

My hackles went up; my lip curled, showing teeth. Well, if he wasn't going to argue with us he at least seemed like he wasn't going to stop us, either. I glanced at Ben and we started to go around him to the front door.

Braun put out a hand and clapped it on my shoulder. Snarling, I batted at him and swerved out of reach, fingers curled into claws. Also snarling, Ben jumped in between us, lunging forward, daring the vampire to strike again. Someone in the line of people screamed.

Wolf rose up under my rib cage, pressing out, ready to fight. When I tried to dodge around Braun again, he went to grab me, but Ben shoved. The vampire backhanded him, and he hit the sidewalk with a rush of breath. Braun came after me, yanking me back so hard my shoulder hurt. He moved too fast for me to get out of the way, too fast for me to see. Even for his size, he was shockingly strong.

I kicked, and he lifted me, my toes just scraping on the sidewalk, to the level of his face. I bared my teeth, and Wolf growled in my throat. I could let her go, I could tear out his throat—

"Put her *down*," Ben growled, crouched, ready to pounce.

Braun looked at him sidelong. "You really want to start something here in front of all these people?" he said, his voice a low purr.

Deep breath. Stay calm. Keep it together. "I need to talk to Angelo," I said, with some growl at the edges.

"You can't," he enunciated and dropped me. Didn't even bother to give an extra shove or smack, just dropped me to the pavement. Ben came to my side, and we faced the vampire together. We could be calm, we weren't going to lose it.

"Well. You mind passing on a message?" Braun didn't say anything, which could have been a yes or a no. Might as well interpret it as a yes. "Tell Angelo I need to talk to him. It's important. Please." Because I could be polite, even if I did bite off the word with a clack of teeth.

The beautiful clubbers in line were staring. They couldn't possibly have any idea what was really going on.

"Come on," Ben said, pressing my back to steer me away. We stalked off without another glance.

"I still have to talk to Angelo," I muttered.

"Of course you do," Ben said. "That's why I'm going to run interference while you sneak in the back."

We owned a bar. Or, we used to own a bar. Never mind. I knew how these buildings worked. Every one of them had a back entrance, a delivery bay, an emergency exit, all of the above. This would teach me to try the front door ever again.

Braun or one of his buddies might be tracking us, making sure we stayed away. Just in case, we circled around a couple of blocks, cut over, and came at the club from behind. I moved fast, trotting easily, channeling Wolf. Ben was at my side.

Psalm 23 wasn't a restaurant proper. Except for the vampires, of course. It didn't have a kitchen with a back door standing open to the alley while bussers carried loads to the Dumpster. But it did have a stockroom, and that door was propped open. A couple of staff—a bartender in a smart shirt and creased trousers, a cocktail waitress in a short dress—were leaning on the wall, talking and smoking over their break. They weren't vampires; they might not even know they were working for vampires. This was just a job at a nightclub.

Ben trotted forward without telling me the plan first. He just expected me to play along, which gave me something of a warm fuzzy feeling that he trusted me. We were a team. We could do this. I stood back, waiting.

"Hey!" he called to the two staffers. "I'm really sorry to bother you, my car died in the intersection. I just need some help pushing it to the curb, do you guys mind?" He gestured over his shoulder and gave them an earnest expression.

It worked. The two stubbed out their cigarettes and followed him around the corner. Coast clear, door open and waiting.

I went inside and took a breath of air—no one was hanging out in the stockroom—good. Slipping in, I found a dark corner, a shadowed space behind a shelf full of boxes of what looked like napkins and other paper products. No one was back here. No one had seen me. The music, standard thumpy Euro-electronic dance music, sounded muted.

Once I got to the main part of the club, I wasn't going to be able to blend in, not in my grubby clothes. The trick in that kind of situation was always to brazen it out and act like you belonged, no matter what. I pushed through the door, down a hallway past restrooms, and emerged into open space. The place was all shadows, blues and chrome, little tables with lights on them, a dance floor tucked away, a couple of bars with lights shining under the bottles. All very chic and sci-fi. This late, the place was pretty crowded.

I couldn't use my nose to find Angelo. The whole place smelled like vampires. I spotted a couple of vampires I recognized, very elegant women with pinned-up hair and complicated makeup, leaning up against a column on a raised section near the dance floor. They scanned the crowd, almost as if they were standing guard rather than looking for a snack. I'd be staying out of their way. I started my circuit going the other direction, cutting through a group of drunk frat boy types and skirting past the front door just in case Braun happened to glance in and see me.

Rick used to hold court at a little bistro table in a back corner, alongside the more sedate of the club's bars. The space of quiet was all his own; he could keep an eye on things and not be in the way. Unobtrusive, understated. Tonight, that table—*his* table, I thought of it—was empty. Whenever I came to see him here he'd offer me a drink. I'd usually take him up on it, and we'd sit and talk. I didn't recognize the bartender tonight. Made me sad all over again.

I finally found Angelo—he *was* here, and holding court in his own distinctive fashion. A little obvious, really. I should have known. He was on one of the raised sections near the dance floor and DJ booth, the first place all gazes would go to when they came in through the front door. A semicircular black leather booth with a chrome table loomed over everything like a throne, and Angelo sat in the middle, babes in skin-tight dresses and too much hair on either side of him, cuddling. He was sipping from a crystal goblet that I was absolutely sure was filled with blood, because of course it was.

I didn't know if he actually enjoyed being ostentatious

like this, or if he did it because he thought this was what vampires were supposed to do. This was what people expected from vampires. Why be subtle?

Even better, the place was arranged in a series of platforms and hidden staircases so there was no easy way to get to him. He'd have plenty of time to watch me coming. Well, that was okay. I marched straight across the floor, sending dancers stumbling in my wake, jumped a railing, hopped up a set of stairs, and stopped in front of his table. I crossed my arms and waited. The women were human. The glass did indeed contain human blood. He probably kept it there to impress and intimidate people. It made me want to pour it over his head.

His smile was stiff, fake. His grip on the stem of the goblet was rigid. He stared right back at me, didn't say a word.

"What happened to New Moon?" I asked. "And where's my pack?"

"I don't know what you're talking about."

I slammed my hands onto the table. "What happened to New Moon? What do you know?"

The two women flinched at the noise, stared at me, and snuggled closer to Angelo, as if he'd protect them.

His expression changed, donning smarm, an oily smile and a lazy, half-lidded gaze. Like cuddling babes was more important than my place burning down.

As expected, he wrinkled his nose, presumably at my unshowered odor wafting across the table. "Are you well? You appear to be having a rough time of it."

"Angelo, *talk* to me, dammit."

He drawled, "I don't know why you expect me to—"

"Stop it. Just—" I put my hands to my eyes, squeezed, counted to ten while Wolf settled back under my ribs rather than jumping over the table to rip his throat out. Out of the corners of my eyes I saw the two women vampires approaching slowly, watching for another outburst. One of the suited vampires was coming up on the other side. I might be able to fight and duck my way past any one of them, but not all of them. "Can we just have a conversation? No posturing, no posing, no accusations. I just . . . I come home to find my bar burned to the ground and I kind of hoped you might know something about that."

He must have practiced that smile. "I'm afraid I don't," he said. One of the girls giggled.

And that was that. What was I supposed to do now? I could whine—Rick would have talked to me, no problem. If Angelo knew something, I deserved to know. But he had all the power. Or he thought he did.

I said, "Mercedes Cook is dead. Dux Bellorum isn't."

His expression dropped, just like that. The arrogant dismissal turned to openmouthed terror. I couldn't help being pleased about that.

He took a long drink of blood from the glass, licked his lips, and shoved the women away from him. "Go, go."

Very inelegantly, for him, he scooted out of the booth after them. Not that there was an elegant way to scoot out of a booth—that was why these guys always made sure they were well situated before anyone saw them.

He waved off his bodyguards. "You can't be here," he said, grabbing my arm.

"Angelo, what's the matter?"

Wrenching my arm, he dragged me toward the front entrance. What was it with vampires manhandling me tonight?

"Angelo, wait, stop—" Growling, I dug in my heels and jerked back. He didn't let go, but he stopped.

He brought his face close to mine. "You don't understand. You've lost. I don't know how to make it any clearer to you, but you've lost. You need to leave."

"Where's my pack? What have you done with my wolves?"

He was scared; his hand on my arm was trembling. "I can't say."

I bared my teeth. I didn't care how many vampires were here, I was going to go for his throat in a second. "Angelo—"

"Leave Denver. Go to ground. You're finished here."

I stared at him wonderingly. "No." A simple, stupid word. My turn to use it as a brick wall.

"Then I can't help you."

"Will you please tell me—"

He shoved me through the door and into the waiting arms of the bouncer outside. Braun was tight-lipped and avoided Angelo's gaze. They would probably be having a conversation later about how I'd gotten past him. Sucks to be him.

Angelo stalked back inside. So he didn't want to talk. Fine. I'd figure this out without him.

I spotted Ben trotting up the sidewalk, gaze narrowed and lips pulled back, ready for an attack. But Braun let me go, with an encouraging little shove toward the street. He crossed his arms and blocked the way back in. I headed Ben off, taking his hand to let him know everything was okay. But I wasn't done with Braun.

"What's got Angelo so spooked?" I said to the bouncer. Because the worst he could tell me was nothing, and I was getting used to that.

He turned to look at the door, after Angelo rather than at me. "I don't think he knows what he's doing," he said. I bit my tongue, just in case he kept talking. "He never wanted to be in charge. He never wanted to be Master." He gave a deep sigh, which for a vampire had to be purposeful and expressive. Normally, they didn't have to breathe at all. "I miss Rick."

That was a hell of a confession.

"Do you know what happened at New Moon? Who's got their claws into him?"

He glanced at me, startled. I carefully didn't look back. Somebody *did* have their claws, fangs, whatever, in Angelo. I'd just made a guess.

He gave a curt nod to the door where Angelo had been. "He ought to be asking, What did *you* do? New Moon—that was retribution."

"Yeah. Figured." I started walking off before he could tell me to leave. "You be careful."

The line of pretty people out front didn't look any different than when I'd come in. They all smelled like overpriced body spray and desperation.

By the time we got back to the car, my hackles had settled and I didn't want to sprout claws anymore. Much. I did slam the door after climbing into the passenger seat. On the driver's side, Ben gripped the wheel like he wanted to break it.

I growled and sank back against the seat. We sat for a long moment, catching our breath, holding on to our human sides.

He lifted my arm, studied a bruise there—it was already fading to yellow with my werewolf healing, but I'd clearly been manhandled. Vampirehandled.

"They're done playing nice," he said finally. "They're not even pretending anymore."

"Angelo's scared, Ben. He acted like someone with a gun held to his head. All the vampires are scared. He told me to leave Denver. I think . . . I think he thought he was looking out for me."

"Don't go convincing yourself he's a nice guy—he's a vampire."

"That doesn't make him a bad guy." Rick and Alette were not bad guys.

"It doesn't make him a good guy," Ben said pragmatically. "This is not the time to be giving anyone the benefit of the doubt."

"I think he knows where the pack is. He just wouldn't tell me."

"We'll find them, Kitty."

I scrubbed my face. I was so tired I could feel my pores.

He started the car and headed out of downtown. "I think it's time to sleep. We're going home."

THE NEXT day, Detective Hardin stopped by to check on Tina and the rest of us. Tina was up and about, still banged up. The bruises on her face had turned some amazing colors, and she expressed gratitude that the next season of *Paradox PI* wouldn't start filming for another month.

"I've filed a missing-person report for Shaun, to start with," Detective Hardin said, pacing across the kitchen, arms crossed, right hand tapping—she was still on her plan to quit smoking, God bless her. "So it's in the system, but until we get a lead I'm afraid there's not much more we can do."

"So raiding Obsidian and arresting Angelo is out of the question?" I asked. Obsidian was a downtown art gallery that doubled as the Denver vampire Family's main base of operations.

Hardin glared. "No probable cause. Sorry."

Ben was at the back window, looking over the property and wild open space beyond, as if he could will Shaun and the others to appear, walking to the house like they'd just gone out for a stroll. We were all anxious, snappish.

"I could try scrying for them," Tina said. "But I'd need to get these painkillers out of my system first. They kind of muddle things up."

"Don't push yourself," I quickly reassured her. "I imagine trying to be all psychic while in pain isn't any more effective than being psychic on painkillers."

She sighed in agreement.

"What's your next plan?" Hardin asked.

Used to be, I avoided telling her things, because so much of the supernatural world fell in gray areas as far as law enforcement was concerned. I'd killed people; Hardin knew I'd killed, but she didn't know how many times. She didn't know about Carl and Meg. Part of her wouldn't see it as self-defense, and would insist that I should be arrested for murder. Usually, I felt the same, that if vampires and werewolves wanted to live in the civilized world, we had to follow civilized laws. But there were exceptions. There were situations that fell through the cracks, and the woman with the badge maybe didn't need to know about those. But she was in this now as much as the rest of us. She'd bent rules for me. She was an ally.

If I'd had a next plan, I would have told her.

I said, "I want to find out what's got Angelo and the vampires so jumpy, but we may have to wait for them to make the next move."

"Well, keep me in the loop," she said, giving us all a thin smile before showing herself out.

Tina managed to eat lunch before going back to bed, and I went to our home office. To think.

For all our efforts, for all our attempts at prediction, we still didn't know what Roman had planned. We assumed he was going to use the Manus Herculei, this spell that caused volcanoes to erupt, to create a massive disruption, and in the resulting chaos he'd collect his allies and enact some kind of global takeover. A massive volcanic eruption would create clouds of volcanic ash, a permanent overcast sky blocking the sun, creating a nuclear winter—a dark world, great for vampires. And demons with a sensitivity to sunlight.

I kept what I called our volcano map pinned to the wall of the office. It was a spectacular geology lesson. The Ring of Fire around the Pacific Ocean was aptly named, an almost regular series of active and dormant volcanoes marking the boundaries between continents and oceans. Island archipelagoes formed by volcanoes stood out. The recent eruption in Iceland of the volcano that no one knew how to pronounce had made me wonder, is this it? Is this what we've been waiting for, the focus of Roman's plans? It had certainly annoyed a lot of people, halting air travel in Europe and across the Atlantic for weeks. But it hadn't been particularly destructive. Volcanoes did erupt on their own; not everything was Roman being a dick. I'd put a big X on that site on the map, just in case. I'd asked Tina to take a look at the map when she first came to the house, to see if she could pick up any particular insight from it. She'd passed her hand over it, and kept coming back to the North American continent, which had plenty of volcanoes, starting in Alaska and running all the way down the West Coast. "That could just mean it's my home and I'm worried about it," she explained.

I couldn't chase the man all over the world. We'd set a trap for him and failed. What now? Pull the blankets over our heads and hide?

Ben joined me a few minutes later. I sat on the floor, hugging my knees to my chest, staring up at the map. I hadn't slept well last night, even with his arms around me and his scent in my nose.

"Figure anything out?" he said, leaning on the door-frame, arms crossed.

"Yeah," I said. "Hiding's not going to do a bit of good."

He donned a wolfish grin. "Fair enough."

"Angelo wants us out of Denver. Whoever's holding the metaphorical gun to his head wants us out. So we don't leave. We wave a red cape at them. We show them Denver's not theirs, it still belongs to us."

"How—ah, right. Got it. It's going to be another long night, then."

Yes, it was.

Chapter 10

W E BEGAN at the house at dusk. I stood at the edge of the yard in nothing but a tank top and panties, dealing with a sense of déjà vu. This was how I'd started out, when I decided to take over the Denver pack. From a human perspective, it was a ridiculous way to provoke a response. But to Wolf's way of thinking, there was no better way to announce ourselves.

I looked over my shoulder. Ben stood on the back patio, shirtless, wearing sweatpants. Arms loose, hands clenched, he had a hooded, focused expression. His wolf, rising to the surface. Close to naked, out in the crisp twilight air—that only meant one thing. We were going running.

Behind him, leaning up against the house, was Cormac. Our backup.

Since the failed trap in Albuquerque, he'd received one e-mail from Roman on the anonymous account. "I applaud your attempt," the vampire had written. "It's a small world, isn't it? Tell Katherine Norville that she cannot win this, and she'll merely destroy herself and everything she loves trying. But I'm sure she already knows that."

Cormac had decided not to send any kind of response. And still, I wanted to poke this guy with a stick. I'd already gone too far to stop.

"Ready?" I called back to Ben.

Cormac said, "You two run into trouble out there, I might not be able to help."

"We'll be fine," Ben said, determined.

"We need you to see what we flush out," I said. "Keep track of what kind of reaction we get."

"You're putting yourselves out there as bait," he said.

"Well, yeah." I grinned. "Or swinging the first chair in the bar fight. Take your pick."

He frowned even harder than normal.

"I'm almost ready to tell you to get your guns," Ben said.

"Naw. Not yet, anyway," Cormac said, which sounded ominous. "You two be careful."

"Yeah," Ben said. He might have been about to say more, but Cormac slipped inside the house, sliding the glass door firmly shut behind him. He didn't want to see what came next. Understandable.

"Ready?" I asked. Ben was looking past me to the foothills.

"I think I'm only going to be happy about tonight if I get to kill something. Preferably a vampire. Preferably Roman."

Alas, werewolves couldn't easily kill vampires. Not unless we chewed entirely through their necks to decapitate them. "Actually, that doesn't sound very appetizing. Venison?"

"That'll do."

We only had to shift on full moon nights, but the monster was always there, ready to be called. The blood called to us. My mouth watered. "Hey," I said, running my finger down his arm. I felt pressure in my hand, then pain, a claw waiting to break through skin. I reached up, kissed him lightly on the side of the mouth, whispered, "Race you." Then turned and ran.

He launched himself after me in the next breath.

I'd had a lot of practice at this. My shirt came off, I shoved my panties down midstride, and my skin flushed against the air. A million needle pricks itched—fur, breaking through. My back bowed, my hips and shoulders wrenched, bone sliding into new shapes, the joints twisting into new angles. It hurt, but not so much if I didn't fight against it. The roiling in my gut, Wolf breaking out of her cage, was power. I could be powerful if I let it flow through me, just close my eyes and let go—

She is running, four strong legs launching her into the wild, the wind of her passage brushing through her thick fur. Mouth open, she tastes the world, chill air from the mountains, a tang of spring, grass sprouting. Some prey. Not much, not yet. Time to hunt.

Pack, where is the pack . . .

Her mate runs alongside her, and her panic subsides. He nips at her shoulder, she bares her teeth in mock anger. They're together, this is right. The two-legged half of her remembers: the pack is in danger, yes, but she must strike back another way. Marking territory, declaring their presence.

She has the feeling that they're being followed. She keeps stopping to look behind, her head up, ears pricked forward, nose flaring, but there's nothing there. Nothing that she can sense.

At the hills, the forest begins. She slows, trots along the edges of the trees, catches her breath. Her mate darts off, golden eyes burning and lips curled to show his teeth. He's stretched out, his nose working. He spins back, circles—then pounces. Sleek and lean, he returns to her with rabbit dangling from bloodied jaws. He drops it at her feet, settles into a crouch. Not the biggest wolf she's ever encountered, not the fiercest. But he is smart, capable, and he is hers. She gets close to him, wuffs breath over him, taking in his scent, rubbing against him, and licking the blood off his muzzle. They nip at each other, playful, a moment of joy.

They share the rabbit, then they run.

They must cover ground, as much as they can. They fan out, come back together, marking as they go, laying down their scent, sending the signal to any others who happen by: we are here, this place is ours, you can't have it.

She climbs a hill, a vantage point into the next valley. Sound carries here. She howls, singing. Her mate has gone ahead into the valley, and he answers her. Their songs make another mark that echoes to the heavens.

He continues, and she races to join him.

If there was danger here, she would smell it. She doesn't, but that doesn't change the feeling, bleeding over from her other side. Something's wrong . . .

She finds her mate and whines, bumping him shoulder to shoulder for comfort. It's late—early. The sky pales. Still, there's time to hunt again, and they're still hungry. Deep in the hills they stalk a deer. She circles one way, flushes the prey into her mate's waiting jaws. He drags down its throat, she hangs onto its haunches until it falls, twitches.

A feast; they gorge. She keeps looking up, waiting for that thing she feels watching.

Nothing there, again.

He's the one who decides it's time to leave, nudging and nipping her until they both run. This is familiar territory, they know where they're going, and soon find the den, a sheltered place where they curl up together, warm in their shared fur and shared breath.

She should revel in this night. She rarely gets to run so far, so long, or feed so much. But the night feels empty without the pack.

Nestling closer to her mate, she sleeps.

* * *

WE ENDED up at the den, just like we planned. I marveled at the amount of ground we'd covered. Through the night, our wolves had traveled miles, straight over the mountains from here to there, where no roads went. I felt the distance in my bones. Waking up after running as Wolf, I usually felt weird and tired. This time, I felt sore as well, through every limb, even around my rib cage. I'd never run so far.

The morning was still, cold. The sun was well up—we'd run until dawn, slept late. I still didn't feel ready to wake up.

I snuggled closer to Ben. Somehow, after curling up together to sleep, I had a vague memory of his tail tickling my nose, and his muzzle pillowed on my flank. Shifting back, we'd ended up with his arms over my back, my face pressed against his neck. We were naked, warm. I smiled.

In response, he closed his arms, hugging me, holding me in place. I looked up at him, combed my fingers through his hair. They still itched, a memory of claws.

He didn't say anything. His eyes shone, his gaze still wolfish, the animal side bleeding into his waking self. He was still hungry—in a sense. He touched my cheek, held my head, kissed me hard, and didn't pause.

His mouth tasted of blood, of the meat we'd killed. So did mine.

Our lovemaking was fierce; I almost couldn't keep up. I held tight and lost myself. Our wolves were still with us, and the world felt wild.

We ended up lying back on the ground, arms around each other, catching our breaths.

"You okay?" I asked, brushing back his hair.

"Yeah," he said, sighing, his human voice finally returned. "I'm just wanting to hang on extra hard to what I've got."

Skin to skin, we lay together for what seemed a long time. I could have stayed there all day. All week. Surely everything would work out without us.

"Do you smell that?" he asked, lifting his head, wrinkling his nose.

"All I can smell right now is you," I murmured.

"Thanks? I think? No, seriously." He nudged me, and we both sat up.

The air was still, quiet. A normal morning quiet in the woods. I breathed slowly, and a prickling tingled on the back of my neck. Something was definitely out there. But I couldn't see it. Couldn't smell it.

"I spent all night feeling like something was watching us," I whispered.

He said, "I don't remember that much. I just remember . . . I couldn't decide if we were running something down, or running away from it."

"Yeah, that's about right." I climbed to my feet, reached my hand to help him up. "You know, if our ride isn't here, it's going to be a long walk back." We were naked. We had no clothes, no phones. No change for a pay phone, assuming we could find a pay phone. I still had dried leaves and dirt in my hair. I ran my fingers through it, trying to straighten it out. As if that would make it all okay.

"He'll be here."

Sure enough, Cormac and the Jeep were at the gravel turnout at the end of the service road. We came into view, and Cormac immediately ducked his gaze and studied the mechanism on the crossbow he was holding.

"Always prepared, I see," I said.

"Always," Cormac said.

A couple of plain wool blankets sat on the hood of the Jeep; Ben picked them up, brought them over to me, and made a show of shaking one loose and draping it over my shoulders. He looked both tired and amused, and I gave in to an urge to brush my fingers through his hair. He had scruffy, brushable hair.

With both of us wrapped in blankets, Cormac could look up again. Toughest guy I knew was also the shyest, it turned out.

Cormac pursed his lips. "You guys accomplish anything?"

Ben and I exchanged a glance, neither of us wanting to answer. Ben finally said, "We made it very clear to whoever's watching that we're not running away."

"And you're sure someone's watching?"

"Yes," I said. Not a bit of hesitation, which depressed me.

"Well. All right then." Cormac wore a sly grin. Like poking the hornet's nest was exactly what we'd wanted to accomplish.

"I need a shower," I muttered, and stalked on to the Jeep and my clothes.

Cormac also brought my phone, which was stuck in my jeans pocket. It beeped a message as soon as we hit the freeway heading back to Denver. I was hoping to see Shaun on the caller ID. But no, it was Ozzie. The station manager at KNOB and my immediate boss. The guy who ran herd on me and made sure that *I* made sure there was a show every week. I supposed I could just ignore him. But I didn't, because I'd have to talk to him eventually. Either that, or just disappear.

"Hi," I said. I managed to sound even more tired than I felt.

"You coming in to work at all this week? Or should I plan on playing folk music during your show Friday?"

Oh yeah. Work. The show. I really ought to think about that. What day of the week was it, anyway? "That depends, are we talking like Bob Dylan pop-rock folk, or British retro-folk like Fairport Convention? Or are you just going to straight-up play Kingston Trio concert bootlegs?"

That at least made him pause for a second. "There are Kingston Trio concert bootlegs? Seriously?"

"Should I be worried that you actually sound interested?"

"Kitty, cut it out. I need you at work, or I need some notice that you're not coming in so we can plan around you."

I glanced at Ben. He was whispering, "Take vacation time."

"Um, Ozzie? What day is it right now?" I had completely lost track.

"It's Thursday, Kitty," he said in a long-suffering tone of voice.

"So when am I going to be powerful enough and untouchable enough that I get to boss you around?"

"I remember when you were a snot-nosed intern who didn't know that the Go-Go's started out as a punk band. So, never."

Figured he'd play the old-man card. Well, tomorrow was Friday, I was upright and in town—of course I was going to do the show.

"Thanks, Ozzie. I'll be in today, don't worry."

I hung up before he could say anything else patronizing and guilt inducing. Looking at Ben, I waited for him to argue and say I shouldn't do the show while all the rest of this crap was going on. Not when I had a target painted on my chest.

What he said: "Wait, the Go-Go's were a punk band?"

Chapter 11

I GOT TO KNOB's building and felt an incongruous wash of contentment. No matter what happened, this was an island. The chaos rarely stretched this far.

The receptionist stopped me on the way to the elevator.

"Kitty, Ozzie wants to see you first thing."

"Is that good or bad?"

"Well, he wasn't yelling. He's not in a *bad* mood."

That was entirely inconclusive. "Wish me luck, I guess."

I got to the offices upstairs. Ozzie's door was open, so I knocked on the frame. I avoided entering his domain, where some fifteen years of clutter reigned. I didn't want to knock over one of the piles of CDs sitting on the floor.

When I first started working at KNOB—as that snot-nosed intern before landing the late-night DJ gig—Ozzie annoyed the hell out of me. He was one of

those smug aging baby boomers with a thinning pony-
tail and a musical aesthetic frozen at 1978 prog rock.
He'd mellowed out over the years since then. Or maybe
I had. He'd supported me. Hell, turning *The Midnight
Hour* into a regular show had been his idea. Syndica-
tion was his idea. I owed him a lot.

He got up from his desk. "Kitty, you're here, good.
Great timing. There's someone here to see you, he's
waiting in the conference room."

I blinked at him, bemused. "Is this something I was
supposed to know ahead of time? An actual appoint-
ment?"

Ozzie winced apologetically. "Not really. It's kind of
last minute. He called this morning, and since you said
you were going to be in today, I told him to go ahead
and come over—he really wants to talk to you in person. I think it's important—it feels big. Just give the
guy ten minutes to hear him out."

Why not? "You coming?" I assumed this was about
the show. As my producer, Ozzie would want to be
there.

"He wants to pitch to you first."

Well, okay then.

Ozzie led me to the conference room, gestured me
in, and was strangely deferential during introductions.

"Hi, Mr. Lightman? Thanks for waiting. Kitty? This
is Charles Lightman. This is Kitty Norville, our star."
His smile was earnest, anxious.

Mr. Charles Lightman had been standing, studying
the bulletin board filled with workplace announce-

ments and concert flyers, colorful and overlapping in archaeological layers. He looked over, brightened, came toward us. He couldn't have been much more than thirty, so baby faced he might not have needed to shave more than twice a week. Fashionably floppy black hair brushed his ears. He was shorter than me by an inch.

Just before stretching out his hand for shaking, he pulled up short. "I'm sorry—werewolves aren't much for shaking hands, isn't that right? I read that somewhere." He had the Hollywood patter, fast and easygoing.

I hoped my smile was gracious rather than irritated. "Most of us are fairly well socialized. We don't mind it too much." I offered my hand to demonstrate. He shook with a strong, dry grip.

Ozzie slipped out without a word, closing the door behind him.

Meanwhile, Lightman produced a business card and handed it over. Business card at the start of the meeting instead of the end—this must be serious. The card was clean, the text straightforward, stating that Lightman ran his own production company. That was what I thought this was about.

"What can I do for you, Mr. Lightman?"

"Call me Charlie, please. How are you today, Ms. Norville?"

"Kitty," I said, dancing the dance. Politely, I waited for the punch line.

He stuck his hands into the pockets of his suit

jacket—just friends chatting, you know? "I've listened to your show—it's a great show. How long has it been running now? Five, six years?"

"Seven, actually." I was proud of that. Sometimes I felt like I'd only been doing this a few weeks. But I was practically established these days.

"You ever think about moving to TV? You ever get any offers?"

"Oh, a few. Here and there. I did a TV special out of Vegas a couple years ago."

"I'm talking a regular slot. This may sound crazy, but I think you should be in a regular late-night talk show slot."

Like, Letterman? Like *The Daily Show*? Was he serious?

"And you're here to tell me you can make that happen?"

"I am," he said, in such a way that made me think he could make anything happen. He had *presence*. He smelled . . . average. Nothing supernatural about him that I could tell. He bathed regularly, his clothes were washed. Professional, male. He drank a lot of coffee.

"I have to tell you, the Vegas show I did was a lot of fun, but I don't know that I could maintain something like that four or five nights a week. Not to mention the full moon plays hell with keeping any kind of regular schedule. I like radio because I can maintain some amount of anonymity. TV brings so much visibility—"

"Kitty, you say you don't want visibility, but you

keep stepping on stage. Excuse me for saying so, but you gave up anonymity a long time ago."

He had me there. "Yeah, well. Life's strange."

"Yes, it is," he said. "But I think you really need to consider what a move like this would do for your career. For *you*. I'm talking the whole bushel here. Top of the game, star billing—this is career making. Life changing. You have to have been working for this all along."

I wouldn't have stuck with the show this long if I didn't have some spark of ambition. I remembered this feeling, from way back when Ozzie asked that question after my first accidental episode of the show—can you do it again? Yes, I'd told him. Yes I could. I used to hold down the night shift every single weekday. Could I do that on TV?

"You're appealing to my vanity, aren't you?"

"Nothing wrong with that, it's how I get things done. Oh, one question though—are you willing to leave Denver?"

My heart did a jump at that. I had never even thought about it. Never even considered. I couldn't picture what my life would look like anywhere else.

"I ask because a show like this, the production facilities and distribution structures are mostly in either New York or L.A. A deal would be easier to make happen at either one."

Leave Denver, Angelo had said. And then this comes along.

"I really don't know. My family is here—" My birth family, my Wolf family . . .

The man ducked his head, smiled, and I bristled because he might very well have been making fun of me.

"I don't think you understand. What I'm asking is: What would it take to get you to leave Denver? Cash money? Executive producer credit? Percentage of the take? What do you want? Think big, Kitty. Heart's desire. What is it?"

Safety, I thought instantly. Safety, a child to raise in that safety. Things I had by necessity given up. To know that my pack was safe, that my family would always be safe. Hell, think big—a cure for lycanthropy? If I wasn't a werewolf, everything else would go away. Giving that up was a wide, impossible chasm. My smile was thin, my gaze narrow. "Mr. Lightman, you can't give me what I want."

"We'll see," he said confidently. "What's your answer, Kitty? Is this something we can talk about?"

No pressure, right? "I've been out of the office for a few days and I'm a little distracted right now. I really need to think about this. Talk it over with Ozzie, and my husband."

"But you're the one who makes the final decision, yes? That's why I wanted to be sure to talk to you first."

"And you've given me a lot to think about, but now you'll have to give me time to think about it. If this is something I have to decide on right this minute I'm going to have to say no—"

He raised placating hands. "No, of course you can

have time to think about it. I just wanted to make sure you knew I was serious. Name your price, we can make this happen."

Deals like that rarely came along. There were always strings. People like Lightman talked fast so you'd forget to ask about the strings. I said, "It'll probably take a little more negotiation than that. But I'll think about it."

"That's all I'm asking. Thanks for meeting with me, Kitty."

We shook hands again. He had the hungry smile of a salesman paid by commission.

I walked him to the elevator and he showed himself the rest of the way out. As soon as the door closed, Ozzie rushed from his office to accost me. He might have been listening at the conference room door the whole time.

"Well?" he demanded.

My brow furrowed. "I'm not sure I trust him."

"He's a producer, of course you shouldn't trust him. But is he for real, is what I'm asking?"

Good question. I'd thought that of Ozzie the first time I met him. "This," I said, "sounds like a job for the Internet."

EVERYTHING I found online about Lightman looked good. Too good, as they said on TV. Good enough to encourage me to say yes, but also to inspire a prickling on the back of my neck. His production company had a website, they had a slate of successes, mostly in the genre of reality TV but also some cable-specific talk shows. Reviews mentioning the company popped up here and there, a few articles in *Variety*. I kept asking myself, what's the catch? There had to be a catch.

Maybe that was because everything else in my life seemed to have a catch these days. If Lightman was serious, if he really did think I had a chance at the late-night talk show audience—the timing was terrible. I couldn't think about that big of a life change right now.

On the other hand, if I wanted to run away from it all, this was a fabulous opportunity.

I had a picture hanging on the corkboard in my office, a sketch of a vision I'd had. Or a hallucination. I supposed it was a vision only if it turned out to be right. In a cave with the vampire Kumarbis and his followers, in the middle of a ritual that was supposed to be the end of all this—they'd kidnapped me, forced me to be the fifth part of their circle, their Regina Luporum. I'd scoffed, but in the middle of that ritual I saw her, just a glimpse over my shoulder. The first Regina Luporum, watching out for me. She was tough, small, with wild hair and fierce eyes. A warrior woman, and I couldn't help but sigh with admiration looking at her.

What would she do? Well, she wouldn't have started a radio show . . . But no. Be serious. She would stay and fight, discover Roman's plans and stop him. She would stand up for her kind, protect her city. Find her pack, bring them home.

I had work to do.

* * *

ANOTHER FRIDAY night saw me back in the studio.

Tonight's show felt like the confluence of several rivers. It felt like an opportunity, but it also felt like a trap. I could play it safe—or I could call out my enemies. I'd be trying to decide which way to go, right up to the moment the On Air sign lit.

Matt was already in the booth when I arrived—he seemed to live there, though he sometimes came out to New Moon with me. He had a girlfriend who was a night-shift ER nurse. Two night owls, cozied together.

I leaned through the door.

"Hey," he said by way of greeting. "All set?"

I took a breath. "Yeah, I think so. I have to warn you though—things may get a little weird tonight."

He raised a brow, because he'd heard this before. "Weird how?"

"Not sure. I just . . . I've been kicking over rocks to see what's there, and what's there may kick back. The show's always a good target for that."

He snorted good-naturedly. "You know your cop friend, Hardin, already called me and said she'll be over if we need her?"

I might have gotten a little teary eyed at that. I could do what I did because of the people looking out for me.

"Matt. Thanks. For sticking with it all this time. You're as much the show as I am."

"Are you kidding? What other gig would be as

interesting as this one? And I love Denver; it's not like I'm going to leave for some other job."

That was something I hadn't thought about when Lightman made his offer—if I moved the show, Matt likely wouldn't move with me. Had Lightman considered all the implications? I was beginning to think he hadn't. He was an L.A. guy; Denver must have looked like a hick town to him.

"Right. Let's get it on."

Tina had offered to come in and help with the show, but she was still recovering from injuries and I didn't want her up late and in pain. We had the recorded interview we'd done, that would be good enough. I had my folder of notes, of innocuous topics of supernatural interest I always kept on hand so I'd never run out of things to talk about. I also had a list—what we knew about Roman, what we needed to know. The show could go either way.

On the other side of the window, Matt counted down. The On Air sign lit, "Bad Moon Rising" spooled up, and we were live.

"Good evening, true believers. Once again you've tuned in to *The Midnight Hour,* shining a flashlight on the things that go bump in the night and watching them twitch. I hope you've all got your phones ready, because I want your calls.

"First off, a news item has crossed my desk that I want to share: Broadway star Mercedes Cook has retired for good and for real. Her publicist issued a statement yesterday that the actress has, and I quote, 'officially retired from public life and would no longer be available for any concerts or other performances.' Unquote. You'll recall that Ms. Cook came on this very show a few years ago and announced that she was a vampire, making her one of the first outed vampire celebrities in the world. Now, theoretically, Mercedes could keep her career going on, well, forever. So what prompted this sudden retirement, without so much as a farewell tour? I called her publicist and was given a rote statement that they will not be answering questions and that, yes, the retirement is for real and permanent." All that was true: Cook's PR firm had issued a statement, and I had called them looking for more information. Mainly hoping they'd let drop a clue about whether or not they knew that she was dead, or if they were just trying to cover for what must have looked like a sudden disappearance. I couldn't tell if they knew or not. I certainly didn't tell them what I knew. I didn't want anyone asking *me* questions about it. As far as the rest of the world was concerned, she'd simply vanished, not been staked to death, and that was that. The mystery would linger.

"Some critics and commentators have suggested that this is how a vampire like her might maintain a career over several centuries—she periodically drops out of sight and reemerges with a new identity a generation later, after everyone's forgotten about her. I'm not sure how that's going to work in this day of Internet searches and pervasive photography, given that everyone knows she's a vampire. Maybe she just got tired of living the

life of a Broadway star, and maybe she really is gone
for good. I'm sure we all wish Ms. Cook well." I managed to keep most of the sarcasm out of my voice.

"Second item of business: I recently ran into a friend
of *The Midnight Hour,* Tina McCannon, costar of the
paranormal investigation show *Paradox PI.* I've seen
enough of Tina's work to know she's onto something
when she talks about being psychic, and to know it's
not as simple as TV would have us believe. I asked her
a few questions about what she's been up to lately, what
she's learned, and where she goes from here . . ."

I signaled the booth, and Matt cued up the recording, which gave me a few more minutes to dither. A
tame fluff interview—this was fine, this was innocuous. For the moment, I felt safe. That bubble of safety
would end just as soon as the show did.

Calls were already coming in, names and cities and
topics scrolling on my monitor. I recognized some of
them—regulars with axes to grind calling about the
same damn things they always did, and Matt put them
through anyway and let me decide, just in case I wanted
to have some fun with them. Some had obviously
called before the show started, because the topics they
wanted to talk about had nothing to do with what was
actually coming out their radio speakers. This was normal, and sometimes I'd start taking calls at random
just to see what happened. Another chunk of calls
actually were on topic: comments about Mercedes
Cook's disappearance, wanting to talk about psychic

abilities, hoping to talk to Tina and ask questions. I could fill up the rest of the show just taking these calls.

The interview ended, then we broke for prerecorded station ID and PSAs. They droned through my headset and I tuned them out because I'd heard them a million times before. Getting up from my seat, I stretched, shook out my hands and legs.

I could make this a softball show, picking easy calls and keeping the conversation light. But I didn't want to do that. Waving a red cape, I'd told Ben. I had a lot of possible red capes. Wolf marking her territory was just one of them. Time for the next one.

Matt called, "Kitty, you're back on in five, four, three, two . . ."

"And, we're back. This is *The Midnight Hour,* and I'm Kitty Norville. I want to thank Tina McCannon for taking the time to answer my questions. Maybe one of these days I'll get the whole *Paradox PI* crew back on the show and they can tell us about some of their recent cases. For now we're moving on, I do have some meatier topics to talk about tonight. Maybe some bloodier topics. That's right: vampires. They never seem to go away—of course not, they're immortal— but what's more amazing to me is no one ever seems to get tired of them. How many vampire soap operas can one person watch in a night, anyway? The answer would amaze you.

"I have kind of a weird question to throw out there. What do vampires want? This might seem like a deceptively simple question. I mean, I know they want human blood—they need it to survive, and fortunately for the rest of us they don't need very much of it. Can you imagine the body count? In another respect, they want what anyone wants—a nice life, a safe place to stay, friends and hobbies. I think a lot of vampires have lives that most mortal humans would recognize—just extended over a longer period. We've had calls from a lot of those vampires. You vampires listening out there—you're a big part of the reason I do the show at all.

"But then there are a few. If they'd remained human they might have run for president or become CEOs of major corporations or the like. What is a vampire going to do with all that drive and ambition? And an unlimited amount of time to spend it on?" Especially the few I was thinking about right now . . .

"Many of them become Masters or Mistresses of cities. I've been thinking a lot about these vampires lately, for various reasons. How much power do they really have? How far do their ambitions really go?" This was a way of talking about the Long Game without actually saying the words. I didn't know where this line of questioning was going to go. I was making noise to see what jumped out to complain. Cormac had his crossbow, Amelia had her magic, Hardin had her badge, Ben had his credentials, and I had my show.

I hit a call from one of the crazy regulars. Mostly because I could predict what he was going to say and had a script for it.

"Hello, you're on the air, thanks for calling."

"Kitty, hi, so great talking to you again, I love the show. Anyway, I mean, aren't you the one who's always saying that vampires are trying to take over the world?"

"Well, sort of," I was surprised into saying. "But I don't think I say that 'vampires are taking over the world' so much as I say that a few individual vampires working together might in fact have designs toward world domination. Just, you know, as a hypothesis."

I'd gotten in trouble before for sticking my neck out about this kind of thing. I'd lost ratings and market share when I crossed the line from "endearingly fringe" to "genuinely crackpot," which hardly seemed fair. It had been a while since I'd gotten this close to discussing the Long Game in the open. I was curious to see how it would go.

"See?" the caller said. "Seems obvious to me, if you're immortal you can put plans in place that work out *centuries* later, and no one will even guess because no one's around to put all the pieces together."

Unless Amy Scanlon meets Kumarbis, the vampire who turned Roman two thousand years ago, and records everything she learned from him in her book of shadows, which we were then able to decode, and I was able to bring together a network of vampires around the world who started comparing notes on Roman . . .

My voice took on a wicked tone. "Ah, but someone has been able to put the pieces together, or we wouldn't be talking about it. Stuff like this doesn't happen in a vacuum. For example, do you know I've heard from a

couple of different sources now that indicate that the
eruption of Mount Vesuvius that destroyed Pompeii and
Herculaneum was caused by a magic spell called the
Manus Herculei? The Hand of Hercules. I know, right? I
have to admit, I get a tiny bit suspicious these days every
time there's a volcano or earthquake or something.

"Let's take another call now, see what else jumps out
at me. Next caller, hello!"

"Well," the guy huffed. "It only makes sense, doesn't
it? Vampires are clearly the next step in evolution.
We're doomed, like Neanderthal."

"Except if mortal humans go extinct what are vampires going to eat?"

"Who do you think is funding all this research into
artificial blood substitutes?"

"Huh. That's an angle I haven't thought of before. So
you think their ultimate plan is to get rid of the whole
seven billion of us? Is that even possible?"

"Two words: viral pandemic. But here's the thing: I
think enough human scientists will figure this out that
they'll engineer the artificial blood to give vampires
cancer! If they try to live on it, they'll all die! We'll all
die!"

"I'm not sure how that's better," I stated.

"Then nature can start over. Fresh. *Clean.* It's like
Noah's flood. Zombie apocalypse. It's *beautiful.*" He
gave a deep sigh.

"And with that, we have veered into another talk
show entirely. I'm cutting you off now." I punched up a
new call. "You're on the air, lay it on me."

"No, it's not going to be a pandemic. It's going to be the weather," the woman said.

"Oh?"

"If vampires can control the weather, they can cause some kind of greenhouse effect that blankets the planet in perpetual darkness. Then it'll be nighttime forever. Sunlight won't be able to kill them. That's how they're going to get us."

This was turning out to be *deeply* entertaining. I ought to be writing these down so I could sell them to Hollywood. Was Lightman listening? "You know that nighttime is caused by the rotation of the planet and not by cloud cover, right?"

A moment of confusion, then, "Wait, so you think they're going to make the whole planet stop rotating? Is that how they're going to do it?"

"Right, moving on . . ."

It went on like that for a while. Then things got a little strange. Stranger.

"Hi, Kitty," said a calm female voice. The monitor said she was Elsa from San Diego. "I'm a vampire. I'm not all that old, but I'm older than some, and I wanted to tell you about something. There are these coins—they're old Roman coins that some vampires wear around their necks, like tokens. No one will talk about them. I've been told not to ask. It's . . . I think it's the sign of some secret society. I just wanted to know, have you heard of anything like that?"

A chill washed through me. But I had to keep talking. "Yes. I have. It's not a secret society as much as it's . . . well. Have you heard stories about a vampire called Dux Bellorum?"

"Yes!" she said, excited, as if I was the first person who'd ever been willing to talk about this with her. "He's this shadowy figure, like something out of a story. Even vampires are scared of him."

"The coins identify his followers. But you can also find coins that have been marked out, cut up, and ruined, basically."

"Oh yes, I've seen those, too! I wondered . . . if it was all some kind of harmless club-type squabbling, or if it was serious. I . . . I've had chances to get one of those coins, but I never knew quite what it meant. It's not harmless, is it?"

"No, it isn't," I said. "The guy they belong to—he isn't a good guy. If it were me, I'd stay away." I *had* stayed away.

A couple of calls later: "Kitty, you're so right. I'm a vampire, and if Elsa's still listening, I just wanted to tell her to listen to you. Elsa, listen to Kitty, stay away."

And then, "You're going to pay for this. Talking about Dux Bellorum in the open like this. You don't know anything, and when the Long Game ends, you will call him Master, if he lets you live."

"Hey!" I answered, pissed off now rather than nervous. "You're wearing one of them there coins right now, aren't you? Yeah. Not worried."

"Yes, you are. I can smell your fear from here."

"Yeah, okay, whatever, moving on."

I took another couple of calls, then the next time I

looked at the monitor, there was a call at the top that didn't list a name or city. The monitor only said, "You really need to take this one." I looked through the booth at Matt—he was pale, biting his lip. Not just serious, but scared. He'd been threatened. Well, alrighty then, what could this be about?

"Hello, you're on the air, what have you got for me?"

"This is Roman. Dux Bellorum, if you prefer."

I went numb, just for a minute. Then Wolf snarled, and my lips parted in a smile. I'd gotten him. Kicked him hard enough he had to come out of hiding. This was a hunt, cat and mouse, and I didn't know which of us was which. I let my radio self loose.

"Roman, hello, thanks for calling in. You have a problem you need solving? Or a comment on what we've been discussing? Hm?"

"At the start of all this you asked what vampires want. What *I* want. Tell me—what do you want?"

I pursed my lips a moment. "You know that's the second time in as many days I've been asked that?"

"Then you've had time to think about it."

"I want what everyone wants. A nice life."

"You aren't going to get that, pitting yourself against me."

Any quip died on my breath. "Yeah. I know."

"It isn't too late for you to drop out of the game," Roman said. "I'm not unreasonable. If you run, I will let you run. I don't like giving myself more work by chasing inconsequential mice. But you have been given so many warnings. You have had so many chances. And yet you're still here."

"I keep telling you, I'm not part of the game, I'm just trying to kick the board over. Scatter the pieces."

"The board and all the pieces are still here. Nice work." His tone cut.

He wasn't wrong. We'd been kicking at each other for years. We were both still here. "Where is my pack, Roman? What have you done with my wolves?"

He answered, "I haven't done anything. I don't know where they are."

He sounded amused, an adult scoffing at the antics of a child. My rage stayed at a low simmer, because I believed him. He didn't know.

I would have been speechless, except I had a microphone in front of me, and after some ten years in radio I was constitutionally incapable of keeping quiet in front of a microphone.

"Something's got to give," I murmured. "You'll screw up, and I'm going to make sure I'm there to see it."

"One last warning, Katherine Norville, and this is the very last one. For you and all your allies. All your deluded listeners. Leave the field quietly, and you can keep your 'nice life.' For at least a little while."

"Just tell me one thing—am I right? About the volcano, about Pompeii and the Manus Herculei—is that right? How close are we to stopping you? Is that why you called, because I'm close enough that you feel like you have to threaten me to get me to back off?"

The line clicked. He'd hung up, he was gone.

"Well, dang, Roman must have had something else he needed to do because he's gone away. And to think I was going to ask him to stick around and maybe take a few questions from my callers—"

But the monitor was blank. All my callers had hung up. Even the regulars.

This was my nightmare—the show worked because people kept calling in. What would I do if people stopped calling? Did it make a difference if they stopped because they were scared?

How much time did I have left to fill, when I just wanted to run home and hug my husband, my sister, my niece and nephew, my parents, and all my friends? When I wanted to turn Wolf and stand before them to protect them? Find the pack, circle the wagons—

Just five minutes. Less time than I thought. More than I wanted. There was a metaphor in there somewhere.

"Right, then," I said. "I think I may leave off there, because how will I ever top that? And I'm a little over-stimulated, I'm thinking, which isn't a surprise, is it? Such prestigious callers! Such intense discussion! All this talk about games, and wants, and taking over the world.

"It's not a game. And not because there isn't actually a board with pieces on it like we're both trying to get enough houses to set up hotels on Park Avenue. That makes it sound so me versus you, us versus them. Good versus evil. And it's not, really. Making it about good and evil . . . misses the point, I think. I'm not fighting for good like some kind of—" A moment of hesitation, as I self-edited the expletive. Radio training, ha. "—avenging angel. I just want to protect my family, my pack, my friends. I don't want too much—I want just enough. And I don't want to have to put up with crap. That's what I want. Is that so hard?

"Once again, and as always, thanks for listening. This is *The Midnight Hour,* signing off. Don't forget to leave a porch light on so you can find your way home after dark."

And that was a wrap. Matt cued up the credits, which played along with a howl—my Wolf, recorded back in the day. A territory signal, a declaration of existence. I wanted to howl back.

I sat back in my chair. I expected to be exhausted, but I felt strangely hyper. The spike of adrenaline was still with me. My shoulders were stiff, my hackles tensed up—Wolf was on the surface, watching. I took off my headset and scratched my head.

Matt had come to the door of the booth to look at me with an expression of concern, and I offered a wan smile.

"Weird, huh? Is that what you meant?" he said. "What the hell was that all about? That guy—I get threatened by callers all the time, that I need to put them on the air or else. I usually just hang up on them. But this one . . ." He shook his head; he had no words.

"That one was a two-thousand-year-old vampire with plans for world domination," I said.

"You're not joking, are you?"

"Nope."

"And you've managed to piss this guy off."

"Apparently." I left out the part about setting a death trap for him earlier in the week.

"Huh," Matt said. Again, wordless, which was why he was the engineer and not the host.

"So . . . are you heading home right away?"

"No, I was planning on sticking around to train one of the new night DJs. Guy's too green to be trusted alone with gear, you know?" He chuckled. The sound was strained. Someone was always around KNOB, twenty-four hours a day. Small comfort.

"When you do leave, get someone to watch you get to your car. Get security to walk you out."

"You don't think that Roman guy is actually going to come here?"

"It's just a precaution." I was going to spend the rest of my life looking over my shoulder. If that was what it took . . . "And, you know, if you have any crosses or holy water lying around . . ." My smile was starting to hurt.

"What about you?"

"Ben's picking me up." I was very glad I'd asked him to come get me, which I'd done because things were already weird. Now I really didn't want to be alone. "He's got a crossbow in the trunk."

"Is it too late to quit?" he asked.

I straightened, panicked. "No, you can't quit, not now, I couldn't do this without you!"

He raised calming hands, chuckling, and the tension

of the last half hour dissipated. "I'm joking, chill! But I want a raise."

"Ask Ozzie," I said, which was the answer I always gave.

I turned on my phone, which immediately beeped with messages. From Alette, Tina, Hardin, and a half dozen others who knew about Roman and who must have been listening to the show, all asking if that was for real and what was I going to do about it. Answer: I was going to do what I always did. Go home and worry about it tomorrow.

Ben had also called, twice. I called him back immediately.

"I'm so happy to hear you," I sighed, even though he'd only said hello.

"Hey, hon? I'm in the parking lot. You need to get down here."

"Like, now?"

"Now is good," he said. He didn't sound worried as much as cautious. Reserving judgment. Something was happening, but his tone didn't tell me anything about what that was.

"On my way." I grabbed my jacket and bag, rushed down the stairs and through the lobby and out the front doors.

The vampires were waiting outside.

Chapter 12

TALL AND imperious, Angelo stood with his courtiers, a dozen other vampires ranged behind him, tense and wary, like they were getting ready for a fight. The vampire eurotrash army, gathered for war. Some I recognized, some I didn't, and I noted again that I'd never known exactly how many vampires lived in Denver. Braun, the bouncer from Psalm 23, was absent, I noticed. A couple of other vampires I knew by sight were missing. So, this wasn't the *whole* Family.

I might hold my own against just one of them, maybe even Angelo. At least long enough to get away. Against all of them? I wouldn't even get away.

They were focused on me, which meant they might not have known that Ben was in the parking lot at the side of the building. I didn't dare glance over, drawing their attention to my mate. Then again, they might have had colleagues keeping watch over the parking lot.

Ben could take care of himself. I had to pay attention to what was in front of me.

"Angelo? What's going on?"

Angelo stepped forward, regarding me with a sad, pitying gaze. "Katherine. Kitty. Are you *trying* to get yourself killed?"

He managed to sound even more world-weary than usual, but it was a put-on. He was anxious; his hands were balled into fists at his sides. His gang of vampires didn't seem casual—they were looking around, keeping watch.

"No," I said. "But I can see how it might look that way."

"I warned you. Whatever else happens, remember that I warned you."

I frowned. "What's going to happen? What do you know?"

"It's not too late," he said. I'd never heard a vampire sound so desperate, without a stake actually pointed at his chest. "You can still leave, and all will be forgiven."

I backed toward the parking lot, step by cautious step. Something was very wrong, and Wolf was howling to get out of here before it was too late. Get to Ben, get into the car, find some stakes, and a cavalry.

Had to keep him talking, to give me time to get to Ben.

"I get it," I said. "You're trying to protect me. You have my best interests at heart—or whatever's left of your heart. That's cool. Except that's not it, is it? You look like someone trying to cover his own ass. You're trying to get rid of me because someone put you up to it. Is that it? You're under orders—get rid of me or else?"

Angelo reached under his collar, pulled out a coin on a cord. One of Roman's coins.

"Oh, Angelo." I wasn't so much disappointed in him as I was disappointed that my lack of faith in him had been confirmed.

He didn't look defiant, or determined, or evil. He looked lost.

"I don't want to destroy you," he said. "If you simply leave, I will not have to destroy you."

Destroy—a particularly vampiric word. Vampires couldn't be killed because they were already dead. But they could be destroyed. A very serious word for him to use.

"Oh, so you're just being lazy, trying to save yourself some actual work," I said, when I probably should have just shut up and run.

What did it mean, that he actually seemed sad when he said, "I truly am sorry for this."

Four of his entourage lunged for me, and they were too fast, like I knew they would be. A whole four—I should have been flattered.

I ran. I'd already been braced for it, and power surged through me, launching me forward. It wasn't enough. One managed to swing in front of me, and when I swerved, another blocked my path. My pulling up to try to change direction gave the two vampires behind me a chance to grab my arms and wrench them back. Another put his arm around my neck to choke me.

I struggled, dropping my weight, yanking with all my strength in an effort to break free. I managed to knock the two holding my arms off balance, dragging them with me. The one around my neck stumbled, but kept hold, so I mostly strangled myself. A pain, as my neck wrenched at an angle it really shouldn't be in.

Werewolves were tough, with almost limitless fast healing. *Mostly* indestructible, I liked to say when I was being snarky. Beheading killed us, high explosives, extreme blood loss. Silver. We were fast, and strong. But vampires were faster. I didn't break free, not that time.

Teeth bared, I snarled. My fingers clenched and I twisted to rake them against my captors. They burned, claws ready to sprout, to tear. My jaw ached, teeth ready to grow.

"Stop!" a voice shouted across the wide space in front of the building. Ben, snarling the command.

And everyone stopped. It was beautiful. I tried again to use weight and speed to break free, but the vampires kept their grips solid, alas.

"Let her go." Ben moved into view, crossbow leveled at Angelo.

For a moment, the vampire's threatening demeanor slipped. "Are you any good with that thing?"

"Wanna find out?" Ben said, lips curling to show teeth.

One of the minions, fueled by pure reactive instinct, growled and charged. Ben shifted aim and fired, and

the wooden bolt struck true, right through the guy's un-
dead heart. The vampire crumpled, knees buckling as
his skin desiccated, his body drying out, decaying, becoming a husk as it hit the ground. He hadn't been terribly old—only a few decades of the grave caught up
with him.

That made everyone pause.

Quickly, cleanly, Ben put his foot in the stirrup
and cocked the crossbow back to reload. He also had
wooden spears lying on the ground beside him.

The scene froze for a moment while the respective
sides considered the next play. Ben stepped forward,
closer to Angelo, the point of the second bolt aimed decisively at his chest. The vampire entourage flinched
back. Someone hissed; it seemed a reflexive noise of anger and frustration, laughably cliché.

"Let her go," Angelo said as if it pained him. His
shoulders slumped, defeated, as if Ben had already
shot him.

The vampires let me go, slipping past me like ghosts,
glaring at me as they drifted back to their entourage
poses. Catching my breath, I shook loose the kink in
my neck and my aching shoulders. I moved to stand
with Ben, wondering . . . might he just up and shoot the
guy? And would I even fault him for it? He was holding steady, for now.

I faced Angelo. "You blew up New Moon because
Roman told you to. Right?" He didn't say anything,
which I took as a yes, so I pressed. "And my pack—
you did something, you know something—"

"No," he said. He smiled, but it was a sour, mean look. "We were supposed to find them. Capture them all and put them in cages to use as hostages to control you. You wouldn't leave Denver or quit the Long Game if we simply *asked*. But you would, to protect them. There could be no better pawns." He chuckled, a bit madly.

Let me go, let me kill . . . Wolf surged with rage, pressing against my control. Baring my teeth, I stepped forward—and Angelo flinched. Small victory.

"But, Kitty, they were already gone," he said. "We couldn't find them. I don't know where they are."

I blinked, confused, because if Angelo and the vampires hadn't done something to the pack, I didn't have a clue what had happened. I had to scramble to think, with Wolf rumbling under my rib cage.

"It's not too late, Angelo," I said softly. "Take off the coin, smash it. It's not too late to come back."

His minions looked at me, looked at him. I couldn't tell what they were thinking, and I couldn't meet any of their gazes, to try to silently persuade them to my way of thinking.

Angelo stepped forward; Ben threatened with the crossbow, and the vampire stopped. But he reached, begging.

"Kitty. Katherine. Please listen to me, you don't understand. I had to do what I did. You told me to protect Denver, and that's what I've done. They're going to *destroy* Denver if we don't do what they say. And they can do it. *They can do it.*"

His job as Master was to protect Denver, and he saw siding with Roman as the best way to do that. And I'd been trying to protect Denver *from* him.

"You should have come to me. We could have stood against him together. Rick would have stood against him!"

Angelo spat. "Rick isn't here, is he? *This* is why he never should have left! I *told* you I wasn't strong enough!"

I couldn't argue with that.

Abruptly, the vampire looked skyward. "And now . . . it's too late." Something had startled him.

I smelled brimstone.

"Ben!" I hissed, grabbing his shirt, prepared to drag him away.

First, though, he fired the crossbow, and it would have hit Angelo if the demon hadn't snatched it out of the air first.

At first I thought it was a stray burst of wind knocking it off course, maybe a sign of weather coming in from the mountains. But the wind was followed by a gloved hand reaching out, a body shifting from blurred movement to visibility. It was as if she stepped through a door made of wind that slapped at the leather straps of her armor as she came to stand between us and the vampires.

"Do you happen to have your gun with you?" I asked Ben.

He was busy cocking the crossbow again. "Yeah. You think it'll do any good?"

"No, but it might make us feel better."

"Cormac would be very proud of you for saying that," he said.

The demon had a silver knife drawn—I didn't want that thing anywhere near us. But she didn't come after us; she had all her attention focused on Angelo.

"The wolf is still alive," Ashtoreth said to the Master vampire. "She is a traitor to her kind—as are you."

Angelo's fangs showed, and his eyes were wide with desperation. "No. No, she isn't. Watch, I will still kill her, I will—"

He rushed past Ashtoreth and flew at me, a shadow with fangs and killing hands. Ben fired again; Angelo swerved midstride. The bolt pierced his arm, but he hardly noticed. His hands closed around my neck, squeezed hard, knocked me over. He was too fast to dodge.

My head banged on the concrete. I choked, then I scratched, clawing at him with fingers that were growing sharp and weaponish.

More vampires were on Ben before he could fire again, biting and punching. He couldn't reach his other weapons. He writhed, flinched, hit, scrambled— managed to stay out of their reach by moving, always moving.

I smelled blood, mine and his. I had a gash on my arm where Angelo's teeth had dug in and I'd pulled away. Another vampire appeared behind me, one of the women from the nightclub. She grabbed my arms, wrenched them back. I hollered and kicked, but she held tight.

"No! I'll kill her myself, I have to kill her myself!" Angelo was so furious the woman just let me go.

I lunged forward toward Angelo, and managed to knock him off balance, but he came right back, grabbing my neck, throwing me down.

Something in my arm cracked. Bone—I'd stuck my hand out to catch myself. There was pain; I tucked my arm close to my body and tried to run. I needed a bolt, a spear, a tree branch, anything.

Angelo grabbed my foot and I crashed to the ground again.

It was chaos, and Ashtoreth stood aside to watch, calmly, unperturbed.

"Kitty!" Ben yelled, somehow breaking free from the three vampires attacking him. He had blood streaming from his face, his arms, and his eyes were golden, wolfish.

I looked up to see a staff lofting toward me. He'd tossed over one of the wooden javelins. I grabbed it with my good hand, forced my broken one to clasp it. Angelo was coming at me. I scrambled to my feet, pointed, thrust as hard as I could, howling, running into the vampire with all my strength.

The point slipped between ribs, right through his heart.

One of the vampires screamed. They all stopped; Ben backed off, a long wooden stake in hand, sweeping to clear a space around him.

I kept hold of the wooden staff, and Angelo fell at my feet, groaning, not in pain or fear but in pure anger.

Hundreds of years old and he wasn't done yet. His body dried out, crumbled, blackening to ash, and his mouth stayed open. Somehow he looked straight at me, caught my gaze, grimacing. "Kitty. Obsidian. Go there, Obsidian. Kitty!" The sound died to a screech, his teeth bared as the lips pulled away, blackened, ash scattering on the breath of his last words. He'd held on long enough to scream in desperation—to scream my name.

I howled, dropping the spear. I hadn't wanted to kill him. I'd never wanted to kill anyone. A coin lay among the ashes of his remains. Belonging to Roman hadn't saved him.

The vampires, Angelo's minions, backed away, staring with shock. They could have kept fighting, but their will, their Master, had been destroyed. And I'd destroyed him. What would they do to me?

They ran. Faster than the eye could see, vanishing into the shadows like puffs of smoke. This wasn't their fight anymore.

And now we were going to have to figure out how to deal with the demon, all on our own, without magic.

"Ashtoreth!" I called. I wanted to see if she responded, and how she felt about me knowing her name.

She looked; her lips pressed together, some indeterminate acknowledgment. Goggles covered her eyes, and I couldn't read her expression. I wanted at least a grimace, to know if I was pissing her off.

"Why are you here?" I demanded. My voice was rough, on the edge of a growl. "Did I do your work for you this time? Were you here to kill him like you killed Mercedes?"

Now, her lip curled. "It must all seem so simple to you. If you just find the right words to say, you will be saved. But you will not be saved."

"Kitty!" Ben called.

I stumbled to his side. The pain in my arm was agonizing, so I kept it tucked in. I squinted; blood on my face made my eyes sting. Ben's shirt was torn, and he was bleeding from a dozen wounds. But we were both on our feet. We'd made it this far.

He held his semiautomatic in both hands and fired at Ashtoreth. Three clear, ringing shots.

They went through her. I saw them hit with puffs of smoke. But she didn't react, didn't even flinch. The leather of her armor seemed to seal back over the wounds. She drew spears off the holster across her back. Two of them, tipped with gleaming silver, flashing like mercury in the glow of the streetlights. She'd throw them at us, and we'd be dead.

Shift, fight, tear her throat out . . .

Not with all that silver.

"Do we have time to run?" I murmured.

"What have we got to lose, I say."

Not that we could run fast enough. In tandem and without discussion, we stumbled backward into the parking lot and toward the car, like a couple of losers in a horror movie. I dug in my pockets for a spare amulet, hoping I'd forgotten something there. A cross, a rabbit's foot, a can of mace, anything.

Ashtoreth was an assassin, and she was unstoppable. We didn't have a whole lot to say about what happened.

Those damned goggles, if I could just get them off . . . I was too far away to go around her reach, and she had too much silver for me to get close. She cocked back her arm, ready to throw both spears at us. We'd split, we'd dodge, we could get out of this.

A car pulled into the parking lot—a nondescript white sedan, the kind you'd rent. Two men sat in the front, silhouettes visible through the reflection cast by streetlights on the windshield. We all stopped to look, even the demon.

I thought maybe I should shout a warning at the newcomers—battle with evil demon in progress, please leave! But I was stunned. The car very smoothly pulled into one of the empty spots, and the engine shut down. Ashtoreth regarded the car with her head tilted, lips pursed, and even lowered her spear.

Now, we rip her throat out . . .

I appreciated that Wolf had so much confidence in our ability to inflict damage on indestructible supernatural beings.

When the car's two front doors opened, and the two men stepped out, one of them held up an object that suddenly flashed. Incredibly bright light filled the lot, like a strobe or a bolt of lightning. Ben and I ducked, coming together and shading our eyes.

The demon hissed in pain. The goggles—the light had gotten through her goggles. Her eyes, acclimated to darkness, couldn't adjust. She hunched over, her arms shielding her face; her expression was wracked.

A blast of wind smacked into us, a choking smell of fire overcame me. A whirlwind, a tornado coming to instant life right over us. Ben fired to where Ashtoreth had been standing, but I couldn't see her anymore. A maelstrom hid her.

Just as quickly, the storm ended. Dead leaves and stray trash skittered across the pavement as the wind died down. Ashtoreth was gone. That was her exit strategy.

I didn't know what to think. I looked over at the car and the newcomers. Two men in suits stood at the open doors, looking over at us with vaguely bemused expressions, as if they were embarrassed to have interrupted a conversation. They looked like two lost salesmen in their dark suits, with their unassuming manners. They looked like—

"You!" I said, pointing, marching toward them. They weren't wearing sunglasses this time; that threw me off. "You were at New Moon, after the fire! You're following me! Why? Who are you?" I only got halfway to them when Ben held my arm and pulled me back. I must have looked like I wanted to rip someone's throat out. Well, I did.

I winced, because my injured arm had started throbbing. The broken bone would heal, but it would take time. I wondered if it needed to be set. Ben and I both stank of blood and sweat.

The driver, the olive-skinned one, very casual like, as if it wasn't the middle of the night and he didn't just happen upon a supernatural battle in the middle of Denver, said, "I'm sorry to bother you, but we're looking for the Brown Palace Hotel—can you tell us where it is?"

I thought about laughing but choked on the impulse. Ben did laugh, and the sound was both relieved and exhausted. He rubbed a hand through his hair and walked off a few steps, burning off energy.

"Are you serious?" I demanded.

"Um. Yes?" the man in the suit said.

I gestured over my shoulder to where Ashtoreth had stood a moment ago. "What did you do to drive her off?"

The passenger, the brown-haired Man in Black, said, "Full-spectrum light. They're quite useful. Vampires don't like them much, either."

Ben returned to my side. His gun was still in his hand, but he held it lowered at his side. It wasn't like these guys were waving silver-pointed knives at us.

"Who are you?" I demanded again.

The driver's smile was far too calm. I wanted to hit him. "Mostly we came to say—your pack is safe. We didn't think your care for them should be used against you, so we removed them from the game."

I took a deep breath—they didn't smell like anything. They didn't have the chill of vampires. They weren't human, either. I couldn't tell if they even had heartbeats.

"Are you Fae, is that what you are?" But I'd smelled Fae before, and they weren't it.

"And where is our pack?" Ben said, stepping ahead of me.

"They're safe," said the driver.

"That doesn't answer the question. You haven't answered any of our questions!" I said.

"I know. It's all very complicated," said the passenger. "Maybe we can explain it later."

"So," the driver added. "Can you tell us how to get to the Brown Palace? Please?"

Oh for fuck's sake. "Take this road, turn right, and in a little ways you'll get to Colfax. Take that into downtown, go left on Glenarm, then right on Seventeenth. Driving that area's a bitch; if you don't want to go on a safari for parking you might want to just use the valet." The suits looked fancy enough they could no doubt afford it.

"Thank you," the driver said. "Is it a nice place? I've heard it's nice."

I blinked. "Yes," I said. "It's also haunted."

He beamed back at me. "Excellent. Thank you very much."

I rushed forward, broken arm or no, and slammed my good hand on the hood of their car. They looked on with casual interest.

"Who. Are. You."

"Friends," the driver said, and climbed back in.

Then they were driving away, as if time had skipped a beat.

The whole parking lot and space in front of KNOB fell still, silent. I looked at Ben, who looked back at me. Finally, he shrugged. "I don't know," he said. "I can't explain it."

"Are they telling the truth? About the pack?"

He considered a moment. "I think they are. I don't know why I believe them, but I do."

I sank to the curb and whimpered. My arm hurt. I wanted some of Tina's painkillers.

Ben sat beside me. "You're hurt—what happened?"

I showed him my arm. Bone wasn't sticking out, which was good, I supposed. He felt it, pressing gently. I winced.

"I think it's already healing. Can you move it?"

"Yeah, but it hurts." I wiggled my fingers for emphasis.

The cuts on his face were healing, fading to pink lines. The gashes in his arm, and mine, took a little longer, scabbing over as we watched. The bone would take the rest of the night to heal.

Ben put his hand against my head, and his warmth was a balm. He kissed my forehead, breathing deeply to take in my scent. "That was close," he murmured.

"That was weird," I said, and kissed his lips in return. Somehow, we'd lived.

I resisted the urge to chase after the Men in Black. I had a feeling we wouldn't find them anyway.

The pile of ashes that had been Angelo was gone, scattered by the wind. He was gone, and it had happened so fast I was numb. Didn't feel a thing. I would, the next time I went to Psalm 23 and he wasn't there. I wondered who the Family had lined up to be the next Master, or if there even was a Denver Family anymore. Not that I cared. I couldn't trust any of them anyway. The Denver vampires wouldn't help us.

It had all happened in just a few minutes, and no one from the KNOB building had noticed. No one came out to see what all the commotion was about. No one else had gotten hurt. Thank goodness.

Ben and I clung to each other. After a moment, and a deep breath, he said, "You get the feeling someone is looking out for us?" he said.

Those guys in the car, of course, who'd also been at New Moon. But they weren't looking out for us, they were just looking. Voyeurs. I didn't know.

"No. I have the feeling we've gotten stuck in the middle of someone else's war."

"Let's get the hell out of here," he said, and urged me to my feet.

BEFORE LEAVING, I looked around at the spot where Angelo had disintegrated and found the coin he'd been wearing. The coin that meant the Master of Denver had been recruited, and the city was now in play in the Long Game. I wished yet again that Rick had a phone number.

Ben had some tools in the back of the car, and found a nice solid hammer to smash the design out of existence, rendering the coin useless.

"If these mark Roman's followers, do you suppose wearing the smashed-up ones might protect us from Ashtoreth?" Ben asked.

"No," I said. "Kumarbis was wearing one when she killed him. I don't know that they do anything once they've been broken." Still, I was proud of the collection of them we'd gathered. Every one was an ally Roman didn't have anymore.

I put the coin around my neck, a talisman against the dark. A reminder.

Sitting in the car, I felt safer. Not safe, just safer.

Ben asked, "What did Angelo say to you at the end? I've never seen a vampire do that—hang on to try to talk. It was . . ."

"Sad?"

"I was going to say creepy. But yeah, that, too."

"Obsidian," I said. "He just kept saying obsidian."

"So we need to look out for volcanic rocks? Is there some kind of artifact? Is that Roman's weakness?"

Nothing so arcane as that. It took me a minute, then I kicked myself for needing that long. "No. Turn around, we need to get downtown. Obsidian—the gallery Obsidian. Go."

Ben swerved, turning the corner and sending us around the block until we were headed back—back downtown, to the vampire Family's lair.

Chapter 13

FOR AS long as I'd known there were vampires, the Denver vampire Family housed itself in the basement of a fancy art gallery and import business, Obsidian. The business was a front, a place to launder money, a public face when one was needed to do business in the world. I didn't think I'd ever seen the gallery actually open. The real action happened down a rough concrete staircase and through a plain door in back to a set of windowless rooms and chambers underground.

When Rick was Master, I could just knock on the door, talk my way in, and have a lovely conversation or three with my friend. Now, I didn't know what was going to happen. Angelo was dead. Something had happened, something had changed, the balance in this Long Game had shifted. I had no vampire allies in Denver.

Ben called Cormac. "It's not like he'll be asleep," he

explained. "And he'll be pissed off if we don't ask him for help for something like this."

He was right on both counts. I listened in, and the hunter answered on the second ring and didn't sound at all sleepy. He and Amelia were night owls. Actually, I wasn't sure Amelia needed to sleep at all.

After just a few words, Ben donned a wry look and held out the phone. "He wants to talk to you."

Great. That meant I'd have to tell him we faced down Ashtoreth without him.

"Was that really Roman that called into the show?" he said. Before "What's wrong?" even.

"Yes. I don't know what it means." I sounded numb. Still processing the last two hours of my life.

"What's happening?" he said.

"Angelo is dead. He ambushed us outside KNOB, and I killed him. Then Ashtoreth showed up."

He hesitated. I got the feeling he didn't know which part of that to be more astonished at. He said, "Not that I'm not happy at how it turned out, but if you faced down Ashtoreth, how the hell are you still here?"

"I'm not entirely sure. Someone flashed a light at her and she got distracted."

"Someone?"

"Men in Black. I don't even know. They said the pack is okay. Somehow." I wasn't making any sense.

"What was Angelo doing at KNOB?"

"Trying to get rid of me. He had a coin, he'd signed on with Roman."

"Jesus. But you killed him?"

"And smashed that coin to pulp," I said, putting my hand on it where it lay against my chest. I didn't tell him about the broken arm. It was getting better.

"Are you and Ben safe for now? Are you being followed? Watched?"

Yeah, Cormac wasn't going to be happy about this. "We're headed to Obsidian."

He paused, and said, flatly, "Why?"

"Because Angelo's dying words were 'Obsidian.' Something's there."

"Yeah, a mess of vampires who've probably gone crazy with no Master to control them. They're going to blame you."

"Yeah. So. Want to come help?"

"I'll be right over."

BEN HAD been hanging out with Cormac long enough that he knew the score and kept a whole kit in the trunk: not just a crossbow and spears, but a spray bottle of holy water, a pile of garden stakes, and wooden javelins. It would be the kind of thing I would tease him about, if we didn't seem to need an antivampire arsenal so often. He also reloaded the Glock from the box of ammo in the glove compartment. Ben was a paragon of practicality.

The front of Obsidian was entirely nondescript: double glass doors between display windows containing antique furniture and gilt floor lamps. The door didn't have an open or closed sign, and didn't display hours.

If it wasn't for the sign above the windows, you'd never know this was a business. I was sure that was the idea. The stairs to the vampire lair were around the corner from a loading dock.

"You know what we're looking for?" Ben asked. He had the crossbow and bolts; I had a couple of stakes in my good hand and the spray bottle tucked under the bad arm.

"No. But it makes sense, if Angelo had sided with Roman, that would give Roman a base of operations here. So we're looking for Roman, the Manus Herculei, the Holy Grail. Whatever. To be honest, I've always wondered what was in the back room of this place."

"What do we do, knock?"

I did so, rapping knuckles on glass. Nothing happened. "We move on to the back, I guess."

"I was afraid you'd say that."

We stepped carefully. A couple of streetlights gave us a pretty good view of the front of the building, but the back parking lot, with its cracked pavement and lone Dumpster, was mostly dark. It was the kind of place I'd been told not to walk alone when I was in college.

His voice dropped to a whisper. "Hey, Kitty—smell that?"

The place was a vampire lair—it always smelled like vampires, so my hackles were already up. But the scent Ben picked up was fresher—and moving. We stopped, back to back, looking around, even though in the dark we likely wouldn't spot them until they were right on top of us. I might have caught a flash out of the corner of my eye, then another. Movement. We were being watched.

Since they weren't attacking—hell, they weren't even appearing to lord themselves before us, all smug and superior like—I kept on toward the back, trying out a service door next to the loading dock. It was locked. Maybe Cormac could break us in when he got here.

The only door left to try was the one to the basement lair. Heading down those stairs would get me cornered, trapped. Besides, I was pretty sure anyone I wanted to talk to was up here, watching us.

"Hello?" I called. "By chance does anyone have the key to the gallery? You know, so I can maybe look around?" Hey, it was worth a shot. "They've got to be just as nervous as we are," I murmured to Ben when nothing happened.

"That's what I'm worried about," he answered.

A cornered predator was the worst kind of predator. We knew that very well. "Hello?" I called again.

A figure broke off from the shadows—Braun, standing at the corner of the building, arms at his sides. I felt a tiny bit of comfort—he hadn't been with Angelo and the others. Maybe he wouldn't try to kill me.

"What do you want?" he asked, suspicious.

Ben turned and aimed the crossbow at him; I put my hand on his shoulder to calm him. I glanced around—other vampires came out from where they'd been hiding, or from where they'd been stalking us. None of the ones here had been at KNOB. Had the Family broken into factions? Should that give me hope?

Ben turned again, watching the others, covering me while I talked.

"Braun, right?"

"Kitty."

"I just want to talk," I said. "You didn't come after me with Angelo and the others."

"No. You got a little banged up, I see. What happened?"

Ben and I looked like we'd done a couple of rounds in a cage fight. Cormac wasn't going to be happy when he saw us.

"Angelo is dead," I said.

He didn't seem surprised. I wondered if they'd felt it, because he was the Master. "What happened? How did you survive?"

"He was trying to kill me—under Dux Bellorum's orders. Did you know that?"

"Some of us didn't agree with him," Braun said. "We . . . we wouldn't stand with him. He said he'd be back to 'take care' of us. I can't say I'm sorry he's gone. How did he—"

"I did it. I staked him."

One of them let out a soft hiss; a couple stepped back. They all looked surprised. And I felt a tiny bit safer—they were scared of me.

I looked. There were maybe half a dozen vampires here in a circle around us, and I recognized most of them, vampires who'd been at Psalm 23 with Arturo, then Rick, then Angelo. They were like coworkers or neighbors you knew well enough to say hello to, but you couldn't name any details about them. None of them had attacked us at KNOB. I still wasn't sure I trusted them. We had enough stakes and bolts and holy water to take a bunch of them with us, but they'd probably get us, and it wouldn't be pretty. But they didn't look like hunters at the moment. They looked wary, unhappy, nervous—lost. They wanted to talk, or they wouldn't be standing here.

I found myself hoping Cormac didn't get here in the next ten minutes to blow everything up. I lowered the stake I'd been holding. At that, Ben relaxed a notch. Just a notch.

"So you wouldn't back Angelo—what are you doing here?"

"Angelo may be gone but he has followers. We have to hold this place, if we're going to keep Denver safe."

"Safe the way Angelo was trying to keep it safe, or safe for real?"

"We're on your side," he said. "I think. Against Dux Bellorum, that's the important part."

I spoke carefully. "Dux Bellorum is still out there, and he's close to whatever it is he's been working toward. Angelo told me to come here, right before he died. I don't know why."

Braun said, "Denver doesn't have a Master anymore. How do you expect us to help?"

I didn't know. I didn't know what they were feeling, or what they needed. "Maybe you could just, I don't know, decide to help? Maybe you could get together and decide what to do next? Maybe elect a new Master? Or do you really need a Master? I mean, aren't you all still a Family without one?"

One of the women to my left gasped, as if I'd suggested something awful. Braun looked tired. "We can't just elect a Master; the power doesn't work that way."

This was the part I didn't understand. Something bound Families together; there was a bond between a Master or Mistress and their followers, and that bond had power. Whatever bond they'd had with Angelo had been broken without ceremony. The power in his blood had turned to ash. They had my sympathies, but I was losing patience. "Well, then you'll have to figure out something else to do about it in the meantime."

Braun said, "This isn't your radio show, you can't just run your mouth and make everything better."

Ben snorted at that. "She can try."

I resisted the urge to elbow him. "Formality, is that it? You want some of that old-school formality and structure? Okay, then. As the established alpha pair of the Denver werewolf pack, we are asking you, the established vampire Family of Denver and our longtime allies, for help. This isn't just to protect the city, it's . . . it's for everything. Will you please help?"

He looked over, and I followed his gaze as it traveled along the line of vampires standing around us. An unspoken vote took place as vampires nodded slightly, or gave brief shakes of their heads. I thought I knew what the problem was, why a decision needed to be made at all: did they want to help us more than they feared what Roman and Ashtoreth would do them? I could understand why someone would want to flee. But my God, I'd managed to stick around, and if I could do it . . .

"Wait here," Braun said, while one of the others, a short, prim-looking woman, went down the stairs into the lair.

The rest of the vampires didn't break position. They reminded me of a wolf pack in uncertain territory, wondering when the attack was going to come. They wouldn't much appreciate the comparison, but it made me aware of my own body language. I tried to relax, loosening my shoulders, taking calm breaths, lowering my gaze. Imagining my currently nonexistent tail dropping. Wolf for *everything's fine, we're all fine here.*

"We're okay?" Ben whispered at me over his shoulder.

"Don't know. I just don't want a fight."

"May not be an option."

"Yeah, but I'm not going to be the one who starts it."

The prim vampire came back up the stairs, dangling a set of keys from her hand.

"Well, that'll make things easier," I said, bemused. I wasn't sure what I'd been expecting, but this was a nice turn.

While Braun and the woman led us to Obsidian's back door, the other vampires drifted away—slowly enough that we could watch them go. Some went to the basement, some moved off as if they'd just been out for a stroll. I sighed, relieved. This wasn't going to turn into a battle—good.

"You can put that down," Braun said, eyeing Ben's crossbow.

"Yeah, I'll just hang on to it," he said, grinning to show teeth.

Braun unlocked the door, then punched in a code in a keypad on the inside wall.

"Huh," I said. "Good thing we didn't just pick the lock, I guess."

"What good's a front if it doesn't function like the real thing? We run this as a business."

"But I never see the place open," I said. "Does anyone even shop here?"

"You ever hear the saying 'If you have to ask, you can't afford it'?" he said.

"You can't afford it," the woman added. She had a faint accent, some brand of European I couldn't identify.

Right. Okay.

For the first time, I looked inside Obsidian. We were in a back room, which looked like a typical back room, with a concrete floor and exposed ductwork, lots of metal shelves with various boxes stacked on them. A doorway in the corner led to the showroom, and I couldn't resist. I knew we were on a mission and didn't really have time for this. But it would only take a couple of minutes. I went snooping.

The front space looked like some old-world nobleman's parlor, which I supposed wasn't far from the truth. On the back wall hung half a dozen paintings in ornate gilt frames: complicated Renaissance art, filled with mythological figures, the paint cracked with age. The only other place I'd ever seen work like this was in a museum. And at the homes of Ned Alleyn, Master of London. Against another wall was a weapons rack displaying swords and spears, angry-looking spiked ironwork bolted to age-stained wooden staves, long grooved blades set in impractically ornate hilts. There were vases, candelabras, tables decorated with scrollwork, straight-back chairs with embroidered seats, faded and worn. It all smelled clean, but old. Dust in the cracks would never entirely go away.

On a pedestal in the back, near a desk with a computer and a stack of ledger books, sat an old Spanish helmet, with arched crown and sloping brims. A conquistador's helm.

"Is this his? I mean, was it his, back in the day?" I asked the woman, who followed me in. No one had to ask who I was talking about. Rick, Ricardo, former Master of Denver who said he'd once followed Coronado. A real conquistador. Retired, now.

"No, I don't think so. Not that exact one, anyway. But I think he has it because it reminds him. It's one of the items marked Not for Sale. There are several."

I wished I'd thought to ask Rick to show me around, to tell me the stories. And even Arturo before him, though I was pretty sure Arturo thought I was a nuisance. He might have told me stories if I'd thought to ask. If I'd had the courage to ask. Burying the pangs of regret, I returned to the back room.

Ben said, "You know what you're looking for?"

"Something old. You know—Roman. Some kind of artifact from Pompeii or Herculaneum."

"So, *relatively* old," the woman said archly.

"Yeah? So how old are you?" I said to her. She just rolled her eyes at me. "Do artifacts from Pompeii ever hit the collector market?"

"Occasionally, but most of them have been acquired by museums."

"I'm not sure this would ever have been catalogued. Really, I don't have a clue what this could be."

"Isobelle," Braun said to the prim vampire with the key. "You're the appraiser, you see everything that comes through—what is there?"

"A crate came in a few days ago that Angelo wouldn't let me look at. Wouldn't even let me open it. He said he was holding it for someone."

"That's it," I said. Looking at her, almost but not quite meeting her gaze, I said, "Thank you."

She gave a quick nod and pointed me to the crate in question, maybe a couple feet on a side, stashed in a corner out of the way so a casual observer wouldn't notice it. A dozen labels were taped over one another on the outside. This thing had been all over the world. If I peeled back the layers, I bet I'd find it originated in Split, Croatia—where Roman had retrieved it, where the thing's existence had first come to light.

So, this was it. Time to dig in. I pried at the edges with my fingers but couldn't budge it. The lid was nailed down.

"Can you help me with this?" I asked the vampires.

Isobelle found a crowbar and popped the lid off with little effort.

With an air of discovery, and more than a little anticipation, we dug through piles of shredded paper used as packing.

"I feel like I've landed in an Indiana Jones movie," Ben observed. His crossbow and the stark overhead lights in the warehouse-ish back room made the whole thing feel like a film set. Braun huffed in agreement, which made me like him a little better. Slightly better.

Isobelle and I kept digging. And digging.

"Bugger this," she muttered, and tipped the crate over. I jumped back, startled. She pawed through the spilled packing material, kicking paper away, until the stuff was spread all over the floor.

Except for the several square feet of packing material, the crate was empty. I must have stared at it for a full minute.

"We're too late," I said.

"Looks like it," Braun said.

"What now?" Ben said.

"Back to square one," I said, leaning against the wall and rubbing my face.

"Is this bad?" Isobelle asked. "This is bad, isn't it?"

"It means whatever he's got planned is going to happen soon," I said. And I had no idea how to stop him.

"I hate to say this, but I think Kitty's right," Braun said. "We have to get everyone together and batten down the hatches if we're going to get through this."

"I thought we could stay isolated," Isobelle said,

crossing her arms, looking hunched in and unhappy. I wondered what her story was: art appraiser turned vampire, or the other way around? "Not have to pick sides, not get involved."

"I'm hoping this will all be over soon," I said.

"One way or another," she answered.

We left the building to find Cormac standing in the parking lot, armed with his crossbow and a dozen stakes hanging off a bandolier. Various vampires were keeping their distance, glaring and waiting for an opening.

"Whoa, wait, stop!" I said, jumping between Cormac and the vampires. He didn't lower his weapon. Maybe because he knew a bolt through my heart wouldn't kill me. Still, I was a little put out.

"Why the hell didn't you wait for me?" Cormac said.

"No good reason," I answered. "But hey, we're all friends here."

His frown at that was very familiar.

Ben finally put away his crossbow, to set an example maybe. He went over to Cormac. "It's okay. I think we're done here." *Then,* Cormac lowered his.

"We'll get out of your hair. Thanks again," I said to Braun.

He made an ironic bow while Isobelle just frowned. They were vampires, immortal; all they had to do was lie low and they'd get through whatever was about to happen. I bet Angelo had thought that, too.

I grabbed the guys and hauled them back to our cars at the front of the building.

"Well?" Cormac said. After looking us up and down he added, "Jesus, you guys got thrashed."

"Sort of," Ben said. "It's healing."

"Yeah, I don't think it's even broken anymore." I stretched my arm; it was feeling better. Cormac narrowed his gaze.

"Did that go how you planned?" Cormac asked.

"About," I said.

"Roman's still out there," Ben said. "And whatever the Manus Herculei is, he's got it.

Cormac glanced at his watch. "It's not long until dawn. He likely can't do much else tonight."

"Not like he hasn't already done enough," I muttered.

"Roman's in town, he has to be. Daylight hours, we'll go hunting," Cormac said. "Meanwhile, I'm going to sleep." He stalked to the driver's side of his Jeep without a backward glance.

"Thanks, Cormac," I said uselessly.

"You sure you guys are okay?"

We didn't answer right away, which was telling. Finally, Ben sighed and said, "Relatively speaking, yes."

Cormac nodded, didn't question further. He made a wave and that tight-lipped expression that passed for a smile.

Ben loaded our gear back into the trunk—except for the crossbow, which he wanted to keep up front with us.

"I can never tell if he's angry," I said, watching the Jeep pull away.

"Naw, he doesn't get angry," Ben said. "He gets even."

IN THE end, sleep was an awesome idea. Cormac was right: daytime was a much better time to be hunting vampires. Evidence said Roman was in Denver. Between Amelia and Tina, maybe we could scry for his location, then flush him out into the sunlight.

All the way home, I was still mulling over the night, chewing like a dog with a bone. Playing the whole scene over again, wondering what clues I missed. I could still hear Angelo screaming my name as he crumbled to dust. Ben waited for me as I climbed tiredly out of the car.

I looked at the coin still hanging around my neck. It had all happened just a few hours ago.

"I can't believe Angelo's gone." He'd worked so hard to stay unnoticed, out of power and therefore out of trouble. I remembered him at New Moon, leaning back in his chair and smirking like we were all beneath him. Playing the stereotypes, but still a reluctant Master. "I can't believe I had to kill him—" I just started crying. Waterworks. All that stress, it just broke.

We stopped, right there on the walk leading to the front door. Ben held me. Didn't say a word, didn't try to say everything would be okay. I sobbed on his shoulder, and he was there through it all.

Finally I cried myself out into sniffles and eye rubbing. Ben's shirt was soaked with tears and snot, and he stood and took it. Then he put his arm around me and we walked into the house.

I DIDN'T sleep well. I kept jerking awake and sitting up, wide-eyed, like I expected to find monsters in my room. Monsters other than Ben and me. But nothing was there, just the usual collection of shadows and ambient light. My arm still ached, but the bone was apparently healing the way it should. In a few more hours it would be back to normal.

Every time I woke up, Ben woke up to ask what was wrong. A couple of times, I awakened to find him already sitting up, studying the room with narrowed, wolfish eyes.

"What the hell is wrong with us?" I groaned at one point, flopping back onto the pillow.

"Too much stress for too long," he groaned back, stretching next to me and wrapping his arms around me, like I was a big, comforting pillow. And that was just fine.

Around dawn, after time had stretched and contracted until I had no idea when it was, the bed vibrated, like someone had grabbed hold of the mattress and shook it as hard as they could. I looked for who was pulling the prank—no one. I grabbed Ben's arm; he grabbed back.

A crash sounded, as something elsewhere in the house fell off a shelf and broke.

Then the shaking stopped. The quiet after was profound.

"What was that?" Ben said. His eyes were wide.

"Was that the house? Is the house falling down?"

Knocking pounded the door. "Kitty?" Tina called.

"Tina, are you okay?" I grabbed my bathrobe and went to open the door. Ben pulled on pajama bottoms and a T-shirt.

She looked a lot better than she had when we got back from Albuquerque, but was still pretty banged up. That didn't stop her from looking panicked, her eyes wide. She said, "That was an earthquake."

Somehow that didn't sound right. "Are you sure?"

"I've lived in L.A. half my life, of course I'm sure. That was at least a five-two. I didn't know Colorado even had earthquakes."

Ben had his phone in hand and started scrolling through news sites until he found a streaming clip. ". . . still waiting for confirmation from the U.S. Geological Survey. The tremors seemed focused in Denver, Arapahoe, and Jefferson Counties . . ." The narration went on, describing initial reactions and warnings to get to a safe place and call the gas company if you smelled gas. I took a long sniff and didn't smell anything out of the ordinary. But all my hair stood on end and the air seemed charged.

"We're on a major mountain range; there are plenty of fault lines," Ben said. "We get quakes, but never anything big, not like this."

The phones started ringing then: Ben's, mine, Tina's, the land line. I grabbed mine and had a dozen text messages pour in. I answered the call from my mother first.

"Kitty, are you all right?"

Yes. Well, no, but not because of the quake. I needed half a second to answer, which probably worried her. "Yeah, Mom, I'm fine—what about you and Dad? Cheryl?"

"Oh, thank goodness. Can you believe it? A real earthquake, here? Your father says to check your roof and foundation. Check the whole house for cracks, you might not see any damage right away, but the house might not be safe."

I wasn't even thinking about that. "Yeah, Mom, I'll do that—"

"Nicky and Jeffy were crying when I called Cheryl. I can hardly blame them, this is just terrifying—"

"But you're all okay?"

"Yes, we're fine."

"I think I need to get off the phone, Mom. I've got about a million messages coming in, we should probably free up the lines for real emergencies. You heard about the gas thing—you guys have any gas leaks?"

Her voice went distant as she lowered the phone and shouted at my father, "Jim, do you smell gas? Is there a gas leak?"

He called back, "Do *you* smell gas? Is there gas?"

"I don't know, I'm asking!"

"I don't know—"

"Mom," I interrupted. "Just stay alert and be careful, okay? I'll call you back later."

"Okay, Kitty. Be careful. I love you."

Ben fielded a call from his own mother—much briefer than my talk with my mom. Ellen O'Farrell was happy with a simple *yes, we're fine*—and then the lines got overloaded and the calls dropped off.

"I can't get hold of Cormac," Ben said after trying half a dozen times to reach his cousin. I thought of his run-down apartment building, built of concrete a few long decades ago, and tried not to worry. Nothing in this town was made to withstand earthquakes.

"He's fine," I said, willing it to be so. He was smart, strong; he could handle himself. Not being able to reach him didn't mean anything.

After dressing, we migrated to the kitchen, where we turned on the TV and started the coffeemaker.

The local news channels were in breaking-story heaven. Every geologist in Denver was getting fifteen minutes of fame. Some neighborhoods lost power, some buildings had been evacuated. I gave silent thanks that ours hadn't, allowing us to have coffee. I desperately needed coffee.

Eventually, I sat on the sofa, hot mug grasped in both hands, watching the TV screen intently and not hearing a word. The images were enough—a ramshackle warehouse in Wheat Ridge had collapsed. A small bridge in Littleton had cracked in two. A fire had started in a house where a gas main had indeed broken.

Angelo had said they—Roman, his followers, the demon, whoever—would destroy Denver if I didn't leave.

Maybe he hadn't been talking metaphorically.

The doorbell rang, and I snarled. I about sprouted claws right there, because I was just so sick of dealing with crap.

Ben made a calming gesture—I really must have looked like a crazy thing—and went to get the door. A moment later I heard, "Kitty? It's for you."

He didn't sound nervous, angry, or confrontational. Instead he sounded nonplussed. My nose flared, testing the air . . . Ben wasn't angry because the smell was familiar.

I arrived just as Ben stepped aside to let our new visitor in. He was either a weathered young man or a vibrant middle-aged one, with a craggy face, close-cropped hair, and gray eyes. He wore a trench coat over slacks and a dress shirt, making him look dapper and poised.

Odysseus Grant.

"Hello," he said, with a hint of a smile.

I hesitated just a moment before wrapping him in a hug, to give him a chance to escape, but he didn't, handling my enthusiastic greeting with patience.

"What are you *doing* here?" I exclaimed. I'd met Odysseus Grant in Las Vegas, where he was a stage magician. His show was self-consciously old-fashioned, keeping alive a host of Vaudeville-era stage tricks. If he mixed some real magic into the show, who would notice? Until Amelia came along, he was my main resource for magical questions and problems. One of my allies, one of the good guys.

He tilted his head. "Would you think it odd if I said Anastasia sent me?" He'd also been a part of the nightmare reality show with me, Tina, and Anastasia. He'd taken a stake for the vampire and lived to tell the tale.

Anastasia—what the hell was she up to? It really did start to feel like I had a guardian angel looking out for me. "Yes. But I wouldn't be surprised. You're not the first."

I led him to the kitchen, where Tina wrapped him in a more careful hug. Along with Anastasia, we were most of the survivors from that adventure.

"This isn't a coincidence, that we've all been brought together here and now," he said.

"It's the earthquake, isn't it?" Tina said. "It's not natural."

"It's natural," Grant said. "But that doesn't mean it wasn't triggered. That's what you've been saying, isn't it? That Roman has some kind of spell to control such phenomena."

I said, "He has a spell that can ignite volcanoes. I don't know about earthquakes. We've been trying to figure out where he'll strike—"

"Show me," Grant said.

I led him back to the office; the others followed.

"Roman's making his move. He's sent people after me, my pack, my restaurant." In the office, he stepped back to regard the map with its tangled pattern of active volcanoes wending around the world like lacework. I continued. "He was in New Mexico just a few days ago, but I have reason to think he's in Denver now. Maybe he did cause the earthquake, but we were sure he'd try to trigger a volcano."

"Yes, that's what Anastasia said." He studied the map, then glanced around sharply, looking for something. "You've missed one."

He found the box of red thumbtacks, pulled one out, and stuck it into the map a mere five hundred miles north of Denver.

"Right there. That's your volcano," he said.

I stared, then sank into a chair as the breath went out of me.

Chapter 14

ROUGHLY EVERY six hundred thousand years, a certain hot spot under the Earth's crust erupts in a massive explosion. This hot spot was currently located under Yellowstone National Park. Geologists had found evidence of past eruptions in a series of craters that tracked westward, as plate tectonics moved the North American continent over that location. In modern times, the hot spot created a region full of geysers and hot springs, more concentrated thermal activity than anywhere else on the planet. Yellowstone Lake, the large body of water in the middle of the park, filled up part of the caldera that resulted from the most recent eruption, which covered much of the continent in meters of ash and spread a toxic cloud over half the planet.

The next eruption was about sixty thousand years overdue. The hot spot was ready to burst. A potential Yellowstone eruption was a favorite doomsday scenario with people who talked about that sort of thing.

An eruption similar to the previous one would cause something like a nuclear winter, shrouding the planet in ash, raining dozens of feet of debris for hundreds of miles, blocking the sun, dropping global temperatures, resulting in the destruction of crops, mass starvation, and disease . . .

If a guy who could trigger volcanic eruptions wanted to destroy Denver, or civilization, he couldn't do much better than the Yellowstone caldera.

I stared at that little red pin while Grant explained, and Ben supplemented with information from one of my volcano reference books. Grant was right, I'd totally missed this, because I'd been looking for volcanoes erupting *right now.* Not doomsday scenarios in my own backyard. I imagined the swath of destruction, painted a mental picture of ash sweeping away from that point in a big black smear. We wouldn't even have time to run, if Yellowstone blew right now.

Was that earthquake a sign of things to come? A warning?

We moved back to the kitchen. The TV news was still running, with all its repetitive commentary and interviews with experts and video of reporters standing on street corners describing the destruction clearly visible right behind them. One was downtown, where a historic old Victorian house had lost part of its front porch, which had collapsed into its yard. Still didn't look as bad as the ruins of New Moon.

I'd given the magician our translated copy of Amy Scanlon's book of shadows, with its tangle of clues and commentary. I said, "Everything we know about the Manus Herculei is in here. Roman apparently went to Split, Croatia, last year to retrieve the spell from where he'd hidden it two thousand years before, after using it at Pompeii—"

"And Herculaneum, you said that's where the name comes from," Grant asked.

"Yes. If Roman went to retrieve it, we assumed that meant he was getting ready to use it."

"Speaking as another magician, I make three assumptions: that he needs to be in the appropriate location in order to use the spell. He cannot cast from a distance. Second, the spell has a timed delay, since I assume Roman intends to survive the eruption. He'll need time to flee."

The floor shook, like someone had installed a coin-operated vibrating bed under it. Dishes in the cupboard clinked, the ceiling fan in the living room swayed, the refrigerator made a disconcerting rattle. It only lasted a couple of seconds, but we all grabbed tables and counters and looked around, eyes wide, wondering if the house was going to fall on us, if maybe we should run.

"Just an aftershock," Tina said when everything went quiet. "Nothing to worry about."

"Yeah," Ben said, lip curled. "Who's worried?"

"And third," Grant said, not missing a beat, "this isn't an easy spell to cast. He used it two thousand years ago to great effect, and presumably put it aside and didn't use it again. Or used it rarely—half a dozen times,

perhaps, if we blame every catastrophic volcanic eruption near a populated area over the last two millennia
on him. He'll need time, space, and resources. We can
use that against him. We don't know enough about the
spell to counter the magic, so we must find *him*. The
source of it all."

"We tried that last time. It didn't work so well," I
said.

The front door banged open, and we all jumped,
again, because every loud banging noise was going to
make us jump for weeks from here out.

Cormac walked in a moment later. My first impulse
was to hug him just as hard as I'd hugged Grant, but I
resisted. Tina got as far as jumping up before restrain-
ing herself. Cormac looked even more prickly than
usual at the moment, frowning, taking in the room at a
glance as if confirming that everything was okay. His
gaze finally rested on Grant.

"You're Odysseus Grant," he said, then looked at me
for explanation.

"Yeah," I said. "Anastasia gave him a tip."

"Anastasia?" He didn't sound confused so much as
disbelieving.

Grant stood. "And you must be Cormac Bennett . . .
and Amelia Parker?"

This time, Cormac scowled at me. I said, "Once I
started calling him for advice about deciphering books
of shadows, I sort of had to explain everything."

He waved me off. "Everybody okay?"

"Yeah," Ben said. "We're just trying to figure out if

this is Roman's next move and what we're going to do about it."

"Same as always, stake the bastard first chance we get."

"I think we're on about our fifth chance," I said. "It's not working."

Grant said, "He'll need to go to Yellowstone, and he'll need help, a place to stay, minions—do you know any of the vampires in that area, who he might call on for help?"

"There aren't any," Cormac said. "At least not any established Families. There might be a few loners, but the population up north isn't big enough to support vampires. Denver's the only city with a good-sized Family in the region."

I stepped back, hand on my head. Thoughts fell into place, rattled me—like an earthquake. "That's why Roman's been so interested in us, why he's worked so hard to get the city under his control." He'd sent minions, vampires, magicians, over and over again, to undermine me and Rick, to put his own people in place. And I thought he was just pissed off at me. "I guess it's nice I don't have to take it personally anymore."

"Well, he's finally got Denver," Cormac said. "At least, his enemies aren't in charge anymore. He's using Denver as his base, he's got to be around somewhere. Kitty, you know all the vampire hideouts in town?"

"Only some of them," I said.

"Then we start there. He's bedded down in one of them. We'll work in teams and cover more ground."

Cormac took charge of what was turning into a physical assault plan. That was his area of expertise anyway.

We collected weapons, discussed tactics. Ben and Cormac shared what they knew about hunting vampires, and it turned out Grant knew something about it as well. I made a list of vampire-owned locations in town. Roman would never bed down in a place I knew about—he'd have a secret lair set up somewhere. We'd run all over the place—in a town that was in chaos from a natural disaster—and never find him. I was daunted.

We were going to need help, so I called Detective Hardin. Her line was busy—of course it was, the police were probably stretched to the breaking point. But this—this was important.

I shouldn't have worried; a few minutes later, she called me. "We're all on call, running around like chickens with our heads off. Please tell me you and the rest of the gang are okay."

"Angelo was killed last night." And I killed him . . . "Roman's probably in town. Want to help us go after him again?"

She hesitated a moment. Probably going over her vast list of fires to stomp out. Which crisis would she move to the top of the list? "Hell yeah, I do. I'll see who I can round up to help."

"Bring stakes."

"You know it."

I hung up the phone and beamed at the others. Maybe I couldn't work a crossbow worth anything, but I had my own resources. "Hardin's in," I said.

Half an hour later Hardin arrived in her sedan and brought a patrol car and two uniformed cops with her. Cormac, Tina, and Grant were going to look for Roman at Psalm 23, while Ben, Hardin, and I dropped by the lair at Obsidian and a couple of other downtown safe houses I knew about. If we found any of the Family's human servants, we'd try to recruit them. We'd hope the aftershocks didn't get worse.

THE GALLERY looked different in daylight hours. Plain, unassuming. Like a hundred other downtown storefronts and businesses that had been here forever. A little run down, a little lonely. Concrete and chipped paint. It seemed smaller. The earthquake hadn't seemed to cause it any damage. I wondered if the tremor had affected the vampires downstairs at all. I supposed the building could collapse and bury them, and as long as they weren't exposed to sunlight, they'd be all right.

"I don't think he's here," Ben said, after he and Hardin and I had made a circuit of the building. The door at the base of the stairs was locked.

I didn't smell Roman. I smelled generic vampire, but the place was saturated with their bloodless chill. In daylight hours, the scent was muted. If he'd come back here after the rest of us had left, we couldn't tell with our noses.

"I didn't think he would be," I said. "But we had to check."

"You said you had a couple of other places to try?"

"Yeah. The Family owns property all over town. A lot of vampires make their money with property investments. The places I know about, it's mostly by smell. But the guy's got to spend daylight hours somewhere."

"Well, let's check it out."

The first address was a small apartment building north of downtown. The upper floors were rented out to regular tenants, but the basement apartments were reserved for vampires. Again, we made a circuit of the building, smelling what little we could. Detective Hardin interviewed the on-site property manager to see if she'd seen anything strange, or what she knew about who lived in the basement.

I hadn't intended on getting separated from Ben. We weren't, really—I was at the back of the building, and he was just around the corner—*just* around the corner—while we studied the blacked-out basement windows. I might have been out of his sight, but I wasn't out of shouting distance. We weren't *really* separated.

I heard something, a snapping of fingers down the alley behind the building. Someone standing around being bored. I went to look, moving around the Dumpsters in the back of the lot to the alley fence.

The last person I expected or wanted to see was there, one hand in a pocket. Charles Lightman snapped the fingers of his other hand, then studied them as if trying to figure out how they worked.

I stared at him. "What are you doing here?"

He squinted up at the sky, as if he wasn't used to the

sun, and smiled like this was a joke. "I was hoping we could chat. It won't take long."

"This *really* isn't a good time," I said, trying to catch my breath, mind stumbling. "In fact, it's a pretty damn awful time. I don't know if you noticed, but there's been an earthquake. And how did you know I was here—"

"Yes, I see, I understand. But I can't sit on this forever, Ms. Norville, Kitty. You knew it wasn't a standing offer. But I'm here now, I'm willing to negotiate. Do we move forward? Think of it—expand your influence, your empire. You'll have the kind of success that brings stability. No more guessing, no more taking chances. You'll get away from all this. The very fact you're stalling tells me you're interested. It's a hard choice, I know, but you've had time to think on it. I need an answer."

Was he serious? He'd followed me in the aftermath of an earthquake to demand an answer? I couldn't believe it. "You know, right this minute, if you really want to make an offer I can't refuse? You know what I really want? I want my pack back home safe, and I want Roman's head on a platter."

This should have been nonsensical to him. He should have been confused. Asked who Roman was, what my pack was. But his smile didn't waver. The light in his eyes turned hungry.

"Ah, I'm afraid I can't do that. I knew your pack would be a great bargaining chip, but my opponents got to them first. Protected them. And you, from being manipulated because of them. And Roman's head? No, I need that right where it is."

My limbs went cold, and I stared. Something was about to go very sideways, I could feel it. "Who—"

"The TV show offer—that was the standard rich-and-famous deal. I didn't really expect you to say yes to it. Truth be told, I expected you to say no right away. The fact you were tempted at all—I find that interesting. Ah well. You can't win them all. This just makes it possible for me to move forward with the next plan. You know what they say about one door closing."

"Ben—" I called over my shoulder, recognizing the need for backup, but it was too late.

A wind blasted me, like someone opened the bulkhead door of an airplane and sucked away the air. I smelled brimstone, fury, and darkness—

"Ashtoreth!" I called out, right as she appeared, stepping through whatever invisible portal had opened. I snarled, braced to fight or run, but the wind pinned me down, hunched over. If I tried to move or straighten it would sweep me away.

She hadn't drawn any of her weapons. She stood before me, expressionless, the lenses of her goggles two depthless holes. Her arms reached for me, grabbed me, and everything vanished.

Chapter 15

I HAD A glimpse of something red hot, a powerful sun bearing down on me, and then darkness fell. We were flying, or falling. Ashtoreth had locked me in an iron embrace and I couldn't catch my breath. A hurricane wind blew around us, sweeping us to somewhere. I might have tried to scream. I struggled, but I was trapped. Unable to make out any of the world around me, I shut my eyes. Even when I tried to open them again, I couldn't see anything. Darkness, all in darkness.

Then the wind stopped, and the demon let me go.

I fell hard, like being dumped out of a fast-moving car. Rolled for a ways on rocky ground, scuffing my arms and face, and came to rest with a mouthful of dirt. I spat it out. Lashing out, I got ready for the fight I was sure was coming, a battle with the demon and her silver-tainted weapons. I swung, kicked, scrambled into a defensive crouch—but no one was there. Ashtoreth was gone; she'd thrown me away, then apparently vanished. I couldn't see her, smell her. Then again, I couldn't smell anything. A rotten egg stink overpowered me. I sneezed and tried to breathe through my mouth. Checked for anything worse than aches or bruises, and took stock of where I'd ended up.

The air reeked, concentrated sulfur in a thick miasma. Noises surrounded me: water boiling, steam jetting from vents. The sound of heat, power, and danger. The ground under me felt hot, but despite the heat my skin broke out in gooseflesh. The air was hazy, chilled. The ground around me was barren, stained and blasted with heat and chemicals. A wintry sunlight made everything seem faded.

Rather than kill me, Ashtoreth had taken me somewhere else—her home, her origin. Capital H hell. Killing wasn't good enough for me, so she brought me here. She was gone now, and I didn't know what happened next. There had to be a way out of here. I straightened, brushed my hands on my jeans, and looked around.

I was only a little surprised to see Charles Lightman standing there, hands in pockets, polished shoe scuffing the chalky ground like he really was sorry. Mostly I felt this wash of horror that things were much, much worse than they looked. At this point, that was really saying something.

Run, Wolf growled in the back of my throat. My muscles tensed, getting ready to do just that. Not that it would help. I stared a challenge at Lightman. It was the only thing I could do, waiting for answers he wasn't giving.

"Is this hell?" I croaked. My throat ached, swollen, as if I'd gone for a week without water. My eyes stung, I was so dried out, and my skin felt stretched. I could still feel that boiling sun roasting me.

"No," he said. He seemed quite pleased with himself, giving a wry wink. "You're in the Norris Geyser Basin, in Yellowstone National Park. It's not quite open for tourist season, so we have the place to ourselves. I thought it would be fun—you can see everything up close when it blows. Should be exciting. A once-in-a-lifetime experience. Ha."

My senses finally cleared enough for me to really look around.

I was on a pale, dusty plain cupped in a shallow valley, surrounded by a pine forest. The few scattered trees on the plain were stunted and bleached, and the plain itself was awash in stinking pools of water joined by wide streams of runoff. Steam rose everywhere, and geysers spit, sloshed, and hissed around me. In some spots the crust was broken, sinkholes dropping through, lined with the orange-tinged washes. Steam rose lazily from pools, other springs bubbled with heat, and water spit noisily from holes in the ground. Yeah, it kind of looked like hell. But I was just five hundred miles from home.

Which meant I could get out of here. After I killed the guy, before Ashtoreth came back. In daylight, though, Ashtoreth wouldn't appear. Neither would Roman. I had time, I hoped, before Roman launched the Manus Herculei.

Lightman kept talking. "Regina Luporum. I hear that's what they're calling you. And you, an American, I thought you all were supposed to be against kings and queens and monarchs and all that. All democratic and egalitarian. But Queen of the Wolves—you're okay with that?"

Who was this guy? "It's just a metaphor. It doesn't mean anything."

"Oh, but it does. Monarchy, authoritarianism, has been the dominant method of organizing people for most of human history. Everything else is an anomaly. A deviation."

This area was ostensibly part of a forest in the Rocky Mountains, but it didn't feel anything like home. None of the smells were familiar. Even the ground felt unstable, boiling just under the surface. Lightman seemed unconcerned by it all. He was just as casual and pointedly charming as he had been back in Denver.

"Who are you?" I asked softly.

"Kitty, tell me—where do vampires and werewolves come from?"

This was obviously a trick question. I took the bait. "Some kind of infectious retrovirus—"

He put up a hand, shook his head. "That's a mechanism. I'm looking for *why*. How about I just tell you? Those stories about how vampires and lycanthropes, all the creatures of darkness, were made by Lucifer to pervert God's greatest creation of humanity? About how

Lucifer made monsters to stand against His righteousness at the end of time? Those stories that annoy you so much when people call into your show with them? Turns out, they're true.

"But there's one thing I couldn't change. One part of His creation I couldn't break: free will. No matter how monstrous I made you, the vampires and were-wolves, my soldiers and my children, I couldn't *make* you be monsters. You still had a choice, to follow me or not. And Katherine Norville. Kitty. You, all on your own, have been convincing a great many of my soldiers to choose the side of angels."

He didn't look like much. That was probably the point. Dux Bellorum was only the general, we'd realized. Who then was the Caesar holding his leash? Ah yes. Of course.

I always told my callers, you can choose. You can decide what to do. Don't blame your homicidal urges or basic assholeness on being a monster, because you can *choose*. God help me.

God, help me.

"Are you saying," I said, gasping a little. Wolf had gone strangely quiet—neither running nor fighting would likely do us much good here. I tried again. "Are you saying, that you, *you*, are afraid of me?" I tilted my head, narrowed my gaze, like a dog who'd heard a far-off noise. But there was just the hissing of geysers and bubbling of hot springs. I couldn't even tell if this man, this being, was breathing, or if he had a heartbeat.

"That's a strong word," he said. "But you did get my attention. That's something to be proud of, I'll give you that."

I could not stop glaring at him. One way or another, I suspected I was not going to get out of this. I could talk, I could fight, I could howl, I could run—and he was Lucifer. I might as well challenge him, because I didn't have anything to lose.

"What now?" I breathed.

"I'll kill you," he said. "Kill all your friends. Smooth the way so Dux Bellorum can finish his work and end the world. That line about it being better to reign in hell? Yeah, not so much. But Earth? I can make myself a worthy hell right here." He gazed around, as if contemplating a change of drapes in a suburban living room. Softer, he said, "Stick it to the Old Man, you know?"

I ran. Then I fell. The earth itself tripped me, with sudden cracks opening underfoot. My foot fell into already weakened crust, and when I tried to push myself back up, my hands fell through, and the earth held me there. I ripped free, spun onto my back—and again the crumbling earth trapped me, locking me in place, bands of soil folding tight over my arms and legs.

Lightman—Lucifer, though I was having trouble calling him that, it seemed so outrageous—strolled over to me. He had a sword in his right hand. I hadn't seen him carrying one; he'd probably drawn it out of thin air. He held it up, looking it over, seeming pleased. Flicked a finger over the no-doubt razor-sharp edge. It was probably silver. Wouldn't matter, because it was big enough he could chop my head off with it just by leaning a little.

"And Kitty—what is up with that? Please tell me that name's an accident and that you didn't decide to call yourself that to *spite* me."

I struggled to break free because I couldn't not, but my limbs were locked down tight. But maybe, *maybe* . . .

Let it go, let it wash over me. I imagined Wolf living behind the bars of a cage in my gut, and if those bars disappeared, I could summon her, and she would rise up, change my body, change me and we would run, escape, run all the way back home if we had to—

Nothing happened.

She was there, I could sense her, a curled-up mass of predator, of monster. Usually she was right there. When we were in danger, she came to the surface, breaking free to fight with her stronger teeth and claws. I curled my fingers, willing claws to break through the skin. But nothing happened. She wasn't waiting to break free. It was as if she slept.

"Oh no," he said, showing teeth as he grinned. "You don't get that power. Not while I'm here. You won't be a wolf for me, you certainly won't be one against me."

Being a werewolf was a disease, a curse. I'd spent most of the last ten years working *not* to shape-shift, to keep it together, to control the urge to turn Wolf and run. But now, *now*, I needed her, I needed Wolf, I needed to shift and fight and flee on her long animal legs.

Wolf slept.

I whined, a breath exhaling on the verge of a scream.

"Yeah," Lucifer murmured. "You're not so tough."

He took the hilt in both hands, held the point over my heart, and a look of blazing hatred crossed his face as he prepared to drive down. I kept my eyes open. I could do that. No life flashing before me. Not much of anything. Just glaring at him, with animal focus.

He stabbed down, grunting with effort—and the point of the sword stopped cold an inch above my breastbone. It didn't move, didn't waver, no matter how hard he pressed. He tried again, slashing at my neck this time, then my face. Instinctively, I winced away. But he didn't kill me. He couldn't even hurt me.

Falling to his knees beside me, he began pawing me. But he couldn't touch me. His hands skittered an inch away from my skin, my clothes. He threw the sword away; it vanished.

His expression went slack, his eyes focusing on the collar of my shirt.

"What are you wearing around your neck? Show me. Show me now."

My right hand burst away from the dirt trapping it. I went to punch him with it, but I didn't get very far with the rest of my body pinned down, and he smoothly leaned away from the hit.

"Show. Me," he said, teeth bared.

"Ha," I said, teeth also bared. "Pissed you off."

"What are you wearing around your neck?"

I pulled at the cord and let the coin hang over my shirt. My wedding ring, which I wore on a chain rather than on my finger most of the time, came with it, but I pushed it aside, hiding it from him. What was left: the marked-up coin of Dux Bellorum, the one worn by Angelo. His betrayal, turned on its head.

He drew back, then laughed. "These were supposed to mark my followers, my acolytes. Identify them to each other, connect them to me. Nothing more. But this? I have no idea what this means." He tried again to reach for the coin, but once again his touch skittered away from me.

I'd spent enough time with Cormac, Amelia, and Odysseus Grant, I thought I knew what they'd say: destroying, marring the coins didn't just negate their power. It was a repudiation. A declaration not just of independence, but of opposition. And there was power in that—a deep, protective magic. Maybe entirely unintentional, but I wasn't going to question it.

"You can't hurt me," I said madly.

He leered back. "No, I can't *kill* you. I'm pretty sure I can hurt you."

The ground under me cracked and collapsed. Finally, I screamed.

Chapter 16

A SINKHOLE OPENED under me, dropping me into an underground pool of steaming-hot water, one of the sources that fed the aboveground geyser systems. The water was so hot it didn't register as heat at first—I splashed in, and felt numb. When the searing came, it was almost from the inside out, muscles flaring then flashing to a burn on my skin.

I was still a werewolf, I was still tough. The burning wouldn't kill me. Whatever happened, I would heal. I kept telling myself that.

Snarling with the effort, clothes dripping, I splashed to my feet and looked for escape. I was in a crevice, a cleft jagging its way across the pockmarked rock. Exposed to air, my burned skin seared as if every cell were on fire. My feet, still in the pool of water, were boiling. I could smell my own flesh cooking.

I ran, but the ground under me shook and I tripped, falling again into the hot stream.

Lightman stood over me at the edge of the crevice, ready to inflict the next blow. He couldn't touch me, but he could affect everything around me. The ground rumbled, edges of the crevice crumbling further, stones pattering down. Another earthquake—he could keep opening sinkholes under me until I baked to death in a pool of magma. And he would watch, grinning that smug Hollywood grin.

He expected me to run; he figured all he had to do was keep me from running away. I couldn't shift, but I still had Wolf's power. She was still inside me, and unthinking I moved with her drive, her fierceness. Scrambling over debris up the side of the crevice, I went straight toward him. Didn't stop, didn't plan. This was a hunt; I only focused on the target.

I could tell by the startled roundness in his eyes he hadn't expected me to run at him. I discovered, gratefully, that while he couldn't touch me, I could touch him. But I wasn't interested in touching so much as grabbing, shoving, and stomping. Wrapping my hand in the first bit of convenient shirt, at the buttons, I yanked, swung him around, and put my shoulder into knocking him over the side, right into the water where I'd been. He made a shout. I didn't look back. I didn't have time. I barely paused, kept moving forward.

Any minute now I expected the ground to open under me. It wouldn't even have been him doing it; it might have just been the soft dirt weakened by thermals. My feet sank a few times, but I scrambled on. Avoided anyplace with cracks or steam spitting out. I made for the trees and the ridge marking the edge of the basin.

When I finally fell, skidding into a bank of ice-crusted snow lingering in shadows, I curled up and didn't get back up again. My skin and all my nerves throbbed. My cheek, pressed into the ice, was the only part of me not on fire, so I focused on that, the soothing chill. The rest of me, though—all my muscles locked up with the pain.

I'd heal. I'd get better. I had to be patient. In the meantime, blacking out would be nice. Instead, I listened for following footsteps, for a suave voice taunting me from beyond the next row of trees. I had to hold my breath, to keep from gasping loudly.

Quiet, all quiet.

I unfolded—carefully, slowly. I didn't want to look at myself. My muscles seemed to pop, and my skin stretched, feeling like it was blistered and falling off. But it was still there, though tender, and probably lobster-red. My feet were blistered, swollen. My shoes were just gone. But I was still conscious. I was still in one piece. Lucifer hadn't found me yet.

I was in the middle of Yellowstone, with no clue what to do next. I patted my jeans pocket—my phone was there. Whether I'd get any reception—No, no I would not.

Run.

The word *run* was sometimes a euphemism among werewolves. It didn't just mean the physical movement of running. It also meant turn, shift, flee to the wilderness. *Run with me,* meant something more.

"You're back," I murmured. "You're awake."

My Wolf stirred, and I felt something like claws press against the inside of my gut. Wolf, awake, wanting to run. *It's time to go.*

Whatever Lightman had done to lock her away, we were out of range now, and he couldn't stop us. We had to get away before he found us.

This was going to hurt.

Even taking off my clothes hurt, so I worked it like a Band-Aid—ripping it off fast rather than prolonging the torture, shoving off my jeans, and dealing with the flaming agony of fabric rubbing against blistered skin. Before I was too far gone, I checked for the coin, made sure the cord was tight and solidly around my neck, pressed it firmly to my chest, and repeated over and over, don't lose it, don't lose it. Maybe Wolf would remember, maybe Wolf would keep the coin safe. We needed it.

Then I let go of the bars of the cage in my gut, and Wolf roared out. My neck arched back, my teeth bared, my limbs stretched. Fur prickled along my burned skin, but I shut my eyes and let it wash through me. I was strong, I was Wolf—

Run, that's all there is. There is pain, but it will pass. The danger is too large to manage. Some hunts aren't worth the effort, so you leave off and wait for better odds. Running means being able to try again later.

This territory is difficult and unfamiliar. It ought to smell like forest and mountain, like home, but there's a stench masking the air, confusing her. Finally, she finds a deer trail, follows it not to hunt, but to find water. A river, close. She heads toward this. It smells safe. Stretching, she lopes faster, her stride covering ground. The pain lessens the faster she goes, as if she is fleeing pain. Wind through her fur doesn't hurt the way air on skin did.

Along the way she smells wolves—musky and alien. She avoids those scents and trails. She's in foreign territory, and she isn't strong enough to meet new wolves, especially ones that clearly aren't like her. Wild wolves, pure wolves.

The daylight is too bright and feels wrong; she's used to running at night.

Something hard and uncomfortable thumps against her chest with every stride. She could stop, scratch it off and get rid of it, but her other self whispers urgently, don't lose it. She must carry it in her teeth if she has to, but she must not lose it. So she leaves it around her neck, and its weight is a reminder of what she flees.

She runs a long time until her tongue hangs out and her breath pants, but she finds a place that doesn't smell of rot and steam, where young pine trees slope down to a clean-running river. Here, she smells prey and other predators, competition. Bear and fox as well *as wolf. She avoids these. Is too tired and hurt to hunt. Isn't even hungry, much. Sleep now, hunt later. Survive, the rest will come. She snugs into a den by a fallen tree, on fresh earth, rich with dead leaves and living forest.*

I HEARD voices, one male and one female, talking nearby. I couldn't understand them because they were speaking a different language. Chinese maybe? Though I was woozy, I was sure if I just concentrated hard enough I'd be able to understand them. Their manner was low and urgent.

I looked, but wasn't sure I was really awake. Somehow I could feel that my eyes were amber, like Wolf's, and saw the world through wavering, hyperfocused senses. But I had human hands, human fingers with hardened, pointed nails—not quite claws but definitely not normal nails. Gray and tawny fur covered my arms. I felt my face—a human face, flat with a small nose, but dusted in fur. My ears were Wolf's pointed ears. I rubbed my arms, ruffling the fur, and shivered. It was like I was caught halfway between forms, stuck between myself and her. *We are the same.*

In a dark forest I saw trees drawn out in hard lines, with movement flickering in the underbrush. The silver cast of a full moon edged it all, but that wasn't right, either—full moon was still a week off. And the moon was too close, filling up a quarter of the sky, like in a drawing or a dream.

I breathed and moved slowly.

They were still talking. My voice came out groggy when I said, "I can't understand you . . . do you speak English?"

They stopped. I felt like the speakers should be right next to me, but I couldn't see them. Their air felt thick, like I had to swim through it.

"She's awake," the male voice said, and I recognized it. It was right at the corner of my memory . . .

"Are we taking her home?" I recognized her voice, too.

"No, she has to stay, to stop the thing. We just have to watch her until the others get here."

"That may overstep our bounds. We can only interfere so much—"

"If that jerk can bring her here, we can watch over her," he said decisively.

"He isn't even part of our mythology," she muttered.

The man was almost cheerful when he said, "Yeah, it's all just a big old muddle now. I blame globalization."

I knew those voices. I knew who they were.

A figure stood among the trees, cloaked and regal, long black hair draped over one shoulder, her dark eyes shining and pale lips pressed in a thin smile.

"Anastasia," I breathed, and ran. I stopped short before pouncing on her for a massive hug because I was suddenly afraid that if I touched her, she would vanish, this strangeness would all disappear.

From behind her emerged the man, Chinese like her, slender, young looking, with wild black hair and an infectious smile. He wore an embroidered silk tunic, a far cry from the jeans and T-shirt I'd last seen him in.

"And Sun," I said. My eyes leaked tears. Sun Wukong. The Monkey King. For real.

"Hey," he said, raising a hand. "You're a mess, kid."

"I know," I whined.

"What a strange road we've traveled," Anastasia said. She had a beautiful face, the finely wrought features of a figure in a Chinese painting. When I knew her, she'd been a vampire, born in the Song dynasty as Li Hua. I didn't know what she was now. She'd followed her goddess Xiwangmu, Queen Mother of the West, into another world. Sun Wukong—we all called him Sun—had been there, too. And now they were here. To help, I hoped.

"Where are you? Where is this? What's going on?" My own voice was low, scratching, like I was getting over a cold, but clearing my throat didn't help. I sounded like a wolf speaking through a growl.

"We're between worlds, of course," she said.

Between worlds, sleeping and waking, human and animal, alive and dead.

"Are . . . are you okay?"

She tilted her head, looking amused. "Are you?"

"I—I don't know. I think I just dumped Lucifer into a geyser. Not that that'll stop him."

Sun said, "There's a war on, and this is only one small part of it. We're all caught up in it. But you're *really* caught up in it."

"I brought it on myself. I could have walked away."

More gently Anastasia said, "I've been sending you as much help as I can."

"Thank you, thank you so much for that." I reached to squeeze her hand, but pulled back, because my furred arms and clawed fingers startled me all over again.

She said, "He's here, he's close, and you don't have time. Remember this: stop the spell, not the man. Stop the spell."

I finally did touch her, to brush her sleeve, to reassure myself, but my hand passed through her.

"But I don't know how, I still don't even know what he's doing—"

Sun was moving back into the trees, into the shadows. "I'll help. Look for me."

"Okay, okay—"

"Stay safe, stay strong." Anastasia's ghostly hand closed over mine. I wanted to grab her, hold her, keep her close. But that didn't seem possible.

"Anastasia—I miss you. I *need* you!" She was the strongest woman I knew. She'd been fighting Roman for almost eight hundred years. The wind ruffled my fur, and a howl built up in my throat.

The wind knocked me over, spat dust in my face. As I'd learned whenever Ashtoreth appeared: when doors opened between worlds, wind blasted through. My fur couldn't keep me warm, my feet didn't stay grounded.

I tried to shout again, but I couldn't see her anymore, I couldn't see anything, and the wind was driving daggers into me—

THEN I woke up, for real.

It was daylight. The same day or the next day, I didn't know. Weeks might have passed, but I didn't think so. The world was still here, the sun was still shining. I curled my fingers—regular fingers, with flat human nails—and they dug into the soft dirt of a springtime forest. I heard birdsong, and everything smelled clean, of rich earth and growing things, air moving through pine trees. I could rest here, curled up naked under a half-rotten tree trunk, just breathing, forever.

When I finally looked myself over, I appeared to have a bad sunburn. The burned places were tender, annoying but not crippling. The blisters on my feet had faded. I ached, but didn't hurt.

In a sudden panic, I clapped my hand on my chest and found the coin on its cord, right where it should be. I hadn't lost it. But I didn't know what had happened to my wedding ring. Back with my clothes probably. I tried not to despair.

I shivered. The spring air this far into the mountains and wilderness was still cold. I could survive it. But really, I needed to find some clothes. And a phone. Right *now*.

Look for me, Sun had said. I didn't know where to start.

The spell, Anastasia had said. Stop the spell. Yes, of course, that was what we'd been trying to do all along. I was in Yellowstone now, and I assumed Roman was, too, so I supposed I was closer. I remembered her smile, the ghostly touch of her hand, and wanted to cry. I needed her—why couldn't she be here to help me?

Because she was summoning allies. She was rallying the troops. That needed to be done, and she could do it. Right.

I moved cautiously, alert for the least sound, smell, or flash of movement, knowing full well that if Lightman appeared, it would be suddenly and with no warning. The coin protected me, but only to a point.

The world around me was soothingly normal. The sky was clear and blue. Nice day out. A river ran nearby—its smell had drawn Wolf, the freshness of it had signaled safety. Some distance beyond it, visible from the slope of the hill I was on, was what looked like a major road, two lanes, well paved. This was promising. I followed the river downstream, knowing that it and the road would eventually lead somewhere useful. I found a bridge to cross and watched for cars—didn't see any. It might have been too early in the season for much traffic in the park.

After a few minutes of walking, I picked up the pace, moving in a Wolfish lope. I didn't have time to waste.

Half an hour later, an old beater pickup truck rumbled past. I was sweaty, grimy, and still naked, so I ducked back behind a tree, trying to decide if I should leap out and shout for help, possibly shocking the driver of said truck to death. At best, the driver might call the police and race away from the crazy naked woman. But it might actually stop, and it might actually have a phone I could use. And maybe a blanket or an extra coat. I wasn't about to go back for my own clothes.

I was still debating when the truck swerved up ahead, did a U-turn, and roared back, parking on the shoulder near my hiding place. So, for good or bad, I'd been spotted. Still unsure, I waited.

The driver got out, shaded his eyes, and peered into the woods. I clapped my hands over my mouth to suppress a squeal.

"Sun!" I said, moving into the open, waving. He smiled and waved back. He was back in jeans and a white T-shirt, and seemed all too normal.

Unselfconscious, I ran to the truck and bounced up against it so we were looking at each other over the hood.

"I had a dream," I said. "You and Anastasia were there. Was that real? That was real?"

"More or less." He winked.

I glared, and he threw me a blanket from the cab of the truck.

"Do you also happen to have a phone on you?" I asked, wrapping myself with the blanket and knotting it in place. Wearing a blanket like a muumuu wasn't much better than being naked, really.

He winced. "You know, I don't. Never been able to get the hang of those things."

"Why bother, when you're a divine being?" I said.

"Exactly!" He grinned.

"You do know we're trying to stop the end of the world here, right?"

"Yes. And there's a ranger station up the road, they'll have a phone. Get in."

So I did.

I SLUMPED in the truck's passenger seat. The vinyl was cracked, stuffing coming out. Rock chips marred the windshield, and the thing didn't appear to have any heat. Sun said it was what he could find on short notice, and besides, he liked it because it had personality. Who could argue with that? He'd been kicking around Chinatown in Vancouver when Anastasia came to him and asked for help. Now he was here.

The sun was getting low in the sky. I didn't even know if it was the same day anymore. I wouldn't *really* worry about Roman until nightfall—he could only come out after dark. He hadn't triggered the volcano yet—obviously. But how much time did we have?

I asked Sun, and he said, "Traveling between worlds like that is messy. Not instantaneous. I'm pretty sure it's the same day you got grabbed—the day of the earthquake in Denver, right? We still have time."

The road widened to a series of small gatehouses,

with what looked like an administration building on the side, painted dark brown and rustic looking. Sun pulled the truck into a tiny parking lot off to the side. I'd spotted a ranger moving around inside the first gate-house. That seemed to be exactly what the immediate situation called for, someone in a uniform whom I could ask for help.

I looked down at myself, bundled in a gray military-grade blanket and nothing else. My scalp itched, and I still looked like I had a wretched sunburn from being dunked in a steaming-hot pool of water. Really, there wasn't going to be a good way to do this. Desperation trumped self-consciousness. I needed that phone.

"You coming with?" I asked Sun as I pushed open the creaking door.

"Wouldn't miss it," he said.

I walked across the asphalt, barefoot, edges of the blanket flapping. Sun walked at my side. He might have been coming along for the entertainment value, but I felt marginally more confident with him here. I knocked at the door of the gatehouse. The woman opened it, and her eyes only widened a moment before she said, "Ma'am, do you need help?"

I took a deep breath. "Yes. Yes I do. Can I use your phone?"

RANGER LOPEZ took us to an office in the nearby administration building. She was thirty-something, brusque and professional, looking stern in her uniform.

She sat us down in plastic chairs and offered coffee, which Sun turned down but I pounced on, politely as I could. I might have looked like a wild woman emerged from wilderness, but I didn't have to act like one. Lopez kept glancing at us sidelong, lips pursed, obviously trying to figure us out. She asked few questions—I told her my name, that I'd gotten lost and Sun was a friend helping out, and it was a long story. I wasn't sure how she'd take it if I said I was a werewolf. I definitely wasn't going to say anything about how I'd gotten here.

She gave me the phone I'd asked for. At the same time, she went to another phone, another line, and spoke softly—not so softly that we couldn't hear. She'd called a supervisor and was explaining the situation, asking what she should do about me. I even heard bits of the reply—had I been doing anything illegal? No, not that Lopez could tell. Did I need hospitalization? Hell, if they tried to take me into custody I could just run. Did Lopez suspect anything untoward going on between Sun and me? Lopez just wasn't sure.

Yeah, I could imagine what this looked like from the outside, but I had more important worries at the moment.

I called Cheryl first.

"Hello?"

"Hey, Cheryl, what's up?"

"Earthquake, can you believe it? The kids are convinced the roof is going to fall. And how about you? Besides frazzled. You're sounding kind of frazzled."

Oh hell, yeah. "Frazzled. That's a word for it. Cheryl, I need you to do something kind of crazy. I need you to get Mom and Dad, Mark and the kids, everyone, into a car and drive south. Get out of Denver, get out of the whole state if you can."

"What? Why? I mean, that is crazy, but why?"

How to explain it all as briefly and sensibly as possible? If . . . when . . . the Yellowstone hot spot blew, the seismic blast would affect a huge area. The debris cloud would reach even farther, raining ash and rock, spreading poison gases. Denver was in that path. I didn't know how much time we had, I didn't know if it was even possible to evacuate everyone who would be affected by this—the entire Great Plains and Midwest, for a start. Selfishly, I figured I could try to save at least one family: mine.

"I think something's going to happen, something bad," I said. "I may be wrong, but just in case, grab the essentials and drive south." South, out of the range of the blast. I hoped.

"Kitty, what's going to happen—"

"A volcanic eruption."

"You're right, that's absolutely crazy." But she sounded stressed. She believed me.

"Do you trust me, Cheryl?"

"Yes. Of course I do."

"Then just do it. If I'm wrong you can kick me later."

"Kitty, are you okay? Are you in danger?"

I was sitting right on top of the volcano. "Don't

worry about me, just get everyone out of Denver. I'll call you when I know more."

"Kitty—"

I hung up, because I didn't have anything else to say. What else was there to say? I didn't want to spend more time going around in circles about whether or not I was crazy.

"We'll stop it, Kitty," Sun said gently and with confidence. "I'm sure we'll stop it in time."

"Yeah. But . . . it'll make me feel better."

I made the next call. The phone rang once, twice, more, and I thought my head was going to burst until finally he picked up. "Yeah?"

"Ben?"

"Kitty! Holy shit, where are you? What happened? I smelled the brimstone but it was over by the time I got to the back of the building, and—are you okay? Kitty—"

"I'm fine, I'm alive," I amended. "There's so much crap going on I don't even know where to start."

"Where are you?"

Another deep breath. I was forgetting to breathe. "I'm in Yellowstone."

"Right, good, okay."

I blinked. "What do you mean, good okay?"

"That's where we thought you'd gone. Tina and Grant tracked you. And Anastasia—I guess she found a way to let them know. We're on the way, somewhere in BFE Wyoming, still a couple hours away. Can you hang on until we get there?"

I started crying, silent, stressed-out tears. "Yeah, I think so. Sun found me here—you remember Sun? Ben, something really terrible is about to happen. I called Cheryl and told her to get the family out of Denver."

He paused and said, "So it's happening, for real?"

"I don't know. I met . . . is Cormac with you? Tell him I met the Caesar commanding Dux Bellorum."

"It's bad, I take it?"

"It's very bad," I said.

"Kitty, just hold on. I love you."

"I love you, too."

I didn't want to hang up, but we had to. I scrubbed tears off my cheeks, and Sun held my hand. By then, the ranger was watching us. She'd listened in on my conversation this time.

She said, "Ms. Norville, what do you think is going to happen?"

The end of the world . . . "You've got a lot of geologists monitoring the park, right? A lot of seismographs. You track earthquakes and stuff pretty carefully, right? Has there been any increase in activity? Has anything changed?"

Her smile was wry and long suffering, like she got asked this question a lot. "I know everyone likes to talk about what would happen if the caldera blew, and I know geologically it has to happen sooner or later. But I really don't think we have anything to worry about."

"Okay, yeah, but say it was going to happen, oh, tonight—would there be any warning?"

"This is all just speculation—"

"I know. Tell me."

"There'd be an increase in seismic activity—earthquakes. There'd be a measurable bulge in the crust, and probably a drastic change in thermal activity."

"Like, the geysers would all go off at once or something like that?"

"Or they'd all stop. My geologist friends say that's when we really need to worry, is if they ever all go quiet."

"And there's been nothing like that?"

"Let me make a call to a buddy over at Old Faithful."

We waited. I chewed a fingernail. Glanced out the window just in case Lightman came striding up the road. He didn't, not yet.

"Hey, Roy," Lopez said. "When's the last time Old Faithful blew? Half an hour ago? So it should go off again around"—she glanced at the clock—"four fifteen, yeah? Great, thanks." She smiled at me. "Geysers are normal. Feel better?"

Oddly, I did. Whatever was going to happen, it hadn't started—or it wasn't about to finish. We had time. While it was still daylight, Roman couldn't be out causing trouble. And Lightman couldn't, not by himself, or he'd have done it already. He needed pawns, Ashtoreth and an army of vampires and werewolves.

In the meantime, I was still snuggled in the office chair, wrapped in a blanket.

"Thank you for not calling the cops on me," I said to the ranger.

"No worries. You just seem lost, not crazy."

Small comfort, there.

Sun asked, "Is there a restaurant or diner around here where we can get something to eat? And maybe a place to pick up some clothes?"

"Yeah, down the road in West Yellowstone. Wait just a sec." She went into a back office.

She came back with spare set of clothes, sweatpants and a hoodie. "This should be more comfortable than that blanket."

I sighed a very heartfelt thanks. "I promise to wash them and get them back to you—"

"Don't worry about," she said. "Just take care of yourself."

Yeah, that was me, crazy enough to elicit worry from strangers, but not enough to actually commit. Yet.

Chapter 17

WEST YELLOWSTONE, a few miles outside the park's
west gate, was a lot like other wildnerness tourist
towns I'd been to, except maybe a little more hopped
up on hype and enthusiasm. A lot of one-story motor
lodges done up to look like log cabins, a lot of billboards
advertising snowmobile tours. They probably offered
ATV tours in the summer.

We pulled up to a rustic diner—fake log cabin siding,
murals of moose and bison hung up between picture
windows—to wait for the others and come up with the
next plan. Maybe Ben and Cormac and the rest had
thought of the ultimate Stop Roman Plan, at long last.
How hard could this be? Two thousand years, and no
one had stopped him yet. That was how hard.

We'd just closed the truck doors and were standing
in the parking lot when the asphalt under our feet
shook, just for a couple of seconds. Having felt this a
few times now, I knew exactly what it was. I put both

hands on the truck's hood for balance and waited. A car alarm somewhere started wailing, glass in the diner's windows rattled, then everything fell still. A few people ran out of the diner and surrounding shops and buildings. There was talk and confusion.

"That's the kind of thing you're worried about, isn't it?" Sun, also leaning on the truck's hood, asked.

"If things get really bad, I don't suppose you can use your divine power to zap us out of here like Ashtoreth does?" I asked.

His brow wrinkled. "Ashtoreth. That one is bad news. Really annoying. But no, I can't. Sorry."

As other diners wandered back into the building, a pair of calm men in smart business suits came out, apparently unaffected by the tremor. They went to a nondescript white sedan a few parking spots down, and one of them glanced up at me.

They were my two Men in Black.

I took a few steps toward them and called, "You!"

The one at the driver's side looked up and smiled widely. "Oh! Hello, there."

"What are you doing here?"

They glanced at each other, then back at me. "We thought we'd try a little early season fly-fishing."

"*Seriously?*" I was sounding a little screechy. "You obviously know what's happening. You have some stake in it, you have . . . some kind of power. So why don't you do something? What don't you stop Roman? Or Lightman?"

They flinched a little when I said the name.

"She's met him," one of them said to the other.

"Things really are bad," his partner answered.

"Then help me!" I demanded, my fists clenched.

The pale one looked chagrined. "I'm sorry, Ms. Norville, but we can't really do anything but watch. Technically, this isn't our world, so our influence here is limited. A push here, a nudge here—you know?"

"He knows," the black-haired one said, indicating Sun.

"Hi," Sun said, waving. "Have we met?"

"No, but I believe Xiwangmu knows us."

"Oh, well, okay then."

I wanted to pull my hair out. I was very tempted to strip naked and run back to the park, but I had to wait for Ben.

"Ms. Norville," the black-haired Man in Black said. "We very much look forward to talking to you when this is all over."

I stared. "Should I be encouraged? That you think we'll be around to talk when this is all over?"

"Yes," he said. "Definitely. There's always hope, don't ever forget that."

"Who the hell are you guys? At least give me a hint."

"Good-bye, Ms. Norville." And just like that, they got into their car and drove away.

Sun had come up beside me and was also staring.

"Do *you* know who they are?" I asked.

He shook his head. "No. But they are totally not human."

"What?"

He crossed his arms, pursed his lips, like he was considering a particularly complicated puzzle. "Don't know exactly *what* they are, but they're *definitely* not human."

"What does that even mean?"

"Since you and I aren't human, either, I wouldn't worry about it too much," he said.

Oh dear lord, I needed a fucking nap.

Inside the diner's front door I used a pay phone and called Ranger Lopez. I absolutely could not wait until I got my phone back, only I didn't know exactly how I was going to do that, since it was in the pocket of my jeans, which I'd left somewhere outside the Norris Geyser Basin, along with my wedding ring. She'd given me her card in case I needed anything. "Hi, yeah," I said when she answered. "How's Old Faithful doing?"

"I'm sure it's fine—"

"Can you just check? Did it go off as scheduled?"

"Just a minute . . ." The line clicked as she put me on hold. A minute later, she came back on. "Yes, it went off right on schedule. Nothing to worry about."

"Yeah, okay. Thanks."

"You're sure everything's okay?"

Not really . . . "There was a little bit of an earthquake a few minutes ago."

"Yeah, we felt that one. Seismologists say it was a pretty good one. But you know we get little quakes up here all the time, right?"

"That was little?"

"Pretty little, yeah. Try not to worry, Ms. Norville."

"Yeah. Okay. Thanks."

Try not to worry, ha. Next I called Ben again, to tell him exactly where we were waiting. And to hear his voice. "There's been an earthquake. A tremor, like in Denver."

"That can't be good."

"Apparently earthquakes are pretty common around here."

"But still."

"I know."

"Just hold tight. We'll be there as fast as we can. I'm glad Sun is there with you."

"Yeah, me, too."

Staying still means being a target.

Yeah, it did. "Wolf wants to run."

"I know. Soon."

A pot of coffee and plate of bacon had already arrived at the booth Sun had claimed. I was starving and hadn't even realized it. I'd run to get away from Lightman, but I hadn't hunted.

Lopez had given me a map of the park, and this was my first chance to spread it out and study it. The Norris Basin was roughly northwest from the middle of the park. The river I'd followed was the Madison. Escaping Lightman, I'd run for some thirty miles. But distance didn't mean anything to him. He could teleport right into the middle of the diner and I wouldn't be able to do anything about it. I wasn't safe anywhere. Somehow, that was easier—if no place was safe I ought to just stop worrying, right?

Sun sat with both hands wrapped around his mug, sipping coffee while watching me. On the other hand, I was slumped back, staring into space. This was a marathon with no end in sight. Well, there was always the fiery eruption of a world-shattering supervolcano. That was one sort of end.

"What are you thinking?" he said. *He* didn't seem worried about anything. He never had.

I sighed, sipped my own coffee because it was there and getting cold. I was still in borrowed sweats and a hoodie. No one seemed to have noticed I was barefoot, because who expected someone to be barefoot in the mountains in spring?

"I need to get shoes, I think," I said. "And a copy of Revelation. And *Paradise Lost*. I mean, now that I met the guy. He'll be coming after me. He has to, right? He was so pissed off."

"So you have to get away," Sun said. "We can do that."

"No, I have to find Roman." I set down the mug and leaned my head in my hands. "It's too much. I'll never find him."

"But you've already made it so far," Sun said. "You're not giving up now, are you?"

Figured, the Monkey King would be the one person more cheerful and optimistic than I was. In some stories, the Monkey King was a trickster figure. Of course he'd be enjoying this.

I turned back to the map. Yellowstone Lake was the park's most prominent landmark, and you really could roughly follow the shape of the ancient volcanic caldera around much of its edge. When you knew where to look, the caldera was obvious, not just in the lake, but in the ridges and shape of the land around it. It might have been covered with trees and roads, but it was still there. Groups of geysers were clustered around its edge. The lake was large, over 130 square miles, with over a hundred miles of shoreline. That was a lot of ground to cover, searching for Roman. Come nightfall, he'd be out there somewhere, casting the spell. Ashtoreth would be waiting with him, ready to teleport him to safety before the whole thing blew. And Lightman would be in the background, rubbing his hands together gleefully.

I wasn't any closer to stopping them than when I'd first heard about the Long Game. We were so far past that.

"If you were going to trigger an eruption of a super-volcano," I said, "what would you do?"

"I'd throw a bomb into the middle of it. You know, like throwing a lighter into a fireworks factory. Kaboom." He made a bursting motion with his hands. He didn't even have to think about it, which was vaguely disturbing.

"You make it sound simple," I said.

"Well, yeah."

Okay, then. Working on that plan in the absence of any other: what constituted the middle of this volcano? "There's the lake. There's Norris Basin—that's where Lightman was, so there might be some connection. But it's outside the edge of the caldera. We need to think logically about this—maybe find the lowest spot in the park, in case he needs to be close to the hot spot for the spell to work? I wish I had my books here."

Sun slumped back in the booth, hands pillowed behind his head, and closed his eyes. Obviously, this was a good time for a nap.

I asked the server for a pen and started making notes on a napkin.

WHEN THE pay phone by the front door rang, I jumped from the booth so fast I banged my knees on the table. Didn't even slow me down.

"Hello?"

"Kitty?" It was Ben, and I sighed happily.

"We're just about in West Yellowstone. Are you still okay? Where are you?"

"The Wilderness Diner. It's on the main drag. Looks like a malnourished log cabin, you can't miss it. Hurry, if you can." I glanced out the front doors—the sky had the golden cast of late afternoon. Not much time before nightfall.

"I'll see you soon."

Back at the booth, Sun really did look like he'd been able to get some sleep. I was jealous. He was sitting up now, and calling for the check and pulling out cash. Which was good, because I didn't have any money. I needed shoes. I needed Ben.

Practically bouncing with nerves, I went outside as a familiar Jeep pulled into the parking lot and stopped in a spot in front of me. I almost hugged it. A second later, Ben just about fell out of the passenger seat and came at me. We ran into each other. I jumped at him, and he lifted me off the ground. I pressed my face against his neck and breathed deep. This was home, this was safe.

"What the hell happened?" he murmured in my ear. "You sure you're okay?"

"I think we're in trouble," I murmured back. It was too much to explain here.

He let me slip back to the ground, but I didn't want to let go. When I let go, I'd have to start moving again. I brushed my hand along his face, which was in the process of graduating from stubble to actual beard. He probably hadn't shaved in the same amount of time that I hadn't slept. Pleasantly scratchy. He leaned into the touch and sighed.

"Hi, guys," Sun said, waving. "Nice to see you again."

Cormac was leaning on the hood of the Jeep. He smirked and shook his head. "This just keeps getting weirder."

"Hey," Ben said. "Let me guess: Anastasia."

"Right in one," Sun said.

Ben shook his head and chuckled.

"I have so much to tell you—"

"Not here," Cormac said. "Let's not talk about this in the open with Roman and his crew running around. Tina and the others are getting rooms." He climbed into the Jeep without waiting for a response.

"You know how you're always saying you want a vacation?" Ben said. "Well, I'm ready."

I hitched a thumb toward the park. "Top U.S. tourist destination, right over there."

"Not the same. Wait a minute—where are your shoes?" His nose wrinkled, as if he was just now noticing my clothes didn't smell like me.

"Yeah," I said. "Did I mention I have a lot to tell you?"

The four of us got ourselves to our various vehicles and took off to meet the others.

BEN FORCED a detour to a sporting goods store to buy me hiking boots, socks, jeans, and a coat. Made things a little more comfortable. He was coddling me, which was sweet, and I gave into the urge to let him, sitting curled up against him, both of us crammed into one seat in the Jeep, while he glared out at anything that looked like it might touch me.

The place where we ended up was one of those old-fashioned motor lodges, two stories tall with all the doors and windows overlooking the parking lot. The Pine Tree Inn. Quaint. The parking lot was half filled with cars. We weren't quite in the tourist season, but the place wasn't deserted, either. And all I could think was: if the volcano erupts, all these people would die.

The others had gathered in one room. Tina gave me a giant hug when I appeared. We both winced—she still had broken ribs, and my skin was still tender. Grant nodded solemnly, and Hardin looked relieved, like she hadn't believed I really was still in one piece. The gang was all here, and I felt a sense of awe at the army I'd gathered.

I introduced Sun as Sun, and nothing more. He didn't elaborate, and everyone accepted him without question. Tina narrowed her gaze when they shook hands; her sixth sense was telling her something, but she didn't say what. We could deal with his identity as a major figure from Chinese folklore later, I figured.

The eight of us—counting Amelia as eighth—gathered, sitting on the pair of beds and pulling up chairs. I remained standing, and I flashed on an image: that drawing in my office, the memory of a presence behind me, looking over my shoulder. People kept calling me Regina Luporum—people like *Anastasia* kept calling me that.

They were all looking at me. Not just waiting for me to explain what had happened to me, but wanting me to say what we needed to do next. It was too big—but they were here because of me. I rolled back my shoulders, settled myself, and told them the story. About Lightman, what he'd told me, our fight among the boiling springs. The powers he'd shown, how I managed to get away, and the dream I'd had—that yes, we had help, at least to a point. And how we had until nightfall to make a plan.

It took time because it sounded crazy, and there was no way to make it sound less crazy. I rambled a bit. When I finished, everyone stared at me.

Cormac leaned back in his chair and blew out a breath. "Well, is that all?"

"I'm not letting you out of my sight ever again," Ben said, squeezing my hand. That was fine with me.

"He's not invincible," I said. "Or we wouldn't have gotten this far."

The gazes around me did not seem entirely certain. I clung to what momentum I had. Otherwise, it would be too easy to curl up on the bed with Ben and never get up again. Just wait for the inevitable.

Cormac turned to his canvas bag and started laying out a familiar collection of objects: amulets, demon goggles, and old books. "You said the coin stopped Lightman?" He spoke with an intensity that made me think it was Amelia. Magical artifacts were her thing, after all.

"Yes. He could hurt me, but not kill me."

Grant looked up. "So it confers some kind of invulnerability."

"No," I added, wincing, because my brain hurt trying to sort it all out. "Kumarbis was wearing one of these when Ashtoreth killed him. So it may only protect us from Lightman. Is that possible?"

"It's magic," Grant said.

Cormac pursed his lips. "Lightman is Caesar to Roman's Dux Bellorum. The coins mark his followers—identifies them not just to Roman, but to Lightman as well. To break the coin, to mark it up, is to disavow them both. And Lightman loses some of his power as a result." Definitely Amelia.

"That actually makes sense," Ben said.

"Right. Everyone gets a coin." Cormac started handing them out. We had six of them, counting the one I was already wearing. I could identify them all, remembering where each one came from: the starving vampire we'd tracked down in Dodge City, Kansas; the one Anastasia had worn; Jan, the Master vampire we'd confronted in London; Kumarbis; Mercedes; Angelo. Each one marked out the long road that had brought us here.

"We're one short," Ben said, after everyone had gotten one—except Sun.

"It's okay," he said. "I don't need one."

Cormac snorted a chuckle, because he knew. Tina looked worried. "Are you sure?"

"Absolutely sure," said Sun, grinning.

"He's got a different set of rules," I said.

Next, Cormac dug into his collection of amulets and drew out the bronzed Maltese cross. "Kitty, you're getting this one this time. Put it on."

"That's the one that reflects spells, right? Why do I get it? You're the one who knows how it works."

"You've got the biggest target painted on you," he said.

Well, shit. Fair enough. Ben took it out of Cormac's hand and hung the cord over my neck without further discussion.

Turned out everyone already had crosses on them. Everyone except Sun, who still wasn't worried.

I looked down at the Maltese cross lying on my

chest, its bronze polished to a mirror shine. I held it up, looked at my reflection. My eyes were shadowed and puffy, my hair an unholy tangle. I wondered what Ben would think if I just shaved it off.

I wondered.

"Tell me again exactly what this thing does?" I said.

"It's a defensive amulet," he said. "It reflects spells back on the one who cast them."

Stop the spell, not the man, Anastasia had said.

"And exactly how does it work?" I asked carefully.

He paused. Stared as understanding lit his gaze. "Just like a mirror. If you're holding that when someone casts a spell at you, the effects of the spell strike the caster instead."

"So it only works for people. Not, say, volcanoes?"

"Don't know." We both looked at Grant.

"*That* is an intriguing question," he said. "Where did this come from?"

"I don't even know. Tracked it back as far as some crazy old prospector a hundred or so years ago. A couple of witches in Manitou Springs said I might need it, so here it is."

"Fate," Grant said. "Good enough."

It wasn't good enough, but I'd take it. I had too many people looking out for me to turn my nose up at fate.

"Well then. Now all we have to do is find Roman and . . . what, stand in front of him?"

"Stand in front of him at the exact moment he's casting the spell," Cormac said. "It only works after the spell's in motion."

"That's cutting it awfully close," Ben said.

"Then we'd better get moving."

"But how do we find Roman?" I said. Right back to the same old problem.

Grant was the one who smiled this time. "Tina and I may have a plan for that."

Chapter 18

W E ARRIVED at the Norris Geyser Basin an hour before dusk, and I wasn't happy about it.

"It's a connection," Grant said, explaining the plan.
"We know Lightman was here, and because Lightman
is connected to both Roman and Ashtoreth, we have a
chance of following that thread back."

"He's probably still here," I complained. "I looked it
up. Early explorers thought this spot was a gateway to
hell. They weren't wrong."

"If he's here, we'll deal with him," Cormac said, like
we weren't talking about, you know, Lucifer. Hardin,
checking the magazine in her semiautomatic and the
stakes hanging in a quiver off her belt, frowned, just as
determined. Tina stood to the side, her arms crossed as
if she was cold.

Technically, the park wasn't quite fully open for the
summer season. That was why we parked in a turnout
and hiked in, avoiding the parking lot and visitors cen-

ter at the entrance to the basin. Maybe we could explain ourselves to some intrepid patrolling ranger. I wasn't anxious to find out.

We came at the area from the side, looping around the parking lot and carefully avoiding the barren, steaming stretches that marked geysers and potentially unstable ground, emerging from the surrounding woods and making our way to the boardwalk that guided tourists safely around the sites. I hadn't noticed the boardwalk my first time here. It made everything seem so much more tame and pleasant.

In semidaylight, this was a weird, blasted landscape, with scoured, crusted soil and stunted vegetation. Footprints and droppings from elk and bison were evident, so wildlife obviously didn't mind too much. I wondered if any of them ever fell into the pools.

My skin itched, thinking of it.

Grant, Tina, and Cormac got to work. The boardwalk gave way to a dirt path in the lowest part of the basin, a wide, flat space that must have seemed perfect for working a ritual. They'd apparently planned the whole thing on the drive from Colorado—it was a long drive, they'd had plenty of time. Grant said he had a spell that would amplify Tina's psychic abilities. Give an extra push when she scryed for Roman's location. Amelia didn't offer any arguments, which meant she must have thought it was a good idea.

While Grant set out candles at the cardinal compass points, Tina sat in the middle of the arrangement and spread the park map open in front of her. She had a pen

and pad of paper on hand as well—they looked like the
ones from the nightstand at the hotel. Whatever information she gleaned from the ether, she was going to
write it down. Her legs crossed, her back straight, she
appeared to have started meditating. It made the scene
even more incongruous: she looked like an ad for a yoga
studio, but the chalky, gritty landscape didn't exactly
bring to mind peacefulness. The geysers and hot springs
made a constant bubbling, hissing noise.

The circle pattern Grant marked out was familiar—
he lit the candles, scratched symbols into the dirt next
to each one. In the wavering flames, the patterns in the
dirt seemed to move. The sun was setting, and the sky
grew shadowed.

Cormac stood by, half watching Grant with interest,
and half watching everywhere else. He was expecting
trouble. Both he and Amelia must have been itching at
all this.

The rest of us: our job was to stand watch. Keep a
lookout in case Lightman was here, in case Ashtoreth
made an appearance. In case Roman showed up. Ben
and Hardin both had crossbows and walked a military-
like circuit along the surrounding paths, watching the
trees marking the edge of the basin. They had weapons
and experience. Hardin also brought along some new
toys: a set of portable full-spectrum flashlights. One of
her colleagues had put them together. I hadn't even told
her about what the Men in Black had done. They didn't
destroy vampires, but they sure slowed them down,

was the report. Vampire mace. She, Ben, and Cormac carried them.

No one tried to tell Sun Wukong what to do. He took a position at the edge of the basin, his arms crossed, his expression still. He didn't appear to have any weapons on him, but that didn't mean anything. He was on watch, as intent as I'd ever seen him.

I didn't have much to do here. Everyone else had weapons, magic, experience, or all three. I had a bundle of raw nerves. So I wandered. I told myself I was patrolling. I let my gaze go soft, my senses expand out. Tried to smell anything past the sulfur stink of the hot springs. Checked in with my allies. Regina Luporum, ha—my friends were my superpower.

Hardin was at the far end of the flat stretch at the bottom of the basin. She was all business. I was almost afraid to talk to her.

"Hi," I said, making noise as I approached, crunching in the gravel so I wouldn't startle her. "How are you?"

"I'm not at work," she said wryly. "It's pretty out here. It's good."

It was. The sky was wide, and if you squinted you could imagine that no one had ever set foot here. This was some artist's idea of an alien world.

"Detective, I just want to say thanks. You didn't have to come here and get involved in all this. I don't know what's going to happen, but I know it probably won't be good. And you didn't have to be here. So, thanks."

It seemed little enough to say, given how long we'd known each other, and how many times she'd gone to bat for me.

With her crossbow in hand, semiautomatic pistol in its holster, and full-spectrum lamp and stakes slung over her shoulder, she looked like some kind of soldier on the frontier. Which was exactly what she was. This was a war, I reminded myself.

"Eh, I had some vacation time coming. And you know, you can call me Jessi."

"Okay. Still, you know. Thanks."

She donned a thoughtful smile, an expression I'd never seen on her before. "When I was sixteen, there was a kid in my class in high school—I didn't know him very well, but he lived a few blocks down from me. One day, his father killed his mother. Beat her to death with a crescent wrench. It was all over the news for weeks. I heard the police sirens from my house. The whole world changed for me that day. That was the day I absolutely knew for certain that the world could be a terrible, awful, evil place, and it was never going to go back to the way it was. It was still a few years before I decided I wanted to be a cop, but I must have started thinking about it then. Being a cop—it just seemed like a way to take a stand. To try to hold the line against all that darkness.

"The story turned out to be a lot more complicated. It's easy to blame pure evil, but the guy had a history of untreated mental illness. After he did it, he grabbed a knife and tried to kill himself. Only reason he didn't succeed is the kid, the one from my class, called 911 and the EMTs got to him in time. Hauled the guy out on a stretcher, and my friend and his brother went into foster care. Never went back to school, and I never did find out what happened to them. But after the whole thing—the world changed for me."

She nodded at Cormac, Grant, and the impending ritual. "This is a little like that. Once I knew all this existed, vampires and werewolves and all that, I couldn't unsee it. I can't pretend it doesn't exist. And I can't sit back and not do anything. I have to take a stand.

"I remember the night we met, and I was so pissed off that you wouldn't press assault charges against Cormac. He seemed like the kind of guy who would beat a woman with a crescent wrench, you know? Then it got a whole lot more complicated. Now—I want to see this through."

"Thank you," I said.

"Let me know if you smell anything," she said, turning back to her watch.

Farther down the trail, at the crest of a hill, Sun nodded at me. He suddenly seemed otherworldy, even in his jeans and T-shirt. He should have been wearing an embroidered silk tunic, like he had in that dream space. He was above all this, and he already knew everything I was going to say to him.

The ritual at the floor of the basin seemed to be progressing. Tina's head was bowed forward, her hair masking her face. Her hands rested loose on her knees. Grant made another circuit of the circle, scratching more symbols in the dirt, whispering unintelligible phrases.

Ben should have been patrolling on the other side of the basin. But I couldn't see him. I scanned the trees, the trails that branched off in opposite directions, and didn't see a sign of him.

"Ben?" I staved off panic by taking a breath—I could smell him, he was here. He'd passed this way just a few minutes ago; he couldn't have gone far. I ran up the slope, following his trail.

He appeared from the trees holding a bundle of clothing. My clothing, from where I'd abandoned them—was it just today? "Found your things," he said, almost sheepishly. He must have seen the panic in my face and was now waiting to see if I was going to yell at him.

I didn't yell. I strolled up to him, pressed myself to him, face to his shoulder, and took him in—his scent, his warmth, his solidity—and sighed.

"Tracked me, did you?" I said.

He kissed the top of my head, the part of me closest to him. "Yeah. Figured I might as well. Your phone's still in the pocket."

"Did you find—"

He held up my wedding ring on its chain, and I breathed a heartfelt sigh. I pulled it back over my neck, another amulet to go with the others. Maybe the strongest. "I should train Wolf to keep a better hold of this."

"Wolf's job is to keep you safe," he said, leaning in

to give me another gentle, reassuring kiss. "We can always get another ring."

"Thanks, hon," I said, returning the kiss.

I gathered the clothes, tucked them under my arm. I'd probably end up throwing them away—they smelled charred and gross. They'd been dipped in a sulfuric, bacteria-laden bath.

"Anything happening?" he asked, looking across the plain.

The ritual—Tina in the center of the circle, Grant working around her, Cormac keeping watch—hadn't changed since the last time I checked.

"Still waiting."

Ben took up his guarding stance. Waiting was hard, when I felt like everything depended on what happened in the next hour. The bubbling and hissing of the thermals had become a comforting background noise, like static.

"Kitty?" Hardin hissed in a loud whisper, walking toward me and pointing toward the ritual. Something was happening.

A shimmering rippled the air in front of Tina, just outside of Grant's circle. Cormac stood nearby, crossbow in both hands but not aimed. Grant was watchful, but didn't seem worried.

The shimmering took on a shape: an animal-like figure, a big humped body, a face low to the ground, wide paws, rippling fur—a bear. It seemed to waver in reality, as if it were made of fog, denser air moving through the thinner mountain atmosphere. Other figures appeared throughout the basin, wherever one of us stood: another humped bear, the long-eared form of a rabbit, a thin-legged dear. The blur appearing before Hardin and me, and Ben when he trotted up to join us, was rangy, canine, with alert ears and a straight tail: wolf. I looked over to Sun.

Hazy shapes swarmed around him, a whole crowd of wavering animals acting like they wanted to rub up against him. Sun regarded the swarm, his arms outstretched, mouth open with wonder, but he didn't seem concerned. Not that he would.

"What is it?" I said.

"I don't know," Ben said, and looked to Cormac. None of us wanted to call out, to interrupt whatever was happening.

From the middle of the circle, Tina reached out a hand. She was speaking, and the bear-shaped blur before her seemed to be listening.

Sun came down the slope toward us, and the shimmering figures followed him. They stood apart, as if they weren't sure about us and wanted to watch. But with Sun, they pressed close.

"They like you," I said.

"Yeah," Sun said, bemused. "It's 'cause they don't know exactly what I am. They're trying to figure me out. It's kind of cool."

"But . . . what are they?"

"Spirits. The Shoshone call them the Ground People." He looked up, scanning above us. "There's probably some of the Sky People around, too." Overhead, a

ripple in the air that might have been a ghostly hawk
sailed by.

Tina moved the map outside Grant's ritual circle. The
bear spirit studied it a moment, then leaned in, touching its nose to the paper. Tina responded with a smile.

I felt relief. We had come to the right place and asked
the right question of the right people. These spirits
knew every corner of the park, knew everything that
was happening. They were willing to help because
we'd asked politely. Sometimes, it all came together.

The bear spirit in front of Tina lifted its head for all
the world, like it was sniffing at the air. The shadow
wolf next to us turned and flattened its ears to its head.
All the spirit animals hesitated, straightening to look
across the basin as if a noise had startled them. I didn't
see anything.

"What's happening?" Hardin whispered.

"Something's here," I said.

"What is it?" Sun said, but he didn't seem to be talking to any of us.

The spirits that had surrounded him disappeared,
their shimmering forms wavering to nothing. The one
by Tina did the same. Just like that, they were gone.

"I think we should get out of here," I said, trotting
down the dusty trail toward Cormac. The sun had set;
stars began to light up the sky overhead. Roman and
any vampires with him would be awake now. "Can we
get out of here?"

"Grant?" Cormac asked.

The magician was blowing out candles and kicking

at the dirt to erase the symbols he'd marked. Tina folded up the map. We all converged at this spot, pensive and uncertain.

"Wait a minute," Cormac said, holding out a hand. "Everybody shut up a second. Stand still."

We all froze. Everything was quiet. Just a peaceful night in the wilderness.

"That's not right," I said. Ben turned his nose up, working to take in the air. Hardin and Cormac took defensive stances. Sun had a staff in his hand that hadn't been there before, and he was ready to use it.

But there wasn't anybody, anything, out there. That wasn't what was bothering me. It was the silence. The geysers, the steaming vents, the bubbling fumaroles—they were all quiet. Still. And that was wrong.

"Sun, you remember what Ranger Lopez said about the geysers?"

"Yeah, that we only had to worry when they all stopped." He was frowning, and the expression seemed so incongruous on him.

We were out of time.

Chapter 19

FOR JUST a moment I stood, face turned up to take in a chill breeze. It smelled wild, otherwordly. The sun had set, the trees surrounding the depression were jagged shadows against a dark sky. This felt like the pause before a scream.

"What does that mean, that they've stopped?" Ben said. If he'd been a wolf, his ears would have been pinned back and his tail up, ready for an attack. As a human, his back was stiff and his teeth were bared.

"All the thermal energy is going somewhere else," I said. "It means something big's about to blow."

"We should move," Grant said. "The spell is only starting, it's not finished. We still have time. Tina, you have a location for us?"

"Yeah, the Ground People were pretty sure he's by the shore of the lake. It's marked on the map."

"Then let's get a move on," I said, marching back toward the path we'd come in on.

A wind struck me hard enough to knock me to the ground and roll me toward one of the wide springs of superheated water. Maybe even the same one Lightman had thrown me into. I dug fingers into the dirt, braced my toes, went spread eagle to slow myself down, and it worked. By now I recognized that out-of-nowhere wind and the brimstone stink that went along with it.

"Ashtoreth!" I shouted, out of anger and sheer aggravation. She was the demon of bad timing, was what she was.

She came down the boardwalk steps snaking along the hill above us as if she were just another tourist here to see the sights. She had a weapon in each hand, a spear and sword, and her usual complement strung on straps and bandoliers. Maybe more metal and silver this time. Very little wood. She wasn't here to kill vampires, after all.

And—she'd brought friends. A dozen or more dark figures emerging from the trees, crossing the wasted plain, descending through the air on funnels of wind. They were silhouettes, hard to see. Tall, powerful warriors holding spears and swords, covered with riveted leather armor and sheathed daggers. Like Ashtoreth, they wore dark goggles. They surrounded us.

This one early section of *Paradise Lost* is a whole list of demons, line after line of poetry describing all the fallen angels, all of Lucifer's followers who'd plunged into hell with him after the fall. I wondered how many of them were here. I bet if I had the book with me I could figure out some of their names.

Not that we had time for that.

Ben was at my side, like he'd been blown right along with me, and pulled me to my feet so we could run. Didn't matter where. Ashtoreth came toward us; her companions waited.

"Nice to have you both in one place," she said, giving a swoop with each hand so her weapons sang through the air. "This is so overdue." She picked up a run, hitting the last step with a giant leap that carried her right toward us. She aimed her weapons down, preparing to stab.

"Hey!" Hardin yelled, turning her full-spectrum light on the demon. Sighting along the beam of light, she fired her gun half a dozen times, probably most of what she had in the magazine. Ashtoreth didn't even flinch at the bullets. But she ducked at the light, raising an arm to block her eyes. I imagined her squinting behind her smoky goggles.

Grant joined Hardin, bringing his magic to bear, hand raised, chanting words I couldn't hear. Whatever it was only seemed to make the demon angry, because she swung her sword, a wide attack meant to disrupt rather than injure. Hardin and Grant dodged out of her range.

The other demons rushed in. Tina shouted the warning, and suddenly we had too many targets. We might have been able to stand up to Ashtoreth, but a dozen like her?

Grant turned back to Tina, who was weaponless, and put himself between her and a rushing attack, two demons with swords out. He held his arm straight up, and an object in his hand blazed a white light—I'd seen Amelia use a similar spell.

Like Hardin, Cormac had a full-spectrum light—neat trick, there. The two of them kept a space open around us, but that space was shrinking as demons guarded their vision and pushed closer.

Cormac arrived at my side, grabbing my arm and hauling me back. Reflexively, I turned and snarled at him—he was being so forceful, and I was so surprised. Just as reflexively, he raised his loaded crossbow and aimed at me, even though it wouldn't have done him any good.

It was all reflexive. I calmed down and he lowered the weapon in the next moment.

He turned to Ben, shoving the park map into his hands. He must have grabbed it from Tina. And where was Tina? I couldn't see her—a wall of demons was in the way.

Hardin shouted; I thought it was in anger, but I looked—a spear stuck out of her thigh. Ashtoreth was drawing another from her bandolier. Hardin, grimacing with pain, didn't fall. She gritted her teeth, pulling at the spear while focusing the light at the demon.

"The goggles," I tried to call out. My voice was choking. "Get the goggles off, they're blind without them." Cormac heard me, I thought.

Behind us, Cormac held up an amulet of some kind, shouted words of a spell. A light flashed, like Grant's, and a demon who'd been charging toward us fell. My vision throbbed with afterimages.

Bright light was buying us time. But it wouldn't drive them off.

Cormac shoved me again, and Ben took my arm.

"Ben, get her out of here. Go after Roman."

Nodding, Ben pulled me toward the tree line. I started to argue, but Cormac had already turned away, and somehow my feet had decided to run with Ben. I took a look over my shoulder to see Grant and Tina surrounded by demons, and Hardin and Cormac back to back, facing several more, including Ashtoreth. Hard to count how many demons there really were. Ashtoreth raised her spear. Tina had somehow acquired one of her own. I smelled blood on the air.

Sun Wukong had slipped behind Ashtoreth and took a running leap, preparing to drive down with his staff in some blunt-force attack that couldn't possibly work. I choked back a cry of denial, because there was nothing I could do. Cormac was right: we had the location, Roman was working his spell right now, and we had to stop him.

I wasn't okay with this, the others sacrificing themselves to give me a chance to escape.

But something else was happening: not all the demons were attacking my people, because some others had joined the battle. I'd missed them at first—they were cloaked, shadowy. Hard to see, like the demons. There were only a couple of them, but they moved lightning fast, engaging the demons with long metallic spears that sparked in the waxing moonlight. I managed to take a deep breath, to see if I could catch a scent around the brimstone and blood. There was a chill on the air, a cold scent of death. Vampire—

One of the shadowy cloaked figures drove a weapon into a demon's chest, and the demon screamed, some prehistoric sound of pain. A second one stabbed another, rushing in, launching over, and away to face the next one.

"Ben, who are those—"

"We have to go, *now*!"

We ran.

Ben was very focused, going straight to Cormac's Jeep—Cormac must have handed over the keys when I wasn't paying attention—getting in, starting the engine, without a pause. I barged into the passenger side and closed the door as we peeled off the shoulder and onto the road, heading south.

Yellowstone Park was big. It was a long drive from Norris Basin to the lake. Now that I had a chance to open the map and study it, the distances seemed immense. The whole place would blow up before we found Roman.

Ben was driving very fast. I decided not to look at the speedometer to see how fast. It seemed moot. He hunched over, gripping the steering wheel with stiff hands, bent like claws. His teeth were bared, his eyes gleaming gold. I couldn't tell if it was the engine growling that hard, or him.

He was close to shifting. In the face of danger, his wolf fought to break free. Our wolves were stronger. My own Wolf responded, kicking, digging claws into my gut, ready to tear through.

I doubled over. If one of us lost it, we'd both lose it, which would be a disaster, speeding down the road. We couldn't afford to lose it. The original Regina Luporum must have gone through something like this, maybe even worse than this. She kept it together. We could.

Steadying my breathing, I straightened. I had to be calm when I touched Ben—our nerves and anger would only feed on each other. I put my hand on his arm, spoke softly, "Keep it together. We have to keep it together."

He slammed a fist on the steering wheel and gave a shuddering sigh. "I know. I know."

The fury in his gaze faded. His grip on the wheel finally relaxed. He put his hand on mine and squeezed. We drove like that for a mile, two, feeding calm to each other, trying not to think about the madness we'd left behind.

"Kitty," he said. "Where are we going? You have to tell me where we're going."

I scrubbed my face, tried to focus. So much depended on what we did in the next few minutes. I turned on the domelight and held up the map.

The place where the bear spirit had pointed showed on the map as a blackened smudge—a noseprint—on the western spur of the lake. This was a region, not the pinpoint location that would have been most useful. But a region of a couple of hundred yards or so was a million times better than trying to search the entire park. I looked for the nearest road, for a label that would help us navigate to the spot.

"West Thumb," I said. "A place called West Thumb. It'll be a left turn."

"Okay, okay, I think I saw that on the sign marker back there. We can do this."

"Yes," I said.

We drove for five, ten minutes.

"They'll be okay," Ben said. "Those five are the strongest people I know, they'll be okay."

We didn't know that. The strongest might not be enough for this. But I said, "Yes, they will, they'll be fine, we just have to do our part now."

It's not like we had a choice.

A dozen miles later he glanced at the rearview mirror, glanced again, then took a brief look over his shoulder to the road behind. I turned to see what he was looking at.

Some distance behind us, visible on the straightaways, I made out a car, a big, dark SUV, driving without its headlights on.

"We're being followed?" I said, disbelieving.

"Apparently."

"What do we do?"

"Frankly, I'm more worried about what's in front of us." What the others had set us to do, and what they were fighting Ashtoreth to give us time to do.

I didn't want to think about what was happening with them right now.

Ben bent over the steering wheel, his focus ahead.

The big SUV kept following us. Another henchman of Roman's? The Men in Black? Who was it? Maybe

just a coincidence? Not bloody likely. We kept ahead
of them, so maybe Ben was right. We didn't have worry
to spare.

Ben saw the sign for the turnoff to the West Thumb
basin before I did, so he was already yanking the wheel
hard, tires squealing on pavement, before I had a chance
to call a warning.

West Thumb was another cluster of geysers like
the Norris Basin, but this one butted right up against
the shore of the lake. There must have been something
about it that made casting the spell easier for Roman.
Or it might have offered the easiest access, with paved
roads and convenient parking. Nice.

After dark, the lot was empty, and Ben screeched the
Jeep to a stop, not bothering with something as prosaic
as parking between the painted lines. In a second he
was out of the driver's seat and had the back open, digging through Cormac's stash of weapons for stakes and
spray bottles of holy water. I looked behind us for that
black SUV, but didn't see it. It had followed us all the
way down the road, but didn't come into the parking
lot behind us.

"Whatever he's doing, it'll be by the shore, I think,"
I said.

"Then we'll follow it until we find him," he said.

"Thank you," I said, out of the blue.

"We're in this together. All the way." Pure statement
of fact. His expression was open and unastonished.
Very practical. Ben the lawyer, doing what needed to
be done.

We trotted to the boardwalk and dirt paths that led past a collection of hot springs to the shore of the lake. Like at Norris, these springs were quiet; no geysers boiled or sprayed. Our wolves were close, feeding strength to our legs, our long strides. Our senses pushed out, taking in the air, listening for the least little sound, anything that would give a clue as to what might happen next. We were hunting. We were also being hunted. It was a strange feeling. Exhilarating, too. This was for everything. Couldn't rest, couldn't slack off, not for a second.

We moved a few paces away from each other, covering more ground, Ben looking right, me looking left, toward the water. No Roman, but no other bad guys, either. I pulled ahead and turned all my attention forward, looking for Roman, determined to find him before it was too late.

The trees gave way to an open plain of chalky white dust and sand, a scoured area where mineral-laden geysers and hot springs had washed over the earth and into the lake. The lake was pewter colored, stretching to a blur of hills on the opposite side. The shore curved and bent in the shape of an inlet. Bits of forest survived, and we continued into the next clump of trees. As far as I could tell, we were still within the range of the marked spot on the map. Still no Roman.

"Anything?" Ben called. We were loping together, the way it should be, me and my mate on the hunt.

It didn't last.

At first, I thought the wind came off the water. It

blasted hard enough to make me stumble, and my re-
flexes recognized it before I did. A moment later the
smell of brimstone came.

"Ben!" I screamed in warning.

He pulled up short and turned on his flashlight. The
beam of light blazed around him. She appeared in a
whirlwind of choking white dust. The light stopped her
briefly, which was good, because she had a spear in hand
and had been reared back in the start of an attack. She
dropped to both feet—between us, separating us—and
took stock.

If Ashtoreth was here, what had happened back at the
Norris Basin? Did this mean she had finished there?
What had happened to my friends? I almost called out to
her, demanding to know what she had done to Cormac
and the others.

Instead, Ben yelled at me. "Go! Kitty, go, keep looking!" He had his Glock in hand. I hadn't even known
he'd had it.

"Ben!" I screamed again, because I had to. He didn't
spare me a glance. He couldn't. All his attention was
on the demon and her next attack. He aimed and fired;
she stumbled back. But a bullet wouldn't kill her.

"Run!" he called again. I did, because I had a job to
do. My ears closed against the noises of the battle behind me, I kept running up the shore, into the next stand
of pines, around the next inlet. Roman had to be here.
All of this—it had to be worth it.

Chapter 20

I RAN, LOPING, unthinking, for maybe a quarter of a mile into the next stand of trees, losing sight of the shore and water. I must have been right on the edge of the marked-out region on the map. Pausing, I steadied my breathing and took a breath of air. And smelled vampire, a chill that was more than just the weather, more than the temperature dropping at night.

That wind roared again, then came that stench, and the shout of a warrior about to make a kill. Ashtoreth pounded into the ground in front of me, landing in a three-point crouch before swinging back in a ready stance. It was like she'd leapt from there to here, wasting no time with something so mundane as running.

She was here, and just like before I wondered, did that mean Ben was safe now, or was he gone?

"Did you kill him?" I said, my voice choking. Her wicked smile seemed answer enough.

I didn't expect an answer, just an attack, but she said,

"You'll never know. You can't win this, you had to know that from the start."

"Yeah, that's why I'm still here I guess."

I dodged, thinking to avoid her, but she moved to block me. I went sideways—I could get to the water and swim to Roman if I had to. But she was there again. No matter how fast I was, no matter which way I tried to sprint, she barred the way.

I tried to double back, but when I broke from the trees she was there, stabbing downward with her spear, slashing with her sword. Wolfish instincts saved me. I pulled up, spun around, launched in the other direction—fast, supernaturally fast. Just fast enough to get away. Dirt pelted me from where the spear hit the ground, right behind my heel. The wind from the sword's sweep tickled my neck.

She was behind me again. She was always right there, and she never got tired.

This was it, then. This realization that I probably wasn't going to make it this time settled over me and lent me a strange sense of resolve. My body felt lighter, my running steps felt longer. I wasn't going to survive this. That was okay, as long as I saved the world first. I just had to get the mirrored cross in front of Roman. Whatever happened after that didn't matter. With only one goal to focus on instead of two—just getting to the water, not doing that *and* surviving—a new burst of energy filled me.

But I still had to get to the shore, and Ashtoreth was in front of me. I was long past thinking, I was only looking ahead and around for a new path, the next route, a possible solution.

A wind blew past me, a racing breeze—and a dark figure smacked Ashtoreth across the face with a staff. She fell back, dropped her spear, and snarled.

I stopped and blinked, confused.

Then it happened again.

Another shadow emerged from the woods and struck another blow while the demon was off balance, a jab to her lower back that made her grimace in pain. Her attention was entirely off me now.

The two figures moved with astonishing grace, slipping around Ashtoreth, always out of her reach, while smacking her with long black staves—not badly enough to drive her off, but enough to distract her. It was fascinating. The two were human, or at least human shaped, but they wore hoods and scarves around their faces, and their clothing was dark and shrouding.

What I could tell about them: they had the chill scent of vampires, they moved with the shadowy stealth of vampires, and they were warriors. Vampire ninjas. I stood in awe.

Then something happened. The attack changed. They stopped simply harassing the demon and moved on to what must have been the next step. Clearly they had a plan, a finely tuned and well-practiced one.

The first one produced a new weapon, or tool, or something. A hook with a wire line attached. The vampire got close, made a leap, stuck this hook into the leather of Ashtoreth's vest, and pushed off to escape her counterblow. The wire trailed out—the other end was attached to a metal stake, which he—she? whatever?—drove into the ground. The second vampire did the same, hooking another line into her other side, pulling it taut, securing the stake.

Then they both did it again, and again. Hooks—big, iron-looking things with jagged barbs—dug into her belt, her back, her sleeves. Some of them might have dug into her skin. It was hard to tell, the vampires moved so fast, and Ashtoreth jerked and thrashed, trying to break free. Quick and efficient, the vampires staked down each of the wires until the demon was stuck. Tied down like a tent, with no give to her bonds and nowhere to go. She looked like a marionette, immobilized by her strings, pulled tight in all directions.

A third figure appeared. This one stepped into view, facing Ashtoreth, regarding her calmly. He didn't attack, but somehow gave off every impression that he was just as dangerous as his companions. In a gloved hand he held a gold spear as tall as he was, with a wicked-looking point, barbed and filigreed. It looked like a harpoon.

The demon bared her teeth, closed her hands into fists, strained to break free and strike. But she flailed, a fish in a net.

The third figure slipped his hood back.

It was Rick.

I gasped, and clamped my hand over my mouth to keep from interrupting.

I didn't think it had been that long since I'd seen

him; then again, it felt like it had been years. Now he looked like someone who had stepped out of another world, gloved and cloaked, a character from a medieval epic, a burning determination in his eyes. He had a conquistador's beard.

"Well," he said to Ashtoreth. "Hello, again."

He might not even have seen me—surely he knew I was here. But he didn't look at me, not even a glance. Didn't acknowledge me. He was busy, after all.

She hissed and kept thrashing, as if it would do some good. "I'll not repent. I will not repent!"

"I wasn't asking," he said. "But, you know, if you wanted to, I'd listen."

"Traitor! You're a traitor twice over!"

"I was never subject to the will of your Master."

"He made you! He made you all!"

"And we owe him nothing for that, thank God. But you—you chose your allegiance a long time ago, didn't you? You fell with him, you'll sink with him."

With a great wrenching heave of her arm, she pulled at one of the cables—and snapped the stake out of the ground. One of Rick's companions jumped to grab hold of the wire and hauled back to steady it before she could yank out any others.

Meanwhile, Rick spoke, reciting something epic in Latin, a prayer or a curse. An exorcism.

Ashtoreth shouted back at him, spitting as she did. I couldn't understand her, but it sounded like yet another language. Not Latin, but obviously something filled with hate and expletives. Rick didn't acknowledge her again. He was on a script. The two other vampires pulled back on the cords that held her, keeping her immobile, locked in place.

The battle of words continued. It was not simple, and it was not easy. Rick braced himself, booted feet dug into the earth, and the two vampires at the lines and stakes were struggling to keep the monster they'd caught at bay. Seconds ticked by.

Then Rick raised the golden harpoon and struck, pulling back over his shoulder and stabbing up into her chest.

Every other time we'd attacked or immobilized her, whether with weapons or magic, she'd escaped before we could do any damage. She called a wind, opened some kind of vortex to whatever world she came from, and vanished, just like that. She had some kind of teleporting ability, and if you could just zap yourself away from anywhere, why wouldn't you, when you were about to lose a fight? But that didn't happen this time.

The harpoon struck, sinking through her leather armor and her chest, like a knife through butter. Ashtoreth threw her head back and screamed, a thunderous, echoing noise that rattled through the woods and across the lake. The harpoon blazed gold, and the light engulfed the demon. She kept screaming, and I pressed my hands over my ears to stop the noise. Heat came off her, the heat from the sun on a bright summer's day. This was sunlight in the darkest night. It was glorious.

Covered and protected in their cloaks and hoods,

Rick and his companions ducked away, and I did, too. There was a boom, then stillness.

I looked, and she was gone. Not even ash remained. The hooks, cords, and stakes were gone. The harpoon was gone, even. The ground where she'd stood was scuffed up, that was all. I couldn't smell a whiff of brimstone, and the air was amazingly still.

"Rick?" I said, my voice taut, and ran out of the shelter of the trees.

"Kitty!" He actually smiled.

I jumped at him, and he had enough wherewithal to catch me and return the hug I gave him. I had my friend back.

We separated, still gripping each other's arms. My mouth opened, but I had nothing to say. Or too much to say. This had taken too long, it had already taken too long. I might already be too late.

His companions joined us after brushing themselves off and retrieving their staves. They'd pulled back their hoods, revealing their faces. The first was a woman, tall and well muscled, strong and supple, with ebony skin and close-cropped hair. Her expression was calm and stern. The second was a man who might have been Arabic, his skin cinnamon colored, his black hair tied in a ponytail. He smiled crookedly, wryly. They stood together, lined up next to Rick. They were a team, and I wondered what he'd been doing for the last year.

"This is your Regina Luporum?" the vampire with the ponytail said. His accent was Middle Eastern, musical.

"Oh, she isn't mine," Rick said. "She is all her own."

Too many questions. So I just stood there.

"Speechless?" Rick asked, clearly amused.

"What are you *doing* here?"

"We've been tracking you all night, but you hardly slowed down for us to catch up. Until now."

"You killed her," I breathed. "Finally."

"No, I don't think I did," he said, and sighed. "She's not dead. But she won't be coming back anytime soon."

"What did it take—that spear, blessed by the pope?"

"Better than the pope. Turns out an entire convent of nuns praying over a thing for a hundred years does give it a certain amount of power."

"Oh, is that all it took." Amelia would be happy to know why her spells never worked against Ashtoreth. She just wasn't holy enough, obviously.

"Kitty. You need to go. We'll talk later."

"Yes. Yes—I have so much to tell you." I backed away, my mind already running ahead.

"Go!" he said, and I ran. I hoped we would have a chance to talk later.

I ran on, following the scent I'd picked up before Ashtoreth attacked.

The land sloped up until I found myself at the top of a rise, looking down to where the forest curved around a stretch of open shore and a gravelly beach. Roman was there.

The vampire knelt, surrounded by lit candles, scratching symbols into the beach with a dagger. Dozens and dozens of symbols. Grant and Amelia were right—this was a complicated spell. He'd been at this for hours.

So. Now what did I do?

Attack, of course.

Wolf was right. Nothing else for it but charge down the rise and across the beach. Maybe all I needed to do was scratch out some of those symbols. Stop the spell, not the man. That was all I had to do, and whatever happened after that didn't matter. I started down at a run.

Roman saw me. He looked up, and even from fifty yards away I could see his frown. I wasn't supposed to be here, he was probably thinking. Ashtoreth was supposed to stop me, to guard him.

He had a dilemma now, I realized: he'd most likely been depending on Ashtoreth to zap him out of here as soon as he launched his spell, so he could avoid the blast and still be around to enjoy his new vampire-friendly world. His escape path was gone. Would he still pull the trigger, launch the volcano, destroy the world as we knew it?

He would. He did.

He stood, and in his hands he held a lamp of some kind, an ancient clay oil lamp, a primitive version of Aladdin's lamp. A thick buttery flame burned from the spout, and the words that Roman chanted over it echoed. This was it—the Manus Herculei. It was the lamp. I was still too far away to stop him, even if all I did was run full tilt and crash into him.

I almost shouted at him to stop, but I didn't even have time to cry out.

Roman lowered the lamp to the water, then below the surface. The light should have gone out. Instead, the flame spread, a sheet of fire pouring across the surface of the lake as if it were oil instead of water. When there was enough, the fuse would light, the caldera would ignite. This was it, all of it, down to one moment.

I yanked the Maltese cross over my head, stretched back, and threw as hard as I could. The piece of bronze flew, turning, flashing the orange of reflected fire-light.

It splashed maybe thirty yards out. It'd been a pretty good throw, with my werewolf strength behind it. But the cross sank and disappeared into the dark water with barely a ripple. I could have howled to the sky, I was so angry, so full of disbelief that I had come so far and failed.

The wall of fire stopped. The flames stopped, wavered, the sheet of fire doubling back on itself, burning waves turning from some invisible wall that had risen up to contain them. Then, the fire roared. Exploded. And I thought this was it, the ground under my feet was about to open up, a million tons of magma bursting around me, and my werewolf healing wouldn't save me this time.

That didn't happen. The flames compressed, flowing into another wall of fire that tightened even further, becoming a battering ram that roared straight back the way it had come. Toward Roman, still kneeling by the shore.

Fire bathed his face in an orange glow. He didn't have

time to register any kind of expression before the explosion, focused like a missile, hit him.

The shockwave knocked me over. It felt like another earthquake, and I wondered if the ground under me would ever feel solid again. Face in the dirt, I wrapped my arms around my head, braced against whatever came next.

When the world fell silent, I lay still for a long time, hardly believing that it might possibly be over. That the world was still here. We hadn't all burned up in a primordial explosion. The air smelled of ash and smoke, burned vegetation. I was covered in a layer of dust, earth that had been shaken loose and had settled back down. I was sore, but not hurt. Battered, but not broken. The cuts and scrapes on my arms and face would heal soon enough.

In a sudden panic, sure that he was right behind me with a weapon in hand, I jumped and looked to where Roman was, where he had been, to see what he was doing now.

The beach where he'd been standing looked as if a bomb had detonated on it. Trees smashed flat, fanned away from the point where the vampire had been standing. The ground was black with soot, scorched like the inside of a furnace, to a distance of maybe thirty yards. The magical signs had all been erased.

Fascinated, I moved forward. I wanted to understand what had happened. I had to see what was left. I stepped on crackling, baked dirt. Puffs of ash rose up from my steps. I coughed at the smell of smoke.

A body lay at the epicenter of the explosion. And the body moved, twitched. Propped itself on an arm as it tried to roll over, then collapsed as the arm lost strength. It was Roman. He wasn't dead. Or rather, he was still alive. But he was a mess, charred over his whole body, bits of skin falling away, scalp peeled back to reveal skull. His eyes still gleamed, and grimacing lips revealed pale fangs.

I heard footsteps and dropped to a crouch, balanced on the balls of my feet and a hand, ready to flee, to spring away in whatever direction I had to. For now, though, I waited to see what happened.

The man who walked over the rise and toward the shore was Charles Lightman. He had his hands shoved into his jacket pockets and seemed to be wearing a wry grin. Or a sneer of disgust. Hard to tell, there was such a fine line between the two.

He was here to see to his general. He stopped a few feet away from Roman. Close enough to kick dirt on him, if he wanted. Roman had stopped trying to sit up and merely lay on his back, arms splayed out, staring up.

"Dux Bellorum. Gaius Albinus," Lightman said. "Nice try, I suppose. I mean, who could have predicted the bitch had a trick up her sleeve? Regina Luporum. Shit."

Lightman paused for a reply, but Roman didn't seem to have anything to say. I could make out a smile on his cracked lips.

I was aware that I was lurking, a wolf among trees,

and that they very likely knew I was here. But as long as they didn't come after me, I didn't move.

The man in the suit regarded his surroundings, a guy out for a stroll, unmindful of the chill. He looked like he was surveying the shoreline for a condo development. The wide expanse of the lake didn't seem to impress him.

"So close," he muttered. He kicked the toe of his shoe into the soot and grime. "Ah well. There's always another time. Always another tool. I'll wait."

He glanced over and looked right at me. Shook his head with a kind of disgust, and walked away.

Go.

Wolf attacked, salivating at the thought of closing jaws around his throat, tearing skin, tasting his blood pouring over our tongue. Didn't matter whether attacking him was possible, whether the guy even had blood. *We will kill him.*

I sprang, claws outstretched, ready to slash—

And fell hard against the ground, stopped cold by an outside force. Roman had grabbed the cuff of my jeans and held tight, pulling me up short.

I snarled, kicked at him. He didn't have the strength to keep hold of me and I broke free. But it was too late. Ahead of me, Lightman had disappeared. I'd missed my chance. Not that I really would have been able to rip Lucifer's throat out. But it would be nice to at least say that I tried. He was just gone, leaving me with his servant—still his servant, even after everything.

I crouched near Roman, jaws locked in a permanent growl. The old vampire didn't watch Lightman go, didn't call after him, didn't say a word. Lying in the dirt, with burned bits flaking off his finger bones, he chuckled. Then coughed, as if the air had caught in his windpipe on the way out. The gleaming eyes flickered in my direction, then closed.

After a long moment of silence I said, "He just left you."

"Of course he did," Roman said, his damaged voice croaking. "That's what he does. He's the Betrayer."

"Why did you follow him, then?"

"I didn't have anyone else."

I sat, hugging my knees to my chest. Not sure what happened next. I wondered what he would do. Maybe that was why I stayed, to watch. For the first time, I wasn't afraid of him.

"Why are you still here?" he asked.

"Because I kind of always wanted to just talk to you. Old vampires usually have such good stories."

"Your standards are low. I've listened to your show." He shuddered.

I had never seen a vampire so injured and still moving. It was a shock, seeing him like this. He was the vampire other vampires told stories about to scare each other. My friends and I had spent years opposing him. And now, weirdly, perversely, I felt sorry for him. He was a horror.

Blood would heal him. If an injured vampire survived

long enough to have a conversation, he'd live. But he needed blood. I'd moved out of his arm's reach for a reason.

"I met Kumarbis," I said.

I couldn't tell this time if he was chuckling or coughing. "So I gathered. What did you think of him?"

"He was crazy."

"He was crazy from the start."

"You probably guessed this, but he's dead. Ashtoreth destroyed him."

"Stupid old man. Thought he heard the voice of God. It wasn't God. He'd been a vampire for four thousand years, did you know that? He couldn't even remember being alive anymore. He didn't remember what his name had been, where he was from. He was a fossil walking the earth."

I'd guessed that he'd been old. Without really believing he'd been that old. How did you wrap your brain around that? "He told a lot of stories. Some of them about you. You must have hated him, after he turned you. You must have been so angry."

"I do not need your pity. I was born a citizen of Rome. We are a race of engineers, of builders. Problem solvers. You choose your road, and you build it straight and strong, to last for generations. Rage would have been a waste. I built a road instead. Archimedes said that if you gave him a lever long enough and a fulcrum on which to place it, he would move the world. Immortality is that lever. I have spent two thousand years placing the fulcrum. Only to have it all . . . slip."

His shining gaze turned upward to the sky, which was growing pale. The landscape around me had taken on detail; I could see the needles on pine trees and ripples in the water. Somehow, the whole night had passed. Dawn was almost here, and I hadn't noticed. That always seemed to happen, that moment sneaking up on me.

In moments, the sun would rise, and Roman was out in the open. I felt a panic at that—but I wasn't supposed to care. I wanted him to die. I would sit here and watch him crumble, and be happy.

"What are you going to do?" I asked him.

"Nothing, it seems."

That didn't seem right, none of it did. He'd failed, the world was saved, he was injured, and maybe he even deserved it. *Do nothing,* Wolf says. And she was right, and she was wrong.

Speaking faster than I was thinking, I said, "I can get you to the woods, we can find a cave, a hollow, something—"

"That isn't what you really want to do," he said. "You only offer because it's the ethical thing to do. The moral thing."

"The right thing."

"The right thing for you to do is let me die. I am your enemy, I have caused great harm to you and yours. You should be lording your victory over me."

"I'm too damned tired," I said.

"You make the offer to save me because you think it absolves you. But you simply sit there."

He was right. I just sat there.

He reached out, clawing at the soil. This time, he managed to turn over, to get into a position where he could crawl. He didn't get far, but he didn't have to. He was reaching for something, and when he grabbed it, he collapsed to his side.

His hand had closed around a broken piece of wood, a thin branch that had been blasted in the explosion. It was naturally sharp on its broken end.

He spoke, his voice growing louder as he gained strength, or will, and he placed the point of the branch on his chest. Like a good Roman soldier.

I scrambled forward, hand reaching to grab the stake. He was so weak, I could have just pulled it away. But I didn't. He met my gaze—I let him catch my gaze. But he didn't use his hypnotic power, either because he couldn't, or because he didn't need to. His message was obvious: let him do this. I pulled my hand away.

"Roman," I said, my voice breaking. "Gaius—"

He spoke softly, reciting something with the quality of a prayer. *"His ibi me rebus quaedam divina voluptas percipit atque horror, quod sic natura tua vitam manifesta patens ex omni parte retecta est . . ."*

I didn't stop him. I bore witness, and that was all.

He shifted his weight, leaned on the point, and his already weak body slid cleanly onto the stake of wood, through the heart. In seconds, his body turned to ash and dust, though it was hard to see through the injuries. Bone turned gray, scattered. His form decayed, collapsed. He kept speaking until the words were lost in a failing breath.

The sun broke, light stabbing over distant hills. Roman would not be finished by something as simple as sunlight, oh no. He wasn't at the mercy of anything.

The light on my face was warm, caressing, and the most joyful sensation I'd ever felt in my life. I was alive. Another day had come.

Standing, I wiped my mud-streaked hand across my face. I didn't know why I should be crying, but I was. I was just tired, that was it. I could sleep now. Go home, sleep. Not worry quite so much.

Amid Roman's ashes lay a hard metal object. When I knelt to examine it, I knew what I would find: a bronze coin, like those he'd given to his followers. The first of them, the master. I picked it up gingerly, trying to avoid the flakes and ashes. I hoped for a wind to come and blow him away, but the air was still. His remains lingered, like the charred bits of an abandoned campfire.

The face on this coin was almost recognizable: a profile, like the old coins with kings and emperors on them. I couldn't tell if this one was Roman or Lightman. Didn't matter, they were gone and it was over. I went to the lake's edge and threw it, hurled it after the Maltese cross. Let it sink to the depths.

When it vanished under the surface of the water, I felt better. Smiled, even. God, that sunlight felt good.

On the shore, partly in the water and partly out, I

found clay shards, broken pieces of the lamp he'd been holding. The core of the spell, the Manus Herculei. Broken, done, gone. I stretched my arms, rounded my shoulders. I could have laughed, I suddenly felt so light.

I turned around to walk back up the rise, but two men stood there. The same two Men in Black who'd been following me all week. I hadn't heard or smelled them approach. My hackles went up all over again. Wolf roared, ready to break free.

I marched toward them. "Who the hell are you?"

"We'd like to talk to you, if it's all right," the olive-skinned one said. Like we'd just run into each other on one of the hiking trails.

"Do you have any idea what's happened here?" I pointed at the lake, which had so recently been on fire, and at the smear of soot that used to be Roman. My gestures were wild, my expression most likely crazy. I could not deal with one more thing.

"Yes, we do," he said simply. And I believed him.

I sagged, put a hand on my suddenly aching head. "Who the hell are you?"

"You can call me Ezra. Call him Jacob. We're Powers," said the pale-skinned one.

"Authorities," said the other, Jacob. "Though that's not really important here."

I stared. "Of course you are." I was sure I had read something about this in *Paradise Lost*. Or someplace else. One of those angelic magic books. Powers, Authorities—they were categories of angels. "The other side of the coin, right?"

"This is such a beautiful place," Jacob said, gazing around at the dawn-lit trees and lake, which glowed golden. "It's such a shame—you see, it's always been collateral damage in our war. A bastion. A prize. Our kinds have been fighting for control of it for a very long time."

"A very long time," Ezra added with a sad smile. "Even though our direct influence is limited. Surprisingly limited, really. Both sides need pawns to do our work."

"But Earth is full of pawns," Jacob finished.

For a long moment I just stood there. Even Wolf didn't have a growl for that. Softly, I muttered, "We weren't fighting for you. We were fighting for ourselves. For each other. So, you know—fuck you."

I started the hike back up the hill. I had to find Ben. Or what was left of him.

Jacob said, "Yes, and it made you stronger than you ever would have been as pawns. Lightman doesn't understand that."

"Kitty. Your friends will be here soon," Ezra said.

I stopped, turned. "They're okay? They're alive? All of them?"

"They're mostly okay, yes."

My heart lurched at that "mostly." I had to find them, I had to get to them now—

"Just one more moment, please," Jacob said, reaching. We have something for you, if you want it."

Ezra pulled something from his jacket pocket, held it up. A carved stone on a gold chain, simple and straightforward. Nothing to be afraid of.

"No," I said, hand up. "I'm sorry, but no. No more amulets, no more talismans or crosses or coins, or . . . or . . . Just no more magic."

"Would you like to hear what it does first?" Ezra said.

I sighed. "Okay."

"It gives you a year and a day. A nice fairy-tale length of time, isn't it? A year and a day."

"To do what?" I said.

"To be healed."

Jacob said brightly, "It's another fairy-tale thing—like the good fairy in Sleeping Beauty. We can't take away the curse. But we can give you a year and a day."

"He—" Ezra nodded in the direction Lightman had been standing, was it just a few minutes ago? "He isn't the only one able to influence these things."

They both seemed very pleased with themselves, waiting happily for my reaction.

"A year and a day," I said, very slowly and carefully. "Without shifting. A year and a day as a human."

"Not precisely. You'll always be a werewolf. But this will give you . . . time."

My hands went to my stomach, which seemed a ridiculously stereotypical gesture. But both men nodded. "Time to be pregnant," I said, just to be sure.

"We thought you'd appreciate it, after what you've been through," said Jacob.

The world had gone sideways. It was like I couldn't see straight, my head was ringing so much. "Like, a reward? I didn't do this for a reward—"

"Of course not," said Ezra. "This is more to say . . .

we like what you've been doing and you should keep doing it. Do you want it?"

A year and a day. I nodded. He came forward and put the chain around my neck. Did something that shortened it, so I couldn't just pull it off again. If I looked, I mostly likely wouldn't find a clasp.

The stone looked ancient, prehistoric. The carving was round, primitive, stylized, eyes and flattened ears on a canine face the only visible features. A wolf. I understood what he'd meant—I wouldn't be human. Wolf would always be here, looking out for me. And that was fine.

A sacrifice, for a child. As it should be.

I wiped tears away with the back of my hand. I was leaking. I didn't say thank you, because there were rules about thanking fairies—you didn't do it, it angered them. I wasn't sure if that rule applied to . . . Powers, or whatever they were, but for something this magical and crazy it seemed best not to take chances. I clasped the stone wolf tight in my hand. A clear gesture of astonishment and maybe even gratitude.

"Have a nice day, Katherine Norville," the pale Man in Black said. They walked away. Just like that.

For what seemed a very long time, I stood still. Long enough for the sun to rise fully over the horizon and bathe me in light. I couldn't move. I couldn't think.

I wanted to find Ben. I needed Ben, right now.

I still didn't know what had happened to Ben and the others. I couldn't form the thought that Ashtoreth may have won, that Rick and his friends might have been a few minutes too late. I couldn't face it. So I stood by the shore of the lake, turned to the direction I'd last seen my mate, put my hands around my mouth and howled. Called his name, but it sounded like an echoing wolf song to my ears.

Ten seconds, I waited. Twenty.

Then heard the responding call, "Kitty!"

I ran. Met him coming down the slope that marked out this inlet of the lake. He looked battered, even with his werewolf healing. Bruises on his cheek, cuts on his arms. But they were just cuts, and he hadn't been poisoned by silver. He smelled safe. I took a running leap into his arms, and he caught me, pulling me close, body to body. I might never let go.

He loosened his grip enough to let me breathe, but we held each other's arms and started talking in a hyperactive, adrenaline-fueled flood.

"We're still here," he said. "Does that mean we won?"

"I think so? Probably?"

"Roman—"

"Dead. Gone. Ashtoreth—she didn't kill you."

"She smacked me—I fell, that's where I got the cuts. Then she went after you. I couldn't stop her, I freaked out, almost lost it—"

"Rick came back! Rick and the vampire ninjas!"

"I know! I ran into them as they were leaving, they've got this Land Rover with blacked-out windows—"

I kissed him, because I couldn't stand there not kissing him anymore. His hands tightened around me; his lips took a second to get over the shock and stress and respond. When they did, I kissed even more, devouring kisses, and my body reacted, legs wrapping around his, locking me to him. I wanted to rip his clothes off. And why the hell not? There was no one around. It was a beautiful morning. I slipped my hands under his shirt, rubbed them up his warm back.

He gave a hoarse chuckle and spoke between kisses, "Not that I'm complaining, but something's gotten into you."

"A year and a day," I said, which I knew made no sense. I didn't care about sense. I did a quick round of math. I didn't even stop to think if I trusted the Men in Black. I didn't much care if this was going to turn out to be another cosmic joke. It was a chance, and I had faith. "We have three months to get knocked up."

He stared at me. "Wait. What?"

"Too much to explain. But there's a chance. We have a chance. Please say yes."

Another moment of staring at me, and I was afraid he was going to make me explain, or he was going to say he didn't want a baby after all, or it was all too much and he didn't want anything to do with me anymore. But what he did, finally, was grab my shirt and pull it over my head, and hitch my legs over his hips so he could carry me to the nearest clear spot of ground.

Between nuzzling my ear and massaging my breast, he found the stone wolf around my neck. "This," he said, his voice husky, "has something to do with it?"

"More magic," I murmured back.

"Figured," he said, and moved on to yanking off my jeans.

My head tilted back, my eyes closed. "Don't you want to know what it does?"

"Not interested in anything but you right now, hon."

And those right there were the real magic words.

Chapter 21

OUR SEX was fast and fueled by adrenaline. It was also filled with love and need and relief. Resting after, the cool air against our skin and the bright sun made this feel like the morning after a full moon. I started giggling out of sheer joy at being alive, and Ben joined in. We'd saved the world. We could do anything.

Over the next rise, the geysers of West Thumb had started bubbling again, a pleasant, distant froth and hissing that reminded me of boiling pasta or a mad scientist's lab. The caldera had settled. Nothing was going to be blowing up today.

Far too quickly, we heard voices and caught the scent of familiar people walking upwind.

"Shit," Ben muttered against my naked shoulder.

I grinned. "They're alive."

We scrambled for our clothes and managed to make ourselves presentable by the time Cormac came over the rise, looking for us. Well, actually, Ben was picking pine needles out of my hair when Cormac, Tina, and Sun came over the rise. Ben might actually have blushed when Cormac stopped, smirked, looking around at the treetops as if examining the foliage.

I took another breath, scanned the group—Grant and Hardin were missing, and my gut twisted.

"Where . . ." I said, stepping forward. "What . . . Grant, Jessi—"

"Hospital," Cormac said. My knees went so weak I almost sat down.

"They're fine," Tina added quickly. "They'll be fine, they just got banged up."

"Oh my God," I muttered, hand on my head. Ben put his hand on my back to steady me.

Sun Wukong laughed. "That's funny," he said. "I mean, considering."

They all looked banged up, to tell the truth. Cormac had a bandage wrapped around his arm. Tina, still recovering from her previous injuries, had new bruises on her chin, her arms. Except Sun—he looked completely unharmed, as usual. I didn't know if anything could hurt him. Rather, I never wanted to face down the thing that could hurt him.

"And you two—you're fine, I take it?" Cormac said, politely not mentioning that we looked like a couple of teenagers caught in the backseat of a car.

"Yeah. Just fine," Ben said, smirking back.

Sun strolled along the shore. "Well, *something* blew up here."

In the daylight, the place looked even worse, very

much like a bomb had gone off, right where Roman had been standing. All the markings he'd drawn in the soil, all the evidence of his ritual had been swept away. The nearest trees were broken, the air still smelled of soot. But the water looked calm.

"The amulet worked," I said.

Cormac went to the smear of ashes that used to be Roman. He recognized a destroyed vampire when he saw one. He kicked at it and turned away. "Good."

CORMAC EXPLAINED that Ashtoreth left the geyser basin right after we did. Her job wasn't to kill everyone—it was to stop me, keep us away from Roman, prevent us from interfering. She hadn't let anything distract her.

The other demons kept fighting, but Cormac and the others quickly noticed that they had help opposing them. We now knew they were vampires of the Order of Saint Lazarus of the Shadows. They meant that the mortal defenders had a fighting chance. They'd been injured, but they won. The vampires had left the scene without stopping to say a word.

When the sun rose and the world was still there—when the geysers and fumaroles started bubbling again—they knew I must have succeeded. They focused next on getting help for the most badly injured. I couldn't wait to see them all again. To thank them. I hadn't gotten my friends killed, and that seemed like the greatest victory. Like Cormac said, I might have had the biggest target painted on me, but it was everyone else who'd stood between that target at the bad guys.

We tracked down vehicles and gathered the caravan together. Sun took off by himself in his beat-up truck. "I have to report back that all is well. That'll be fun!" The whole thing might have been a jaunt for him. I gave him a hug, asked him to say hi to Xiwangmu and Anastasia.

I found my phone. I still had a loose thread that needed to be cleared up before I would feel entirely good about this morning. We waited outside the Jeep, Ben listening close while the dial tone rang, and rang.

Then Shaun finally, finally answered. "Hey! Kitty! Holy shit!"

I might have started crying. Just a few tears of relief. "You have no idea how good it is to hear you."

"Oh, I think I do."

"Are you okay? Is everyone okay, have you seen everybody?"

"We're here, we're all fine. What about you, we went to the house but no one's there, and New Moon—shit, have you seen what happened to New Moon?"

"Ben and I are in Yellowstone. We're fine. At least, we are now."

"Yellowstone. Wait, what?"

"Yeah. Long story."

"Tell me about it. Kitty, I have so much to tell you. You're never going to believe it."

I laughed. "Oh yeah? Not if you don't believe me first."

"You're on."

And astonishingly, all was right with the world.

WE STAYED in the Yellowstone area another day, to wait for Grant and Hardin to get patched up. She had puncture wounds in her leg and chest, and gashes that needed stitches. Grant also needed stitches, and had a concussion. But they were both conscious and smiling when I finally saw them. With some persuasive fast talking, they were able to get themselves discharged from the hospital. And without filing a report with the police. Because how would they explain any of this?

We rolled into Denver at nightfall.

The city seemed both brilliantly serene and totally worn out. We were returning to an old battlefield at the end of the war. I finally felt safe—might have been the first time I'd felt safe since meeting Roman and learning of the Long Game. But it was over now. It was really over.

I made more phone calls. Cheryl had managed to get the family out of Denver by cooking up some story about wanting to see the Grand Canyon, and didn't a spontaneous family trip seem like fun? When I called to tell her everything was fine, she sounded relieved, but not about the world not ending.

"Oh thank God, I was running out of excuses, and I have spent way too long in one hotel room with the kids. Kitty, what happened? Is everything really okay?"

"Yeah. It is now. A bad guy was trying to blow up

the Yellowstone caldera, and it would have destroyed Denver. But we stopped him."

"If anyone else said that, I'd laugh. But you're serious?"

"Yeah, 'fraid so. But everything's okay now." Everything, everything would be okay.

"Well, the plus side is we had a nice trip. The kids love the Grand Canyon."

"You know, I've never seen the Grand Canyon," I said absently. I wondered why.

"Well then, you should go. It's pretty cool."

Yeah. My to-do list had pretty much cleared up for the near future. Maybe I could go see the Grand Canyon.

SUNSET MEANT calling all the vampires, at least the ones on this side of the globe. I half expected Alette to already know everything because of her network. But she sounded surprised, and pleased.

"And Dux Bellorum is really, truly dead?" she asked. "You saw him die?"

"I did. He fell on his sword. Figuratively speaking."

"That . . . is somehow deeply appropriate."

As happy as I was not having to worry about the guy anymore, I was still just a bit sad about the whole thing. "There's always another tool," Lightman had said. Roman had known he was a tool the entire time, and he must have been satisfied with the role.

I didn't tell anyone beside Ben about the stone wolf

that the Men in Black had given me, because I didn't know how to explain it. If anything came of it, there'd be time enough to tell. I didn't doubt that Ezra and Jacob were exactly who they said they were: angels. What I doubted was what it meant. What the entirety of Western civilization believed angels to be, and what they *actually* were, were two different things, I suspected. That there was a war on between their kind and Lightman and Ashtoreth's kind I didn't doubt in the least. Was it a war in Heaven?

That mythology was a faulty interpretation of something I didn't understand. We were looking at it through frosted glass, or Flatlanders trying to comprehend three dimensions. I let it go. Hamlet was probably closer to the truth: "There are more things in Heaven and Earth, Horatio, than are dreamt of in your philosophy." What I had seen of them seemed entirely too mundane for the mighty epics written about them. Driving cars and wearing suits, pouting when things didn't go their way.

Maybe they would think twice before using Earth as a battleground, at least in the near future.

TINA AND Grant went back to L.A. and Las Vegas, respectively. They both still had their shows to do. I asked Tina if *Paradox PI* would cover what had happened, the Long Game, the Manus Herculei, any of it. She thought a minute, then shook her head. "The evidence is pretty much obliterated. And you know, technically, we're supposed to be about entertainment. Not fundamental existential crises of faith."

"Yeah," I said. "You say that now."

Grant had the understated satisfaction of a professional who'd completed a difficult job well. I asked him what was next, and he had to think for a minute. "I think I might take some time off. The world can take care of itself for a little while, I'm sure. But—call if you need anything."

"Of course," I said.

Jessi Hardin couldn't really tell anyone at work what had happened. For all that she was the head of the Denver PD Paranatural Unit, this was outside her mandate. She merely claimed that she had an accident and needed time off. She took a week. When we dropped her off at her place, she asked me not to call her for a month.

I hadn't seen her reach into her pockets for a pack of cigarettes in days.

A WEEK later, we were still debriefing, unpacking, talking, speculating—and trying to convince ourselves that it really was over. Cormac was here for dinner, Ben was cooking, and I was drinking water. You know, just in case. We sat at the counter in the kitchen, talking.

"We've gone back over everything," Cormac—Amelia, rather—explained. "Even knowing about the clay lamp you saw him use, there's nothing to determine whether Manus Herculei refers to the artifact or the spell itself. You're sure you don't remember any of the symbols he drew?"

"Sorry," I said. "I recognized some Greek letters and astrological signs, but it all happened so fast. I still don't know enough to be able to describe it well."

"Ah, well. It ultimately doesn't matter. I expect no one will be able to reconstruct the spell again."

"You almost sound sad," Ben said, quirking a smile and pulling steaks out of the broiler.

"We're not sad," Cormac said, with a decisiveness that was all his. "The less of that kind of magic in the world, the better." His inward grin suggested Amelia was expressing a different opinion. What in the world was it like, being the two of them? Just another bit of strangeness that had become normal. Even if Cormac could find a way to separate himself from Amelia, I wasn't sure he would anymore.

A few news stories still trickled out about damage the earthquake had done, and about aftershocks that had rippled up and down the Rockies. The seismic activity had settled, and geologists hadn't connected it to anything other than normal, expected earthquake levels. Old Faithful hadn't even missed an eruption—it had lagged behind a few predicted times, that night we'd confronted Roman. But it hadn't stopped. The caldera still bubbled, and people still made doomsday predictions about it.

However, no one would be using it as a magical weapon.

"What are you guys going to do about New Moon?" Cormac asked when the meal was half over.

Ben and I glanced at each other, and Ben said, "We're still working through what the insurance is going to pay out, but I think we're going to find a new site and reopen."

The building had been condemned, and the owner took the insurance payout rather than try to rebuild. If we wanted a restaurant again, we'd have to move. I brought up the idea of just letting the place go, but Shaun and Ben both nixed it. Shaun I expected to want to keep the place going; it was mostly his baby anyway, Ben and I were just the backers. But Ben had the best reason of all.

He explained, "One of the reasons the Denver pack is so stable is because of New Moon. It's what you always wanted it to be—a second home, neutral ground. We give it up, I think we'd have to work that much harder keeping the pack together."

He was right. So, one way or another, New Moon would be back. It would be different, but somehow, that seemed okay, too. This was a new era.

The doorbell rang then and we all straightened, looking at each other. The anxiety came back so quickly—wondering what was wrong, what battle we were going to have to fight next. Who was after us this time. I needed a deep breath to settle myself.

"You expecting anyone?" Cormac asked.

"No," Ben said, moving out to the front door. I followed close behind.

"Hello, Ben," I heard, after he opened the front door.

Rick stood there in his familiar black trench coat, smiling. He said we'd talk later, and here he was. I waved happily from behind Ben's protective stance.

Standing behind Rick were his two companions, the vampire ninjas from Yellowstone. I got a better look at them this time, mostly because they weren't dressed in their ninja outfits, cloaks and hoods and all. In fact, they wore modern, normal street clothes, which seemed incongruous. The man with the ponytail was half a head shorter than Rick, compact but obviously powerful, holding himself at the ready. The woman was much the same, tall and serene, regarding me with a dark, hooded gaze. She didn't seem to like me. Was it because I was a werewolf, or because I was me?

"It's good to see you, Kitty," Rick said, smiling his calm smile. "May we come in?"

Ben stood across the doorway, blocking it, like he was going to tell the vampire no. If we didn't invite them in, they couldn't come in, that was the rule. I glanced at Ben; we exchanged one of those looks. He stepped aside.

"Come in," I said. "And your friends, too, I guess?"

Rick came inside, and I caught him in a big hug. He had that vampire chill, but his hug was warm and heartfelt. Rick was back.

His companions entered, but politely hung back until Rick was ready.

"I didn't get a chance to make introductions before," he said. "These are my colleagues, Ibrahim and Ruth."

They each nodded. They had that old-world civility that a lot of older vampires had, all nods and bows rather than an enthusiastic American handshake. They seemed watchful, cautious, and I wondered how old they were.

"Hi," I said, hiding any doubts I might have had about inviting them into my house.

"Your name really is Kitty," Ibrahim said, tsking like he didn't believe it. "I heard the rumors. Now I believe them. You look like a Kitty." This was said with a good-natured smile, a wry wink. Maybe he was just trying to be friendly?

"Thanks, I think?" I led them back to the kitchen, where we could sit and talk. "I'm sorry I can't offer you anything to drink. You know how it is."

"It's quite all right," Rick said. It was an old conversation, familiar and comforting.

"I didn't get a chance to thank you before. Thank you. We couldn't have stopped Roman without you."

"No one could have stopped Ashtoreth without our kind of help," Rick said. "I'm sorry it took us so long to reach you. We were almost too late."

Cormac was the kind of guy who always carried a stake stashed in a pocket or slipped up his sleeve. He usually kept it hidden. Now he sat back and flipped it in his hand, tossing it and catching it, then again.

"Mr. Bennett," Rick said, amiably enough. Cormac didn't say anything.

Ruth glared at him. "Do we need to worry about this?"

Rick raised a brow. "Do we?" He didn't seem worried, but he knew Cormac. Then again, the last time they'd been face-to-face, Cormac had had a stake pressed to Rick's chest, and the vampire had threatened to kill him.

I rolled my eyes, because I did *not* want to have to worry. "Do you have to do that?" I asked Cormac. "Please?"

He slipped the stake back up his sleeve like he was putting away car keys. He'd made his point, apparently. No pun intended. Besides, the odds were not in his favor here.

I was still studying Ibrahim and Ruth, without looking like I was studying them. Ruth had her arms crossed over a tailored suit jacket, dark brown, but not as dark as her skin. Her silk shirt, trousers, and shoes were equally high quality. Her hair was cropped close to her head, giving her an elegant, intimidating profile. Ibrahim wasn't quite so polished, in shirt and trousers that seemed expensive but thrown together. That was probably the point, to make people underestimate him. I knew much of Rick's story, but what about theirs? Where were they from, and how did they end up with the Order of Saint Lazarus of the Shadows? The three of them seemed so comfortable with each other, like they'd been a team for years—centuries. They'd certainly fought like a well-practiced team. But Rick couldn't have been with them for more than a year. I wanted to know everything, but I didn't know what to ask to unlock the stories.

"Kitty, ask your question," Rick said.

"Hey. I was trying to be polite."

"Rick warned us about you," Ruth said. "I for one am not going to tell you how old I am. It's rude to ask."

"Yeah, apparently," I said. "So how about I ask about Yellowstone. How did you end up there? What have you been doing since you left Denver? How—I mean, what is this?"

"You know about the Order of Saint Lazarus of the Shadows," Rick said. "It's larger than you might think, a diverse group from all over the world. We find our ways there by different paths, or we're recruited. But we're there because we can't abide Dux Bellorum and people like him. We're beings of darkness, standing against the dark."

"That's a hell of a sales pitch," Ben observed.

"You didn't stop Roman," Cormac said. "Not in the end. It was us. It was Kitty."

"Don't think we didn't notice," Ibrahim said.

I said, "It was all of us. We all needed to be there."

"Yes," Rick said. "A lot of people noticed that." He was eyeing the wolf amulet, which I'd had under my shirt, but the collar was low enough that it fell out. I tucked it back.

"So," I said. "Please tell me now that everything's done you're back to take over the Family. You have no idea how stressed out everyone was when you were gone. Angelo—he wasn't a disaster, but, well . . ."

"He was wearing one of Roman's coins when he died," Ben said. "He was a disaster."

It wasn't his fault, I wanted to say. I hated speaking ill of the dead. Most of the dead, anyway.

Rick frowned, and my heart sank.

"Our work isn't finished," he said, meaning the work of the Order of Saint Lazarus and his cohort. "There are a dozen cities in Europe and the Middle East whose Masters were loyal to Dux Bellorum. They'll be in chaos now. We—all of us in the order—will need to sort them out."

"But you can start with Denver, maybe? Find a new Master, someone who won't freak out."

"I hope to," Rick said. "Any suggestions?"

Ruth looked sharply at him, and I had the feeling that asking advice from a werewolf should have been beneath him. But this was Rick.

"Braun. He kept his head, helped us out when push came to shove. I think we can get along."

"I'll consider it," he said.

He told us that he'd been keeping an eye on Denver—mostly through Alette's network of contacts. We were reporting in with each other regularly enough that she had most of the news. They'd already been in the States since they'd tracked Roman here. They were waiting for him to make a move, and it turned out the bombing out of New Moon was it. I tried to get mad at him for not telling me he was in the States, but I kept quiet. He'd been working, he'd had his reasons. I was supposed to trust him. After all, he'd been there when I needed him most.

They hadn't literally followed us to Yellowstone, but

they'd known to go there. They looked for us, but they could only do so at night, and Yellowstone was really big. Eventually they'd found us. Rick recognized Cormac's Jeep.

And then they had to go. "We're scheduled to be in Europe by tomorrow night. This work, following up with Roman's people—it can't wait."

"No. I really don't want to see what it looks like if someone tries to step into his shoes."

"Exactly."

Rick and Ben shook hands. Rick and Cormac didn't. Ibrahim and Ruth nodded farewells before heading outside, and I walked with Rick to the door.

The other vampires entered the familiar black Land Rover, but Rick and I held back, lingering by the front door, darkened by nighttime shadows.

"Please say you'll call every now and then this time," I said. "You don't know how many times I've wanted to talk to you, how crazy it's been."

"I know," he said, touching my shoulder. "I'll call this time."

His hand moved from my shoulder to the chain holding the stone wolf. I let him lift it out, study it. "What is it?"

"I got it from a couple of Men in Black who said they were angels. They said it'll give me a year and a day."

Rick's brows lifted. He knew what it meant immediately, and I didn't think I'd ever seen him so startled.

"There will be a price for that, later on," he said.

They told me I'd already paid it, I wanted to argue,

but I knew he was right. As the angels had said, this was a fairy tale, there was always a price, and they would come for my firstborn.

No.

"I'll deal with that when we get there," I said, my smile wan. "I figure it's worth a shot."

"Yes, I think you're right. Good luck."

"Thanks. Rick, do you believe in God?"

He didn't say anything right away, which was shocking to me, because Rick's faith was part of what defined him. He'd gone on an honest-to-God crusade, becoming this warrior priest. I had expected an unmitigated yes.

"That's a more complicated question than most people imagine," he said lightly, smiling. "Ten thousand years of human civilization, all of it burdened by religion trying to figure out what it all means, and I think we still don't understand. But ultimately the answer is yes. And what about you, Kitty? After all you've been through?"

What I had seen lately of gods and angels and demons made me think of how you feel as a kid when you catch adults behaving badly. This? you think. This is what being a grown-up is all about?

"I believe that the full moon comes around once a month, and that the sun rises every morning," I said. "And I believe in the pack."

"Amen," he said.

Epilogue

ON THE 366th day after Roman's final destruction, the stone wolf shattered. I woke up to a popping, cracking noise, and crumbs of gravel scattered across my chest. The chain turned to ash in my hands. I gathered the pieces and stared at them a long time, not sure what to think, unsettled at the trace of magic still lingering. Really, I didn't feel sadness about the thing. I was even a little relieved it was gone. The reminder of the Men in Black wouldn't be attached to me anymore, and it had done its job.

We'd even had a month to spare.

The 367th day was a full moon.

Ben held the door of my sister's house open for me, diaper bag slung over his shoulder, baby carrier in his other hand, while I came in holding Jon cradled in my arms. He'd been here a month and I still couldn't take my eyes off him. He was round, pink, bald, with pudgy arms and amazing little fingers, and tiny lips that opened into big, gummy yawns. He had Ben's chin and my eyes. He smelled like sunshine. At least he did when he was clean and sleeping.

Cheryl and the kids greeted us loudly—along with the golden retriever barking from the backyard. That dog had never gotten used to us. Everybody was very enthusiastic about the new baby, and fortunately for me Cheryl was happy to baby-sit. Or she said she was. Nicky and Jeffy wanted to see their cousin. I mostly stood still and let the chaos roar around me.

Ben had taken well to fatherhood, which didn't surprise me, but I often caught him with this bemused look on his face, like he was wondering how he ended up holding a diaper bag and baby carrier. But he was usually right there before I even asked for help, and I also caught him sometimes holding the baby on one shoulder, his nose pressed to Jon's soft baby head, just breathing, taking in the scent.

Tonight was a full-moon night and we couldn't linger. I could feel Wolf scratching at my gut, a hint of things to come. Disconcerting. I hadn't felt her anticipation in a year, and I had forgotten how to deal with it, how to keep it together. Wait, just wait, I kept murmuring, and her growl answered me.

The first full moon after I'd gotten the amulet had been strange. Half believing the thing wouldn't work, I'd gone out with the pack to our mountain den. Just in case. But Wolf hadn't been there. Or she was there, the strength and power I had as a werewolf still curled up inside me. She didn't wake up, didn't claw at my guts

trying to rip through my skin for her one night of free-
dom. It was the strangest thing. I thought about her,
opened my mind in the way that usually let the Change
wash over me. But no fur pricked on my skin, no claws
burst from my fingers.

Around me, the wolves in my pack shifted into their
furry, lupine selves, howling and snapping, running off
into the nighttime woods to hunt. And I sat on the
ground, hugging my knees, feeling like I had fallen into
an alternate world.

Ben took it badly. He waited to shift until he couldn't
anymore, resisting until he fell, grunting in agony as his
wolf overtook him. As a wolf he lingered, rubbing
against me, nuzzling me, licking my face, nipping my
fingers. His wolf didn't understand that I wouldn't be
going with him this time.

Burying my face in the ruff of his neck, I murmured,
"It's okay. You have to go without me. I'll wait here for
you." I cried, and he whined deep in his throat. Since
his very first full moon, we'd only been apart a couple
of times.

Finally, because the blood and the hunt called, and
the rest of our pack was howling for him, he ran. I
watched him, and he stopped to look back a couple of
times before disappearing into the nighttime woods. I
felt very alone in that moment.

I got a blanket from the car, wrapped it around me,
and sat up against a tree to wait. I woke up a few hours
later with Ben's great furry body shored up against me,
snuggling under the blanket, as if he was sure he could

keep me warmer. Hugging him hard, I went back to sleep with wolf fur in my nose, and woke up at dawn with my husband back in my arms.

I went out with the pack every full moon of that year and a day. I may not have had Wolf for the time being, but this was still my pack. It wouldn't have been right to stay away. Even when I was eight and a half months pregnant and huge and grouchy, and Ben's wolf was even more frantic at leaving me than he had been that first night, I sat by that tree, wrapped in my blanket, the baby kicking like he knew something was up. He couldn't get comfortable, I couldn't get comfortable, we didn't sleep at all. Wolf was quiet the whole time.

Now, Wolf was back. My nerves, head to toe, were churning, and Ben could sense it. When I lost it, I was going to really lose it. My shoulders were bunched up to my ears, and my sister kept asking if everything was okay, and I kept saying yes, yes, while clutching at Jon as if he were about to fall off a cliff.

When I was pregnant, we'd wondered: Would the baby be born a werewolf? Would he have some supernatural quirk, would he have magical energy bursting from his fingertips? What price were we going to have to pay for having him at all? Did we have to worry? Had anything like this ever happened before? I called Dr. Shumacher, Alette, Ned, and Marid, who was the oldest vampire I knew. Nobody knew what was going to happen. Nothing like this had ever happened before. But none of them seemed worried. "You're Regina Luporum," Ned, Master of London, had said. "Of course strange things are happening to you." He'd had a laugh under the words, like he'd been joking.

Now that he was here, we both watched Jon carefully, and we both smelled him. He was human. He didn't smell like a lycanthrope, he didn't smell strange or magical. He smelled like a sweet, healthy baby.

It was just his parents who were monsters.

"Can I hold him?" Nicky asked, and though my gut said no, of course not, my mouth said, "Yes, here, just like this," even though she'd held him before and done just fine, and knew how to support his head and everything. She didn't even need to sit on the sofa while holding him. She was becoming so grown up.

My arms felt too light without him. I kissed his head one more time, and Ben gently touched my shoulder and steered me toward the door. "We really need to get going." His own wolf was close to the surface, showing gold in his eyes.

"Thank you again," I said to Cheryl. My voice held an edge of desperation. I wouldn't be able to do this without my family.

"Don't worry," she said. "I'll call in the favor someday." She gave me a quick hug and pushed me out the door, into a night that felt very huge.

My baby was only a month old and I'd just *left him*.

It's time. I knew that. My guts were turning inside out. I hugged myself. But I managed to get into the car.

"You okay?" Ben asked, pulling out of the driveway and heading toward I-70, which would carry us into the mountains.

"I'd forgotten how much it hurts," I murmured. No—I'd gotten used to how much shifting hurt. The calluses of it had all worn off over the last year. I had to get used to it all over again.

He took my hand, squeezed it. "Keep it together."

How many times had I said those words to him in the early days of his infection, when he was still learning how to control his wolf, when the panic and rage took over? I said those words because they were what TJ, the werewolf who'd helped me, had said. I felt like I was right back there, my very first full moon, the first time I shifted. I took a deep, shuddering breath, because I was about to start gasping. Ben drove a little bit faster.

Everyone else in the pack was already there. Ben must have talked to them—gotten the support network together, made sure I had as much help as I needed. Having everyone in the pack in one place was one less thing to worry about. Shaun, shirtless and in sweatpants, came to the car as Ben was shutting off the engine, and he helped me out. He had an expression of concern. So did Becky, standing behind him, taking hold of my other hand.

"How are you doing?" Shaun asked.

"I don't know," I said, wiping tears from my eyes, and I didn't know if it was because I was afraid of what was going to happen, or because I'd only been away from Jon for an hour and I already missed him, and felt like my heart was being stomped on. Why had no one warned me about this part?

Then Ben was beside me. Hand in hand, we walked

past the road to the edge of the forest. "Take the others," he said to Shaun and Becky. "Go on ahead."

Some of the pack had already shifted, and they came up to me, nudging me with their noses, licking my hands—saying hello, we're here for you, and we love you. Their smell filled my nose, pack and night and hunting and blood.

I dropped to my knees in the dirt and Ben was right there with me, kneeling behind me, his arms wrapped around me, an anchor.

"Ben, I don't think I can do this." I didn't know how to shift anymore. I didn't know how to let go. It was like the first time all over again. *Let me go, it's time, it's time, it's been so long . . .*

"It's okay, Kitty, you can do this. I've got you, just like you held me that first time."

He pulled off my shirt, and the chill night air hit my skin. I gasped, and a million needles stabbed my skin. My hands were changing, my bones slipping, and still I tried to hold on.

"Let it go, just let it go," Ben murmured in my ear. And I did. My skin opened, and Wolf leaps out.

I tip my head back and howl.

Author's Note

Once upon a time, I did not intend to be the kind of writer who embarked on a fourteen-volume series (fifteen, counting the short story collection) featuring the same character. I was not a reader of long series. Series annoyed me! My God, how could one possibly keep it all straight after that many books?! Plus, I am easily distracted.

You know, I never did put together a useful series bible.

However . . . I just kept getting ideas. The ideas didn't all fit in one book. Or two, or three, or seven, or ten, as it turned out. Werewolf talk radio show host? It was so gimmicky, an idea like that would never have legs.

Did you know wolves can travel great distances, loping for hours at a time without rest?

As it turned out, the idea of a werewolf talk radio show host didn't limit what I could write about—it expanded the possibilities, almost without end. That ended up being a great joy. Exhilarating. Fourteen books. A dozen-plus stories and counting. I have become a

werewolf advocate in the world of urban fantasy—
another thing I didn't predict. ("Have you always
been interested in werewolves?" I'm often asked. No,
actually . . .)

I would never have done any of it if readers hadn't
kept asking for new books. It started with the great Gene
Wolfe, who wrote to *Weird Tales* after the first Kitty
story was published, asking if there would be another.
(And when Gene Wolfe asks for a story, you write him a
story.) It continued with my publishers asking, can you
write two? Four? Seven?

And I've been getting e-mails for ten years now:
Will there be another book? When is the next book
coming out?

Speaking as someone who wrote three novels that
ended up in the trunk without ever getting published,
having complete strangers e-mail wanting to read *more*
is heady motivation indeed. It really does make writing easier, knowing someone is waiting for the finished
product.

Thank you. Thank you for taking this ride with me,
for your enthusiasm, for falling in love with Kitty, for
"getting it."

Until now, the answer to "Will there be another
Kitty book?" has always been yes. I've also always said
that the series will end someday. It's hard to let go, but
I'm a fan of endings. Series—books and TV—have
natural lifespans, I believe, and it's better to have a big
finish than to peter out. It's time. There are scenes in
this book I've been planning almost since the start, and

it was a great feeling to be able to write them, to be able to bring Kitty's story to that closure.

There are two topics that have been by far the most popular topics that readers send me e-mails about: the first, about why Kitty and Cormac should hook up, why didn't they, when will they, etc. The second: will Kitty have a baby? Oh, the many, many solutions people suggested to me about how Kitty could have a baby! Yeah, boyfriends and babies seem to be the things that really hit people in the soft spot. I've known all along how Kitty would have a baby. I've been keeping that secret for a long time. I hope my solution satisfies.

So, this is the end. Or is it . . . ? I've learned to never say never. After all, once upon a time I said I would never write a series at all. One of the building blocks of the Kitty series is the fact that I'm not very good at world building and I decided early on that any story I wanted to write about vampires and werewolves necessarily had to be set in the same world. Coming up with two sets of rules for these things is way too much work! So I won't declaratively say that this is the end. Any more stories I want to write about vampires and werewolves will, I'm sure, be set in this very familiar world.

And I'm pretty sure that Cormac fellow is getting into trouble somewhere right this very minute . . .

Acknowledgments

I have a lot of people to thank. Too many. I'll leave people out, which makes everybody sad. But I'll give it a go anyway: A big thank-you to my editors, Stacy Hill, David Hartwell, and Jaime Levine, who all helped make the books better than they would have been. Marco Palmieri, Devi Pillai, and many other editors, assistants, publicists, and sales folk have been there along the way to make this journey much easier. In this day and age when people wonder why an author would choose traditional publishing over self-publishing, these people, right here, all of them, are my reasons. Thanks to my agents, Ashley Grayson and Carolyn Grayson—and Dan Hooker, who unfortunately passed away just after *Kitty and The Midnight Hour* came out. I still think about him and dearly wish he could have seen what a great big avalanche he started when he took me on.

Craig White has done the cover art for all the books, and I am so grateful to him for giving the series its consistent, kick-ass look. It's more than I ever hoped for, and definitely contributed to the series' success.

I have a lot of writing workshop friends who helped me: Jeanne Cavelos of Odyssey, all my 1998 Odyssey classmates. James Van Pelt and the folks of the WACO critique group. Walter Jon Williams and Rio Hondo—my summer camp for grown-ups. Daniel Abraham was the beta reader for many of these books, and the series was better for it. Ty Franck, Paolo Bacigalupi, Diana Rowland—I don't know what I would have done without you guys being there for me. Margaritas and gin and bad movies, always.

Paula Balafas has been an invaluable resource for the police work in the series, and in the development of Jessi Hardin. Brian Whitehead happily let me recruit him as a research assistant, which became extraordinarily helpful in the later books when I was trying to remember things like who'd been shot when. I've done so much research, traveled to so many places, gotten so many ideas and had so much help from tour guides, books, conversations. If books are like children, then it really does take a village to raise them. Especially fourteen of them.

Max, Yaz, Anna, Rhoanne, Tatia, Geoffrey, and Tim were all my roommates at various points in my early writing career and all put up with me during that manic phase when I was writing the first Kitty stories and despairing that I would ever have a career. They had no clue what they were getting into, but we all survived, and they made my life better.

And my family: Mom and Dad and Rob, who were